A WOMAN'S AWAKENING

Embarrassed, moved by unfamiliar stirrings, Holly stammered, "I'm just not interested in things like men . . . romance."

Scott raised an eyebrow, his lips turning up in a teasing smile. "Not interested, Holly? In things like . . . this?" He pressed his mouth against hers, gently at first, then his kiss became warm, seeking, lips parting to move provocatively as his tongue began to probe hungrily.

One part of Holly screamed to push him away, to twist her head from side to side to escape his tantalizing lips, while another urged her dizzily to cling to him, to answer that fiery kiss. She could now feel the flames spreading beyond, downward into her loins.

Suddenly, she tore from him, attempting to wrench away, but he held her, arms tightly wrapped about her to crush her and hold her against his rock-hard chest. She trembled, afraid that he could see to the depths of her soul as he sternly told her, "You don't want me to stop, Holly. You want me to make love to you, show you what it means to be a woman . . ."

Other Avon Books by
Patricia Hagan

DARK JOURNEY HOME
GOLDEN ROSES
LOVE AND GLORY
LOVE AND WAR
PASSION'S FURY
RAGING HEARTS
SOULS AFLAME
THIS SAVAGE HEART
WINDS OF TERROR

LOVE'S WINE

PATRICIA HAGAN

AVON
PUBLISHERS OF BARD, CAMELOT, DISCUS AND FLARE BOOKS

Verse quoted on p. 325 is from "The Vine" by James Thomson.

LOVE'S WINE is an original publication of Avon Books. This work has never before appeared in book form. This work is a novel. Any similarity to actual persons or events is purely coincidental.

AVON BOOKS
A division of
The Hearst Corporation
1790 Broadway
New York, New York 10019

First Avon Printing, July 1985

AVON TRADEMARK REG. U. S. PAT. OFF. AND IN OTHER COUNTRIES,
MARCA REGISTRADA, HECHO EN U. S. A.

Printed in the U. S. A.

WFH 10 9 8 7 6 5 4 3 2 1

For Erik, who shared the discovery that love is not trapped in fantasy . . . but awaits those who dare to sail the turbulent waters of reality.

❧ Chapter One ❧

HOLLY stood before the shattered window and
stared pensively at the lawn sloping gently
down to the riverbank.

The warm breeze of evening danced through the
shards of glass to caress her gently and blow long
strands of auburn hair about her face. Evenings, she
reflected somberly, had always been the loveliest
time, but that was before the war. Then, the lawn
had been a carpet of thick green grass, the air
scented by the pungent sweet magnolia trees that
bordered the lawn.

There was no velvety emerald grass now. Now
the earth was red and raw, as parched and dead as
all of Mississippi since the Yankees had come.

Neither were there any more ivory blossoms on
the blackened tree limbs. The trees had burned
along with everything else that had thrived there
once.

Holly turned from the window and its fragments
of glass hanging from the cracked and splintered
frames. As her gaze swept the room, she blinked
back tears. It was so hard to recall how the parlor of
her home had once looked. Silk tapestry of watered

1

shades of peach and gold had adorned the walls, stretching up to the high, intricate walnut molding at the ceiling's edge. Thick coral velvet had gracefully draped the tall, narrow windows. Now everything hung in shreds, ripped by plundering Yankees.

The furniture had been dragged outdoors to feed huge bonfires as the Yankees cooked and ate the livestock during a three-day occupation. After that, they had torched the inside of the house. Only a sudden, furious rain had kept the house from being destroyed.

Holly squeezed her eyes shut to obliterate the flashing images of the nightmare, but it was all still livid, alive in her mind forever. . . .

Two years had passed since that late spring day in 1863, but Holly could remember everything. She and her mother had been sitting on the front porch making lint bandages to be sent to the Confederate hospital in Vicksburg. Her mother made a social event out of everything in her life. Twyla Cunningham and Nolia Pope had traveled from Port Gibson, twelve miles south. The ladies, like everyone else, knew there was a constant threat of Yankee invasion, but life had to go on, and no socially concerned woman within riding distance of Magnolia Hall ever turned down an invitation from Claudia Maxwell. So they had come that morning, enjoying the feeling of helping their beloved boys in gray, enjoying the gossip as well. And there was the tantalizing aroma of Mammy Portia's fried chicken from the kitchen house out back, and the sweet smell of strawberry pies cooling on the windowsills.

Holly remembered so clearly Twyla Cunningham lamenting her fifteen-year-old's decision to join the Confederate Army. Billy Ray was at home packing his things that very day. She was glad, she'd said, to have an excuse to be away, for she could only watch him and cry, and that made Billy Ray and the rest of the family feel so bad. To change the subject, Nolia asked Claudia when she'd last heard from Major Maxwell.

Claudia's face glowed as she spoke of Papa and how relieved she was to know he was just up the road in Vicksburg. He came home at least once a month to see how things were at the Hall. It was really to see her, Claudia had confided with a giggle, like a young girl caught up in her first love. Grandpa Maxwell kept an eye on things at the Hall, so his son had no worries on that score. True, Grandpa refused to live in the lavish house with his family; he loved his isolated fishing shack in the slough of the river to the northeast, and he wouldn't leave it.

Holly had always felt a rush of warmth at the mere mention of her beloved grandfather. Why, if she'd had her way, she'd have been living down there with him. She loved the tranquil beauty, the mysterious swamps. He'd taught her to fish and swim and shoot and hunt as well as any man. Her mother had tolerated it when Holly was a child, but when Holly began to blossom into young womanhood, her mother had begun to object.

Holly distinctly did not share her feelings. Why would anybody prefer to spend hours reading poetry when she could be exploring the wonders of the swamp and the forest? Why would anyone rather learn needlepoint than sit in a boat watching the sun go down, munching corn pone and listening to Grandpa's stories?

It had been at that precise moment, that blue and gold day in May when the war seemed too far away to be real, that moment when Claudia spoke of Grandpa, that he came loping out of the woods to the northeast, waving his arms and yelling.

The women dropped their bandages, standing up in fearful apprehension. Holly grasped the porch railing and bolted over it. Landing solidly, she broke into a run. Grandpa's cries rode to her on the wind and she halted, frozen. "Yankees! Yankees in Port Gibson!"

He reached her, drawing her against him protectively as he approached the women. Quickly he told them about the man traveling up the river on his boat to warn everyone he could. "Get what valuables you can carry, Claudia," he ordered brusquely. "You, too, Holly. They won't be able to find us deep in the swamps."

He nodded to Twyla and Nolia. "You ladies come, too. You can't go home now."

Claudia turned to go inside the house, calling over her shoulder, "I'll get Mammy to get Zebediah and help bury the silver. Holly, you come with me and help gather our good jewelry."

Twyla Cunningham suddenly cried, "I've got to go home. My children . . . oh, dear God." She swung her head from side to side, eyes wide with terror.

Grandpa reached out to grasp her arms. "Miz Cunningham, there's nothin' you can do. Just calm down. Stay with us, and when it's safe, I promise I'll take you home myself.''

But Twyla Cunningham was beyond reason. She had but one thought, to get to her family. Nolia Pope was in the same state of mind, and with both of them hysterical, Grandpa Maxwell could do nothing but watch as they headed for their wagon.

He looked at Holly, shook his head, and told her, ''They're doin' what their hearts are tellin' 'em to do, girl. I tried. Now let's you and me go help your mother.''

They buried the silver tableware and candlesticks and bowls and platters under the outhouse, where Grandpa figured the Yankees wouldn't search. Then they gathered up their jewelry and ran for the woods after telling Mammy to order the servants to hide. . . .

What had followed, Holly would always remember as a glimpse into hell.

They hid deep in the swamps for almost three weeks. Grandpa slipped out to hunt for rabbits and squirrels so they wouldn't starve, and sometimes he encountered others running from the Yankees who told him what was going on. He learned that the Confederates at Raymond, twenty miles northeast, had been defeated by General Grant and his troops were headed for Vicksburg. A few days later, he heard that Vicksburg was under fire.

Holly watched, stunned, as her mother fell into sobbing despair. She could not bear to be around her, realizing, to her surprise, that she resented her mother's lack of strength. Why didn't Claudia burn with anger, as Holly did? Why couldn't she do something—anything—instead of lie on a pallet and cry for her husband? Did she have no spirit without him? Holly vowed she would never be so weak as to transmit her own personal strength to another person. She would never let herself disintegrate like that.

Holly sneaked out of the swamps on her own, hiding in the woods until she could creep up on her house. To her horror, she found Magnolia Hall occupied by Yankees. Her home was being ransacked.

Grandpa found her there. "Don't torture yourself, honey," he coaxed. She didn't take her eyes off the bonfire, and he knelt beside her as her own mahogany four-poster was carried out and thrown into the bonfire. "Come on, Holly. It's dangerous here," he pleaded.

"You knew, didn't you?" she accused, hot tears of bitterness and rage streaming down her cheeks. "You knew the Yankees were here, and you didn't tell us."

He nodded miserably. "What good would it have done? Just like it ain't doin' a bit of good for you to be watchin'. There's nothin' we can do, nothin'. You come along, now."

"Why?" Holly demanded, fists clenched. "Why are they doing this to my home, Grandpa? Why?"

"It's war, honey. War destroys and nobody ever really understands why it happens but it does. But look at it like this." He drew her close to him. "They can burn the furniture and the house and everything on the land, but they can't destroy the soul of that land. When it comes right down to it, land is the only thing that's eternal, that lives forever, and when all this is over with, that land is still goin' to be there, and your papa can build another house and start over again. Land lives forever, Holly. Don't ever lose it.''

When the horror over what had befallen their home subsided a little for the three of them, something far more devastating happened.

Major Wesley Maxwell was killed during the siege of Vicksburg.

He was brought home, and they buried him in the family cemetery beneath a grove of pecan trees now standing with blackened limbs outstretched grotesquely, companions in death.

A few neighbors and friends came to the burial, but Twyla Cunningham and Nolia Pope were not among them. They had been killed on their way home that terrible day, caught in crossfire. Holly felt no defined sorrow for them because, in the abyss of grief that had become her whole life, each new tragedy merely blended with the rest.

Papa was gone. Magnolia Hall was ruined. Life would never be the same.

There would be no more abundant cotton crops at summer's end or gathering of pecans. No gala balls in the splendid house or barbecues on the lush lawn.

Holly and her mother had nowhere else to go, so they moved into Grandpa's shack. There was no way of fixing Magnolia Hall.

Time passed. Grandpa's trips out of the swamp to gather news became less frequent, for the news was too sorrowful to be endured any longer. Claudia spent her hours in a protective stupor, so Holly and her grandfather became even closer, thrown entirely on each other.

Over and over he told her how the South would

surely rise and whip the Yankees all the way to hell. Again and again, he told her that land was the most precious thing a person could have. If you had land, then you had a piece of eternity—even if only for your time on earth.

One evening as Holly sat beside the fire and stared at her almost constantly weeping mother, Grandpa reached out to caress Holly's cheek with his fingertips. He whispered, "Don't sit in judgment, girl. You don't know what she's feelin'. She loved your pa more'n anything in this world, and she's hurtin' somethin' fierce."

Holly shook her head. "I just never knew before how weak my mother really is. Love should make a woman stronger. She shouldn't give all her spirit to a man, not if this is what happens when she loses him."

Grandpa gave her a shrewd look. "That's awful big talk for a snip of a girl who ain't never been in love."

Holly snapped, "Then I hope I never fall in love. I don't want to be weak."

This time, her grandfather didn't scoff. "If you feel all that strong, maybe you'd better think about a lifetime of tendin' your land instead of gettin' married and havin' young'uns. It'd save you—and some man—a lot of misery."

Then came the day an old trapper chanced by and told them General Lee had surrendered the Army of Virginia. The war was over. The South had lost.

From that time on, Holly watched her grandfather die. Every night she sat by his bed, holding his hand, urging him to regain his spirit, but he slipped further and further away.

"Promise," he implored over and over again, "promise me you won't lose this land. It's our piece of eternity. I'm going to die, Holly. You hang on to the only piece of eternity I knew in this world."

Holly promised. She held his wrinkled, gnarled old hand night after night and made the vow again and again, and he smiled and closed his eyes and drifted into a peaceful sleep each night.

Then one morning, he did not wake up.

"They did this to him," Holly hissed between clenched teeth. She knelt beside his body and finished making her transition from innocence to cold, smoldering rage at the world around her. "The Yankees did this. They killed Papa and Grandpa, destroyed my home, and may God damn every one of them to eternal fire and damnation!"

Claudia cried, "Stop it! I won't have you behaving this way, Holly. Your grandfather was old, and—"

"Papa wasn't!" Holly snapped, glaring at her defiantly.

Claudia stared at her in wonder. This was no longer her obedient, loving, eighteen-year-old daughter. This was a woman, a bitter, strong, woman . . . and a stranger.

The sound of wagon wheels churning against dry earth brought Holly's attention back to the window again. She saw her mother approaching in Grandpa's old buckboard, the lazy old mule pulling. How happy she looks, Holly reflected resentfully. How happy and pleased with things. Her mother had declared the war over. The wounds should be allowed to heal, she declared. Everyone had to work together and rebuild. And that, Holly thought bitterly, meant cozying up to the damn Yankee carpetbaggers swarming all over Mississippi and the rest of the South like buzzards on a carcass.

The Yankees, her mother said, were no longer enemies. Now they were "sentinels," trying to restore the glorious union.

Hogwash, Holly told herself as she watched her mother draw the mule to a stop and alight to the ground with a youthful spring. She was a beautiful woman, with limpid hazel eyes and milk-white skin.

Claudia began to call to her as she picked her way carefully up the crumbling steps. "Holly? Where are you, dear? I know you're in here. Heaven knows, you hang around this depressing place every day. I don't want to have to look for you." She poked her head through the archway to the parlor, eyes narrowing as her gaze adjusted to the shadowed light. "There you are. Really, Holly, it just isn't healthy for you to pine away here. I know it isn't pleasant at the shack, dear, but—"

"It is *very* pleasant at the shack," Holly interrupted coldly. "I love it there. It makes me feel close to Grandpa. I come here because I never want to forget what they did to him, to all of us." She turned away, washed once more with the fury and rage that had become her vital force.

Claudia sighed. "I have good news. Two bits of good news, in fact. First, I think I've finally worked it out for us to move to Vicksburg."

Warily, Holly turned to face her.

Claudia ignored the storminess of her cinnamon eyes and hastened on. "Ben Cunningham came to see me this afternoon. Bless his heart, he's been through so much, coming home from the war with one leg gone, finding Twyla was dead. He's tried to pick up the pieces, and he just can't. Goodness, he's got those small children to look after, and—''

"What does all of this have to do with us?" Holly asked impatiently. Her mother was very nervous about something.

Claudia walked into the room, pressing her hands tightly against her bosom. "Ben brought me word from his sister, Abby, in Vicksburg. She's all alone in that big house. You did know she lost her husband toward the end of the war? She says we're welcome to come and stay with her as long as we want, till we decide what we want to do."

Holly's lips tightened. She had no intention of moving and said so. "I know what *I* want to do, Mother, and I intend to do it. I'm going to stay here and rebuild Magnolia Hall. Maybe you can walk away and not look back, but I can't. I owe it to Papa and Grandpa . . . and myself." She turned to the window once more. "I promised Grandpa I'd never give up his land, and I won't."

Claudia hurried forward and held Holly by the shoulders. "Believe me, Holly darling, I know how you feel, but we've got to go forward. We can't cling to the past. There's nothing for us here. How can two helpless women keep this land going? We can't even pay the taxes, so in a few more days this land won't even be ours anymore."

Adamantly, Holly said, "I'll find a way. There's the silver we buried, and the jewelry. We can sell it to pay the taxes." The odd silence that followed caused Holly to turn slowly to her mother, who couldn't face her. "You sold it, didn't you?" she whispered. She gestured helplessly to the stylish gray velvet riding dress Claudia was wearing. "I should have known. The way you've been dressing lately. Oh, why didn't I realize? You've sold our things, haven't you?"

Claudia turned away and began to pick absently at the shreds of peach satin that clung to the wall. "I had no choice, Holly. It isn't just the clothes—though heaven knows, we've been in rags. We had no food. I didn't get much, anyway. The Yankees have money to buy all the silver they want, and the Southerners need food, not silver, on the table. But the jewelry . . . I can't part with that. It's all I have left that your father gave me."

"What clothes, Mother? And what food? I've caught fish, trapped squirrels and rabbits. Last week I shot a deer. We haven't starved."

Claudia whispered hoarsely, "We both need clothes, Holly, so we can return to a decent life. I ordered gowns made for us both. They're being made at the dressmaker's, and that's the other good news I have for you. We must move to Vicksburg at once." Her voice rose with renewed confidence. "Jarvis Bonham has finally invited us to one of his fancy parties. I was in Vicksburg today at the dressmaker's, and then I had tea at the hotel with Ben's sister. He was there—Jarvis, that is—and we talked." She reached for Holly's stiff hands, ignoring her daughter's cringing reaction, the marble coldness of her skin. "Jarvis is such a wonderful man, Holly," she gushed. "He's doing so much to help build things up again. Why, already he's got a large lumber mill going. He's providing jobs for so many people. I know you'll like him, if you'll just meet him and give him a chance.''

Holly was struggling to restrain her temper. This was, after all, her mother, and she loved and respected her. No matter that she was weak, and, yes, selfish. No matter that Claudia was the daughter of a dirt-poor sharecropper and had used her beauty to marry into one of the richest and most prominent families in all of Mississippi. Maybe she had married her father for his money and social position, but she had loved him later and made him happy, Holly knew that. She bit her tongue to keep from saying anything she shouldn't say.

"How is it you know Mr. Bonham so well?'' she asked.

Claudia averted her gaze, then forced a nervous smile. "I . . . I do go into town a good bit, dear. You know how I hate that wretched shack. I have tea with old friends, and . . . and . . . they tell me things. I'm told Mr. Bonham is becoming the social leader of Vicksburg.''

"How did you meet him?''

Claudia's answer was quick, almost defensive. "I went to a tea one afternoon and he was there. I liked him. He's quite charming.''

Instinctively, Holly knew it was more than that. It had been two years since Papa's death. It was only natural that her mother would be thinking about her future, the company of men. "He's a widower?''

Claudia nodded. "A fever. Some years ago.''

"Children?''

"A son. Several years older than you.'' She stared at Holly, desperate for some morsel of understanding, and cried, "Oh, Holly darling, please understand. I've been so lonely. It's been a terrible time. I don't want to wither away out here in squalor and poverty. Don't condemn me."

Holly saw a glimmer of tears in her mother's eyes and felt a true sympathy for her misery. "I don't condemn you, Mother. I want you to be happy. It's just that I can't forget as easily as you can. Or forgive. I won't interfere with your life if you show me the same respect." ·

Claudia brightened. "Oh, I will," she said, "but if you'd just come to the party, Holly, and give yourself a chance to meet new people, you'd make me so happy. I'm having a gorgeous gown made for you. Green satin. It will be so lovely with your hair."

Holly shook her head. She did not want to go.

Claudia persisted. "Jarvis is having the party to welcome the new officer assigned to command the Reconstruction army. It can be sort of a debut for you into Vicksburg society. Please?"

Holly hated the desperation in her mother's eyes. "I have no interest in meeting men, particularly Yankees. I've heard of Jarvis Bonham. He's a carpetbagger. He came to Mississippi like a vulture after carrion, taking advantage of the starving. You do what you feel is right for you, Mother, and give me the same privilege, please."

Claudia shook her head fiercely. "I won't let you have that opinion of Jarvis. It isn't fair. He didn't come here to get wealthy. He's wealthy already from his many businesses. He wants to be my friend . . . our friend. He's brought money *to* the South, not taken it out." She paused, pushed a strand of hair back from her face, and gathered a little more nerve. "Very well. Perhaps it's best I tell you now. Jarvis is buying Magnolia Hall for the taxes owed on it—taxes we can't pay. He's going to rebuild it, create a house even more magnificent than the original. He understands how much it means to me to know I won't be losing my home to a stranger. Why, he's even agreed to pay me a small sum so I won't feel that I've lost everything."

Holly saw the hope in her mother's eyes and knew Claudia was begging for understanding, but she couldn't stand any more. "Mother, you can't let him take our home. He's nothing but a dirty, greedy carpetbagger!"

"I have no choice. What else can I do? You should be grateful to Jarvis. He doesn't have to give me anything. All he has to do is pay the taxes and he can take over the title to this property. There is *nothing* I can do about it."

Holly trembled with her rage. "He's not taking Grandpa's place! It's mine! Grandpa left it to me. I promised him I'd never give it up, and I won't. Maybe I can't do anything about this place, but I'll fight with everything I've got to keep what's rightfully mine."

Claudia stiffened. "Can you pay the taxes, Holly? Jarvis says he's willing to take that parcel as well, so he'll have the entire estate."

"He'll be damned to hell, and so will I, before I let that happen."

With burning, defiant glares, they turned away from each other. Finally, Holly was able to speak calmly. "There is no point in our discussing this any further. I'm not moving to Vicksburg, and I will find a way to pay the taxes on *my* land. I'm staying."

She started away, but Claudia caught her arm and spun her around. Never had Holly seen her mother so angry.

"How do you propose to do that?" Claudia demanded furiously, but her daughter refused to say. She shook loose of Claudia and kept on going, outside, across the lawn, through the woods. Damn the Yankees, and damn Jarvis Bonham and his money.

🍂 Chapter Two 🍂

HOLLY took a deep breath and entered the office of the Vicksburg tax collector.

Early morning light struggled through window-panes dusted with red clay from the street beyond. There was no furniture in the small office, only a long wooden counter the length of one wall. A tall, balding man stood behind it searching through leather-bound volumes of tax records, the pages grimy and yellowed.

Holly took her place in line, ignoring the stares of the others waiting. She knew she looked strange. She was wearing an old pair of Grandpa's trousers, tied at the waist with a length of frayed rope. She had rolled them several times at her ankles to keep from tripping. The shirt had belonged to Grandpa, too. Her hair was twisted into a single braid. She supposed she did look a sight, but what did a young lady wear to town when she had to ride a mule? She felt like posing that question to the rudely staring man in front of her.

At last, she took her place in front of the counter and found herself staring into the disapproving eyes of the tax clerk.

18   *Patricia Hagan*

"Yes?" He spoke crisply, eyes narrowed, as though accusing her of being somewhere she had no right to be.

Well, here goes, Holly thought. "My name is Holly Maxwell. I want to know the amount of taxes due on my land."

Raising an eyebrow, he exchanged an amused glance with another official who had just come in. "Well, now, Miss Maxwell," he looked down at her once again. "You're going to have to give me more information than your name."

Holly bit back an angry response. "The land may still be listed in my grandfather's name—Daniel J. Maxwell. He died and left the property to me. It's adjacent to my father's land—Wesley Maxwell's land."

The clerk's eyebrows shot up at once. "You're Wesley's girl? Daniel's granddaughter? Well, now." He mellowed, reaching for one of the worn volumes. "Knew you when you was knee-high to a billy goat, girl. Sure didn't recognize you, though. Let's see now. Maxwell. Yep." He nodded. "The deed is still in your grandpa's name. No trouble to get that changed, though. Just bring me his will, showing you're the rightful heir." Then suddenly he leaned over the counter to whisper, "Listen to me, honey. I hate to tell you this, but the taxes on that land haven't been paid since before the war. Adding on the interest, the amount comes to quite a lot. Almost two hundred dollars. You don't have that kind of money, I know. Lots of folks with land more valuable than this are losing it right and left, and—"

"I am well aware of how the carpetbaggers are

taking advantage of people's misfortunes, sir,'' Holly interrupted. "I will get the money to pay the taxes.''

She turned to go, and the clerk called after her, "Today's Tuesday. The tax sale is going to be Friday on the courthouse steps. So if you don't have that money in here by midnight Thursday, it'll be sold. You'd be smart to not waste your time worrying about it, 'cause I hear Mr. Jarvis Bonham is going to buy all your daddy's land. Your grandpa's, too, I reckon.''

Holly turned around slowly, withering him with an icy glare. "You can tell Jarvis Bonham it will snow in hell before he or any damned carpetbagger takes my land.''

She hurried out, slamming the door. Swiftly, she made her way to Garrington's jewelry store. The place was empty. At the sound of the bell above the door, a squat little man hurried out from behind velvet curtains. His anticipation quickly dissipated as his eyes swept over Holly in her ragged clothes. "I'm not giving handouts,'' he informed her with a repugnant wriggle of his long nose. "But if you're really hungry you can go around back and my wife might find something for you.''

He turned to disappear behind the curtains, but Holly rushed forward and called, "Wait. Are you Mr. Garrington? I have business with you.''

He paused, then asked warily, "What kind of business?''

Reaching inside the pocket of her trousers, she brought out the carefully knotted handkerchief. Mr. Garrington waited impatiently as she untied it. She held out the emerald brooch. "It's beautiful, isn't it?'' She forced a smile past the lump in her throat. "It belonged to my grandmother. I want to sell it."

The jeweler snatched the brooch from her outstretched hand and turned it over carefully, then stepped behind the counter and picked up his magnifying glass. Finally, he lifted his gaze to her. "It is a magnificent piece. The stone is genuine. Excellent workmanship. Where'd you get this, girl?'' His eyes narrowed.

"It was my grandmother's. She left it to me, and I need to sell it . . . to pay the taxes on my land," she added quickly, "and if you aren't interested in buying it, then I'll find someone who is."

She held out her hand for the brooch, but he drew back. "I didn't say I don't want to buy it. I just asked where you got it."

"And I told you." She continued to hold out her hand.

He looked through the magnifying glass again, then murmured, "Lovely." He put the glass aside and flashed her a bright smile. "Tell you what I'm going to do. You obviously need money badly, or you wouldn't dream of parting with such a sentimental piece. So I'm going to be generous. I'll give you fifty dollars."

Holly snatched the emerald away. "Sir, you can't be serious. Fifty dollars? That . . . that's crazy," she stammered, stunned.

He scowled. "Listen, girlie, there's no money in secondhand jewelry. Especially when folks around here haven't got any money to start with. I'm doing you a favor. Take it or leave it. Don't make no difference to me."

Holly turned on her heel and started for the door,

but he was out from behind the counter in a flash. "A hundred," he said. Names of wealthy Yankees had begun to occur to him. "A hundred. Not a penny more."

Holly pushed on by him. He bolted in front of her. "Now wait a minute. How much do you want? Maybe we should go from there. But I warn you, I can't go but so high. I'll try to be fair."

Holly knew what she had to have but also knew how to bargain. Grandpa had taught her well. "Four hundred," she told him evenly.

Willis Garrington's mouth dropped open. That was the price he'd figured he could probably get by selling the brooch. "That's crazy. I'll give you a hundred."

Holly smiled. The man was no fool. He knew how to bargain too. "Three hundred."

He slammed his fist on the counter. "Two hundred and I swear, girl, not a cent more."

Holly pursed her lips, pretending to give the offer serious thought, then nodded slowly. "Two hundred. I want it right now."

Mumbling that he had to be out of his mind, he disappeared behind the curtains and returned a few moments later with the money. He scowled. "I hope you know you robbed me, girl."

Holly grinned. "No, I didn't. I just didn't give *you* a chance to rob *me*."

It was only with great effort that Holly was able to walk, not run or skip, to the tax collector's office. Entering once again, she smiled and nodded all around. When her turn came, she laid the money on the counter and declared, "I'll have my receipt. This is one piece of land the Yankees won't get."

The astonished clerk stared from the money to her, then leaned forward. "Is it honest money?" he whispered hoarsely.

Holly stiffened but kept smiling. "How I got it is none of your business. Just give me that receipt so I can get out of here."

He took care of the transaction, and Holly watched him. She didn't notice the darting glances he sent to the well-dressed man who had quietly entered the office. She took her receipt and left as soon as she could.

The man stepped forward, and anyone in his way moved aside. Dressed in an expensive maroon coat, gray trousers, and shining black boots, he was about the only wealthy-looking man in town. There was a tight set to his jaw, and his eyes were narrowed, brooding. "That is the young lady you told me about?" he asked the clerk.

The clerk's head bobbed up and down. "Yes sir, Mr. Bonham. Soon as she left, I sent for you, 'cause I knew you'd want to know. I knew you and your daddy were interested in that land, but there wasn't anything I could do. She came in here with the money, and I had to take it," he finished nervously, apologetically.

Roger Bonham touched gloved fingertips to his neatly trimmed mustache. "Of course you did, Hubert. She paid the taxes on the northeast tract?"

"Yeah. Said she inherited it from her grand-daddy."

"Anyone see where she went earlier?" Roger asked of no one in particular.

A man standing near the door spoke up. "She

was going to Garrington's. Only reason I noticed her was 'cause she's dressed so scruffy.''

Roger left the tax office and walked down the street. As he moved along, men stepped out of his path and tipped their hats, ladies smiled. They all believed his smile was a smile of greeting, unaware that he smiled only with smug self-confidence, without any real regard for them. He knew the townspeople of Vicksburg held him in high esteem. Why not? He had planned it that way. Each word, gesture, every act since his arrival had been calculated to win them over. He had succeeded beautifully, as expected.

He opened the door of Garrington's jewelry shop and stepped inside. At the sound of the bell, the owner appeared, grinning broadly at the sight of a prosperous customer.

Roger got right to the point. "A young lady was in here a short while ago and sold you a piece of jewelry. I wish to purchase it.''

Mr. Garrington's smile widened. He slipped back behind the curtains and returned with the brooch. Handing it delicately to Roger Bonham for his scrutiny, he said, "It's a lovely piece. Of course, that young woman robbed me,'' he added with a nervous laugh. "I felt sorry for her. I tell you what I'll do. I'll let you have it for the same price she sold it to me. You'll get a bargain. Four hundred dollars.''

Roger's eyes mirrored contempt. "You fool,'' he said. "You think I got where I am by being stupid? You paid her two hundred dollars and two hundred dollars is what I'll pay you.'' He reached for his wallet.

Mr. Garrington coughed, swallowed, and attempted to maintain control. "Well, sir, that's ridiculous. Begging your pardon, but you can see the brooch is worth a good deal more than that."

"It was you who robbed her," Roger snapped, counting out two hundred dollars and dropping the money on the counter. "I intended to offer you something for your trouble, but you attempted to insult my intelligence, so this is all you're getting."

Roger flippantly gave the brooch a toss, caught it in midair, and put it in his pocket. He turned on his heel and walked out of the store. And now, he thought, for the formidable young woman, Holly Maxwell.

❧ Chapter Three ❧

HOLLY sat on the riverbank, knees hugged tightly against her chest. It was a day of golden sunbeams and enticing, mysterious shadows where the land rose or fell sharply. Weeping willow fronds moved in the warm spring air. A gentle breeze wafted in from the sleepy river beyond. It was a heavenly time in Holly's special, secret world.

She laughed at a turtle lying on a rock at the water's edge, and delighted at the plump catfish swimming teasingly within arm's reach. "I'll get you later," she warned him.

Leaning back against the willow trunk, Holly felt awash with relief all over again, remembering how she had eluded her mother. Not only had she managed to rise early and go into town and take care of all her business, but she had managed to return in time to pack her haversack and escape to the swamps before Claudia returned. Now, this time, this place was hers and hers alone. She intended to hide away for three whole days and contemplate her future without any interference.

There was much planning to be done. It would

not be easy to take her living from the land and the water, but Grandpa had managed and so could she. He had taught her well. There were catfish and rabbits and wild turkeys and deer. She knew the soil where Grandpa had planted his garden was rich, hungry for seeds. She would net crayfish to take into Vicksburg and sell when money was needed. And there was a not-too-distant dream of having her own fishing boat, so the catches could be larger and more profitable.

Life was going to be good once again, she thought with a sleepy sigh. No, there would be no move to Vicksburg for her. Mother and the other spiritless Southerners could cozy up to the Yankees. Holly preferred the tranquillity of her beloved private world. She was free there and she always would be.

Yet she had to come to terms with her fears, too. What lay ahead was as frightening as it was desirable. She would be alone, truly alone, for the first time in her life. Her mother was still beautiful and would have no difficulty finding another husband. Holly had no one.

Suddenly, she sprang to her knees and crawled forward to the water's edge to stare at her reflection. *Am I pretty? Papa always said so, but fathers never think their daughters are plain.*

Her mother had always lamented that Holly didn't make the most of what God gave her. Sometimes, she'd said, women had to work at being pretty.

Holly touched the single braid, which had tumbled forward. Sunlight caught the red highlights of her hair and it glistened. Would she be more attractive if she brushed it to wisp about her face? Or used Mama's curling iron to make ringlets?

Stop being so vain, she told herself. What difference did it make how she looked out there in the wilderness? She settled back against the willow. For now, she wanted only to revel in her first victory of independence—paying the taxes and making the land truly hers for always and always. No one could take it away now, no one. . . .

The sun was sinking when Holly awoke. Rose shadows danced mysteriously in the forest as she got to her feet. There was much to be done before night set in—wood to find for a fire, food to be found. She quickly began to gather dry limbs and twigs, stacked them, then picked up Grandpa's rifle and made her way into the woods.

She had not gone far when a movement in the brush caught her eye. Unafraid, for Grandpa had taught her that fear makes a person weak, she crept forward silently. She stiffened at the sight of a man bending over a trap.

She was shaken with fury. She hated traps. They were so unnecessarily cruel. Like Grandpa, she believed that if animals had to die, they should do so as quickly as possible, with the least amount of suffering. Who, she thought fiercely, would dare set a trap on her land?

She raised the gun and pointed, then stepped out into the open and called in an unwavering voice, "Back off from that trap, mister. Get those hands high or you're dead."

He turned his head ever so slightly. He made no move to obey and his tone reflected no fear.

"There's a fox caught. I'm trying to set him free. Take it easy with that thing."

"You set the damn trap to catch something, didn't you? Well, you caught something. Just back off, and I'll get him out."

He shook his head curtly, and Holly started in surprise. Men weren't supposed to argue with you when you had a gun on them. What was he, a fool? "Hey," she quickly informed him, "maybe you think I don't know how to use this thing, but I do. And I will if you don't back your smart ass away from there right now."

She was quite surprised to hear him laugh. "Now where'd you learn to swear like that? Maybe you need your mouth washed out with lye soap, so you'll learn to talk like a lady."

Holly tensed, finger tightening on the trigger. "You're going to find your mouth shut for eternity, mister, if you keep running it. I'm not telling you again. *Move your ass!*"

He turned back to the trap. "I'm going to set this little fellow free, and then I'll oblige you."

She watched, dumbfounded by his bravery or whatever it was. He sprang the trap, and the fox limped away as quickly as his injury would allow, without stopping to contemplate his brush with death.

The stranger stood up and dusted his faded brown trousers. "No bones broken. Now what's all this about? I don't like someone slipping up behind me with a gun."

Looking at him closely, she felt a strange rush. He had the most unusual eyes she had ever seen, so dark they were almost black, but narrow, as though his lids were partly closed. But he could see her very well anyway. Sleepy eyes, a deep, thoughtful gaze. And the way he was looking at her with those strangely beautiful eyes made her feel very odd indeed.

His face was rugged, but nice. His lips were firm, yet looked soft. His hair was as black as the water at night, damp, clinging to his neck, sideburns tapering in front of his ears. His trousers were tight against firm thighs, and the way his shirt stretched across his chest and arms, he surely had rock-hard muscles. His shoulders were broad and strong, too.

He let her stare at him as long as she wanted to, and then he said, "Put that gun down—unless you plan to use it. If you do plan to use it," he gave her a crooked smile, "make the first shot count, because you won't get a second."

She held the gun steady. "This is my land and you have no business here."

He took a step closer, and she realized that the top of her head came barely to his shoulder. Why did she like the sudden protective feeling that his exuding strength gave her?

He held out his hand. "You don't want to shoot me. You have no reason to. My name's Scott Colter, and I'm just passing through."

"And you swear you didn't set that trap?" she asked, staring at his outstretched fingers.

He shook his head. "Believe me."

She laid the gun aside and shook his hand. "Holly Maxwell. Sorry about the gun, but what was I to think?"

"What are you doing out here in this wilderness?" he asked.

She stared up at him, chiding herself for the feeling of vulnerability overcoming her. "I told you. This is my land. I live here."

"Your land?" he echoed.

She tilted her head defiantly. "This is one piece of land the damn Yankee carpetbaggers didn't get. It's mine. My grandpa left it to me, and I paid the taxes this morning. Nobody can take it away from me."

He continued smiling, which infuriated her. "What are you doing here?" she demanded.

He studied her face. "I was in the war. I wanted some time to myself, to get my thoughts together after all the killing I've seen. I didn't realize I'd get somebody's dander up just being here."

Holly snatched up the gun again. "Are you a goddamn Yankee bastard or did you fight for the South?" He laughed, and she said sharply, "Keep laughing. You're one word from being blown to hell, and that word is 'Yankee.' "

Scott Colter thanked heaven that he had never lost his Texas drawl. "You really do hate Yankees, don't you?" Then, without giving her time to answer, he went on, "It's strange, a pretty young girl so bitter."

"What were you laughing at?"

"Your language," he murmured. "You still need your mouth washed out with soap."

Holly wouldn't let herself be deflected. "Are you a Yankee bastard, I asked you." His eyes narrowed, but he said nothing. "I won't ask you again, mister." She raised the gun.

Moving so quickly she didn't have time to stop him, he grabbed the gun and tossed it aside. Towering over her, he said, "I told you, I don't like guns pointed at me. Now, if it's any of your business, I'm a Southerner. I'm from Texas."

Holly shrugged. "All you had to do was say so."

"Would you have shot me if I weren't a Southerner?" he challenged. "The war is over. Can't we live in peace now?"

Holly laughed. "You sound like my mother. I hate Yankees and I always will. That's why I'm living here, in the swamp, where there aren't any, thank God."

She walked over and picked up the rifle. He made no move to stop her. Without looking at him, she murmured, "I've got to go," and she started back toward her campsite.

"Where are you going?" he called. "Where do you live?"

She didn't turn around. "Never mind. You just go now. Get off my land. I don't like strangers nosing around."

He fell into step beside her in a few long strides. "I never knew a woman who lived in the swamps before. Mind if I come along? I'd like to get to know you better."

"Yes, I do mind," she snapped. "Go away."

"I think I like Yankee women better."

Holly stopped. "What's that supposed to mean?"

There was a mischievous gleam in his dark eyes. "Well, this is your land, but you aren't offering me any hospitality. I haven't eaten since yesterday. I lost my haversack when I tried to cross a lagoon on a log and lost my footing. I don't know these parts as well as Texas, so I haven't been able to find any food.''

Holly smiled. ''Some folks eat foxes if they're hungry enough.''

''Yeah, but he was such a cute little fellow.''

They both laughed, and the tension began to drain away. ''All right,'' she conceded. ''Come along and we'll starve together. I wasted the rest of the daylight on you, and now I don't have anything to eat, either. But I've got firewood and coffee.''

He followed her through the brush, and she motioned for him to sit down while she got a fire going. When she turned toward him a few moments later, he was gone. Fine, she decided, despite a surge of disappointment. Let him go. She didn't need him.

She set the coffeepot to one side of the fire and settled down beneath a tree. This was, she mused, the best time of the evening, when fireflies were beginning to sparkle among the shadows and crickets began their nighttime serenade. The air was cool, and the sky faded from misty purple to charcoal.

The sound of footsteps crashing through the brush brought her out of her reverie. Quickly she reached for her rifle.

''Don't point that thing again,'' Scott Colter yelled before he appeared. He stepped into the clearing a moment later, grinning down at her in the fire's glow.

She gasped as she saw the two dead rabbits. ''Where did you—''

''I'd already made camp up the river a ways. I had to decide whether you were worthy to share my supper before I offered it.''

Holly laughed. It was a good, warm feeling. "So you've decided I'm worthy?"

"As long as you watch your language."

She knew he was serious despite his manner, and although she was the first to admit that she overdid the swearing sometimes, she'd picked it up from Grandpa and it didn't really bother her. But it did bother him. "Okay. I promise to be nice."

He set about skinning and cleaning the rabbits, and she asked, "How long will you be around here?"

"Two or three days. Isn't it my turn to ask a few questions?"

Warily, she nodded. "I suppose."

"To start with," he gave her a brief glance. "Why are you still fighting the war?"

She picked up a stick and began to draw random patterns in the dirt. It was none of his business. Why should she pour out her feelings to a stranger? On the other hand, who else did she have to talk to? Maybe a stranger was just what she needed.

She began to talk, telling him, little by little, everything. When she talked about the devastation of Magnolia Hall, tears began. By the time she told of Grandpa's death, she was crying freely.

Pausing to take a deep breath, she then gave him a long, searching look. "It's over now," she said. "I can't forgive and I can't forget. It's best I stay out here and make a life for myself away from all the reminders."

He was silent. He placed the rabbits on a spit and then came and sat down beside her. "I think," he said finally, "you're doing yourself a grave injustice, hiding like this. You're denying yourself any chance for a normal life. What about getting married, having a family?"

Coldly, she said, "My mother tells me Vicksburg is now filled with Yankee men. You think I'd marry a Yankee?"

He laughed softly but not unkindly. "Who says you have to marry a Yankee? Not all the Southern men were killed in the war, you know."

She gave her long braid a toss. "Who says a woman has to have a man? I don't have to have a husband," she challenged him, cinnamon eyes sparkling in the golden firelight.

He reached out to touch her hair, and she drew back. "No. Don't move," he commanded tersely, deftly unfastening her braid. He ran his fingers through the strands to loosen it, and her hair fell softly around her shoulders.

Holly shivered. Why was she reacting so strangely? Why could this man provoke her with just a touch?

His hand dropped to her shoulder and he gazed down at her warmly, so warmly. "Pretty. But you try not to be. Why?"

Embarrassed, Holly squirmed like a child. "I don't. I . . . mean I'm not," she stammered. "I'm just not interested in things like . . . romance."

He smiled. "Not interested, Holly?" He pressed his mouth to hers, gently at first, and then his kiss became warm, seeking, lips parting as his tongue began to probe.

Holly meant to push him away, to twist her head from side to side and escape his tantalizing lips, but something deeper urged her to cling to him, to answer that fiery kiss. His lips were setting hers on fire, and she felt the flames spreading wildly.

Suddenly, she pulled back, trying to wrench away, but he held her tightly, wrapping his arms around her to hold her against that rock-hard chest. "No, we mustn't! Please!" she gasped.

His eyes searched hers. She looked at him just as boldly, and knew herself lost.

He brushed his lips against hers again and she trembled, afraid. "You don't want me to stop, Holly," he told her sternly. "You want me to make love to you."

She said nothing, and he asked, "Have you ever been with a man?"

She shook her head, and he trailed a gentle fingertip down her cheek. "I thought not. You little hypocrite. You just wanted to be able to say, later, that I forced you. You want everything you know I can give you, but you won't admit it."

His hand slipped to her breast, and she came out of her stupor. Slapping his hand away, she hissed, "No! You're wrong! Now let me go, please. This shouldn't have happened. We shouldn't have . . ."

He released her but continued to gaze deeply into her eyes. "If I've offended you, I'm sorry. You probably need time to grow up." He added, "I've never had to force myself on a woman, and I'll be damned if I'm going to start with a kid."

Nodding toward the fire and the roasting meat, he asked, "Would you like me to just take my portion and go?"

"No. Stay," she said quickly. Then, softly, she added, "I enjoy talking with you. I'm just not interested in . . . other things."

He smiled at her and suddenly the tension was gone again. They sat side by side and ate the succulent food, then sipped hot coffee and talked easily together. Holly told him of her love of the river and the swamps and the woods, and he tried to describe his Texas homeland. They skirted conversation about the war. Night settled in, a thick shroud over everything, and they were consumed by darkness, their faces illuminated only by the soft, flickering flames.

Holly was completely relaxed as she leaned back against the tree and closed her eyes. Scott's voice droned on, fading away as, finally, she succumbed to the sweeping hand of sleep.

Sun was streaming across Holly's face, and she stretched in the warmth. Then it all came rushing back and she sat up, looking around. He was gone.

"Did you miss me?"

He stepped into the clearing, carrying limbs and twigs, which he dropped on the dead ashes of last night's fire.

He smiled in that mysterious way. Was it a genuine smile, or was it arrogance? "Don't worry. Nothing happened. When it does, I want you awake to enjoy it."

She was about to inform him that nothing was going to happen between them, but she kept quiet. He said he'd be grateful if she would show him around, and she saw no harm in that.

They spent the day together, Holly acting as guide. She explained to him that some people referred to that part of the state as "South Mississippi," but to those who lived there, it was the "piney woods." Scott listened to everything, memorizing the landscape. At midday they visited an old fisherman Holly had known all her life, and he treated them to creamy oyster stew and hot, crusty hoecakes.

The afternoon hours were spent trekking the boundaries of Maxwell land—what would soon not be Maxwell land any more.

Holly's bitterness surfaced completely as she talked about Jarvis Bonham, and Scott tried to pacify her. "All of this was yesterday, Holly. Yesterday is gone. Tomorrow may not come, so just enjoy now. Don't let anger spoil the only thing you can be sure of—today."

But Holly's tirade wasn't so easily brushed aside. "Jarvis Bonham is just a small part of what's happening. The whole state is being taken over by Radical Republican carpetbaggers and white trash."

Scott finally led her away from what was left of Magnolia Hall, back to the beauty of the swamps. As the day drew to a close, they found themselves on the banks of a crystal clear inlet.

Scott marveled. "What? No brackish waters? It's hard to believe a place like this exists near the muddy river."

Holly explained that it was fresh water, fed from an underground spring. It would stay clear until it found its way to the river beyond. "This is where I come to swim, because the water is always clean and fresh and cool."

"Then what are we waiting for?"

A stab of fright went through her. She wore no undergarments beneath Grandpa's old shirt and trousers.

Oblivious to her discomfort, ignoring her silence, Scott stripped off his shirt. Holly couldn't stop looking at his broad chest, the dark mat of hair curling downward.

He was moving to unfasten his trousers, and she tried to protest but all she could manage was a soft, strangling sound deep in her throat.

Scott didn't turn around to face her, but he knew what she was thinking. "Swim with me, Holly," he said gently. It was neither a request nor a command, but a declaration.

The water glistened, ripples dancing in the raspberry sheen of the distant sunset.

He held out his hand to her. "It's up to you, Holly. This can be one of the todays I told you about—the only times that matter."

She wanted to. Yes, she wanted to reach out and take his hand and let him lead her to whatever glory awaited them. But wasn't it wrong? Wouldn't giving in make her an immoral trollop? The realization gave birth to a wave of anger. A man could seek his pleasure without condemnation. Why should it be different for a woman?

He was looking at her beneath lowered lids in that mysterious way she found so irresistible. "It has to be your decision, Holly." His voice was a husky whisper. "With no regrets later. I promise you nothing except pleasure."

With the trust of a child taking its first step, Holly shyly held out a trembling hand. He clasped it tightly, drawing her against him. His warm lips kissed her eyelids, moving down her cheeks to claim her mouth.

Her breath came in quick gasps and she threw her

arms around him, pulling him closer. With deft fingers he unfastened the buttons of her shirt and pulled it open. Her breasts fell free, and he lowered his face to kiss each breast in turn. They quickly grew taut beneath his flicking tongue.

He peeled her shirt from her trembling body and tossed it aside, then worked at the rope tie of her trousers until they fell. Lifting her in his arms, he carried her to the water's edge and laid her down. The water moved languidly up their bodies, lapping at them sensuously.

"Today," Holly whispered, trancelike, as her lips moved across his face. "Today is all that matters."

He took his time, igniting every fire in her. His fingers danced where no man had ever touched before, caressing between her thighs to create a frenzy of longing within the velvet recesses of her most intimate self. Needles of pleasure pierced into her belly and she whimpered and writhed.

Suddenly, she felt a new sensation building, as though she were about to explode. Her teeth sank into his broad shoulder. He withdrew his probing fingers and she cried, "No, no, don't stop, please . . ."

"Stop?" he smiled down at her. "Oh, my darling, I have only just begun."

He carried her up to the moss-covered bank. The sun was low, casting shadows of silver and rose.

He lay hovering over her and gently drove into her, slowing as she stiffened with pain. Quickly, her longing for fulfillment took over again and she clung to him, nails digging into his hard back. She wanted him to consume her. Nothing else mattered.

She reveled in this first sweet taste of passion. There was no other world but this, no other time but now. . . .

Much later, when Scott lay beside her, his arm across her possessively as he slept, Holly wondered at the sadness of it. Today would end, wouldn't it? Yet how could any woman forget such glory?

🎋 Chapter Four 🎋

DAWN spread a misty, golden haze across the waters of the cover. The feathery pink blossoms of a mimosa tree bobbed in the gentle morning breeze. Crickets sang their last choruses, while birds began their day songs.

A velvet-nosed deer crept from the green shadows of the forest to drink at the water's edge. Spying the man and woman asleep on the mossy bank, he stared for an instant, then bolted back to safety.

Hearing his crashing sounds, Holly awoke. She stared down at Scott, so peaceful beside her. Staring at the lean, hard lines of his perfect body, she thrilled at the memory of their night. What did she feel for this fiercely enticing stranger? Love? The desire to become his wife, bear his children? No, she told herself firmly. He was returning to his world, and she must remain in hers.

As though the thundering turmoil within her could be heard, Scott Colter awoke and smiled up at her lazily. "I like to wake up next to a woman and see her looking happy," he murmured.

Holly stiffened. He sounded so pleased with him-

41

self, and the idea that his loving might have been a performance chilled her.

She moved away from him, glad she had pulled on Grandpa's shirt during the night. Slipping quickly into her trousers, she tied the rope belt. He watched her. "What's wrong, Holly?" There was an edge to his voice. "You don't have any regrets, do you?"

"Last night was last night." Her voice was sharper than she'd meant it to be. Then, more softly, she said, "This is the tomorrow we thought might not come, Scott. It did. Now life has to go on. You'll be returning to Texas, and I've got my life here."

He did not, she noticed, seem to mind his nakedness, for he made no move to reach for his clothes.

"You really were a virgin."

She stared at him. "What did you expect?"

He rolled over on his side. "All of this has been awfully strange. I meet a pretty woodland sprite, spend one of the nicest days I've had in four years, then one of the most passionate nights. For someone who's never been with a man, you cast aside inhibitions very easily."

"You make me sound like a trollop!" Hot tears stung her eyes. "Besides," she added hotly, "you're obviously *very* experienced. You just made me . . . weak, that's all." Her voice trailed off, and she turned away, washed with embarrassment.

He sprang up with the litheness of a panther. He gripped her shoulders and spun her around to face his burning gaze. "Don't do this to us, Holly. Don't make me sound like a seducer, and don't let childhood teachings mar our memories. It doesn't have to end, you know.''

She gave her long, tangled hair a toss. "Oh, sure. We can do it again today, can't we? Maybe tonight, too. We can do it till you have to leave for Texas. And then what?''

He raised an eyebrow, hands falling from her shoulders. "I can't offer you anything else, sprite. Not now. Maybe one day—''

Cinnamon eyes flashed. "Don't call me pet names, Scott, I'm not a child. And did you think I was hinting for you to make a decent woman of me? I don't want to marry you or any other man.''

He chuckled. "You're so damned independent. No, I wasn't insinuating that you were after a husband. All I'm saying is that I'd like to get to know you better. If you'll let me.''

"All right. I'm sorry. I shouldn't be so defensive," she apologized. "But you *are* going to Texas and it *does* have to end.''

His jaw tensed and a shadow fell across his face. "I may stay in Vicksburg for a while.''

She blinked. "Vicksburg? With the damn Yankee soldiers and carpetbaggers? Well, you won't see much of me then, sir, I promise you that. I don't plan to go near that place if I can help it. My mother can cozy up to those bastards, but I can't.''

He reached out and gave her a shake. "Damn it, Holly, do you have to hate every Yankee? You're going to let bitterness ruin your life. You can't keep on hating. Sooner or later hate will destroy you.''

She knocked his hands away. "Then so be it. I'd rather be dead than compromise my beliefs!''

He was silent for a moment. Then, with a resigned sigh, he told her, "Very well, Holly. There was something I wanted to try to explain to you, but now isn't the time."

"Can we just enjoy the morning?" she challenged, exasperated.

Slowly, fighting something inside himself, he nodded. "I'll have to leave this afternoon, but the morning is ours."

After they bathed in the cool water, they made their way down to the rolling Mississippi River. Another fisherman Holly knew, a friend of Grandpa's, obliged them with fried catfish cakes and cold potato soup for lunch. They washed the tasty fare down with cups of sweet strawberry cider. By then, she and Scott were easy with each other, enjoying the wonders of the wilderness at its most serene.

Scott asked to visit her grandfather's shack, and Holly was puzzled but led the way. After he had inspected the one-room place, he asked bluntly, "How can you plan to live here after growing up in the luxury of Magnolia Hall? Can you get used to this?"

She shrugged. "Actually, I spent more time here than I did at home. I loved it here, and I never minded the lack of comforts because I was with Grandpa."

He nodded thoughtfully. "But I don't think this is what you really want, Holly."

The tension returned.

"I think I know what I want better than you, Scott, and I don't want to discuss it."

"Maybe you need to discuss it with yourself," he said. "It isn't this cabin, or a simple life in the wilds that you want. You want escape, because you aren't woman enough to face life. So you retreat to the woods and hide out like a little girl. You may have the body of a woman, and the passion, but you're still just a little girl. Maybe you always will be.''

Lips trembling, she cried, ''I don't give a damn what you think, Scott Colter. And don't concern yourself with me. You live your life and I'll live mine, thank you.''

Gazing down at her tenderly, he said, ''I suppose you're right. I told you this morning there was something I wanted to explain to you, but I see now it wouldn't make any difference.''

Suddenly, so there was no time for her to resist, he grabbed her and kissed her, deeply. And just as abruptly, he released her and walked away, disappearing into the woods.

Damn him to hell! Who the hell did he think he was, to *seduce* her, preach to her, and then just walk away?

Her scream reverberated through the still swamps. ''I hate you, Scott Colter. You're no better than a goddamn Yankee!''

Later, forcing Scott out of her mind, she walked around the cottage, taking inventory of her new world. Grandpa had made the furniture. There were two beds, one fitted neatly on top of the other, each frame nailed to tall wooden posts. Grandpa had always slept in the lower, because she loved the adventure of scampering up to the high bed.

A fireplace made of river stones was set in one wall, large enough for a big iron pot to cook tasty catfish stews.

Grandpa's old, worn rocking chair sat to one

side, and Holly placed a loving hand on the sampler across the back. *God Bless Our Home* had been embroidered so long ago by her grandmother, and the stitching and colors were as faded as Holly's memory of the woman who had died when Holly was five.

The center of the thin plank floor was dominated by a long wooden table, benches along both sides. Here she had sat, captivated, by the hour, listening to Grandpa's stories. He'd made everything so alive, so real.

She acknowledged silently that there was little comfort here except for memories.

She walked slowly to the door and looked at the inlet beyond. "A stone's throw from the water," Grandpa had often declared. "I never want to be farther from the water than that."

She stepped outside onto the porch and saw Grandpa's old cane fishing poles propped neatly against the log wall of the cabin. Buckets, now empty and rusting, were for minnows and worms.

She sat down on one of the three stone porch steps and watched the sunset, determined not to think, not to let anything intrude on the quiet.

The stillness was broken a few minutes later by the sound of horses' hooves and wagon wheels. She jumped up and ran around the cabin to the front. Her mother was alighting from a smart carriage. Warily, Holly asked, "Where did you get that?"

Claudia's face flushed only slightly as she brushed at the skirts of her new blue taffeta day dress. It was very becoming, with a high collar edged in delicately tatted lace, tiny embroidered pink satin rosebuds dotting the bodice. The wide, white-ribboned waist was just right for Claudia.

Lifting her chin, she met Holly's challenging gaze with her own hard stare. "I will ask the questions. I will start by asking where have you been for the past two days. I've been frantic with worry." She paused for an angry breath. "Where did you get the money to pay the taxes on this worthless piece of land? The story is all over Vicksburg. People are wondering where a young girl got that kind of money."

Holly checked her temper. The showdown was bound to come sooner or later. "I sold Grandma's brooch."

Claudia clutched her throat. "Dear heavenly Father, tell me you didn't!"

"I did. I paid the taxes, and this place is mine. No one is going to take it from me, including your carpetbagger friend, Jarvis Bonham."

Claudia shook her head from side to side, the ribbons on her straw bonnet whipping around her face. "How could you? The brooch was yours. There were other things you could have used the money for. And you can't stay here anyway. I won't allow it. It's not safe or proper for a young girl to live alone."

Her mother moved toward her, but Holly stood her ground. "I mean you no disrespect, Mother, but my life is my own to live as I choose, and I choose to live here. I made Grandpa a promise on his deathbed. I promised I'd never lose his land and I've kept that promise."

Claudia nodded. "Yes, yes, darling, I know. But you've *kept* your promise by paying the taxes. The land is yours. That doesn't mean you have to *live* on it." She glanced around. "Move into Vicksburg with me. Abby's house is large. You can have a social life again, friends, young men to court you. The people of Vicksburg are sick of war and anxious to start living normally again. You'll be happy there. Don't be stubborn, Holly. There's no life for you here."

Holly shook her head defiantly. "There's nothing for me in Vicksburg. For the time being, everything I want is here. One day, maybe I'll feel differently, but I need time, Mother. Please understand."

Claudia sighed, knowing full well that her daughter had inherited her grandfather's and her father's stubbornness. When her mind was set, there was no changing it. "I suppose there's nothing to do but let you see for yourself how miserable you're going to be. Sooner or later, you'll come to your senses. In the meantime, I'll pray nothing terrible happens while you're here."

Holly looked beyond her mother at the carriage and asked again, "Where did you get it?"

A mysterious little smile touched Claudia's lips. "Jarvis was nice enough to lend it to me."

Holly thought for a moment, then surprised Claudia by saying, "If he's a friend of yours, and he's being nice to you, then I won't be rude about it."

"He wants to be your friend, too," Claudia said hopefully, relief buoying her hopes.

"Don't rush me into anything, Mother."

Cautious again, Claudia ventured, "I'll be honest with you, dear." She touched Holly's shoulder in a fond gesture. "I want to show you off. I want you at

Jarvis's party. You're so pretty, and if we do something with that dreadful hair, you'll be beautiful. We need to have your dress fitted, and—oh, Holly!'' She shook her head. ''You aren't even listening to me, are you?''

''Daydreaming,'' Holly said quickly, guiltily. Her mother would surely have a spell if she knew what her daughter was thinking about. Her daughter . . . with a man? Lying naked and moaning with joy?

Quickly, Holly said, ''If you really want me to go to Mr. Bonham's party, I will.''

Claudia hugged her. ''You've made me so happy, Holly. I don't want us to quarrel. I love you.''

Holly nodded. ''I love you too, Mother. We'll try to get along. I promise I'll try my best to behave and make you proud of me.'' Inside, Holly felt her demons rumbling, and she knew it would take every bit of self-control to behave. For her mother's sake, she had to try.

When they reached the outskirts of Vicksburg, Holly felt the familiar sadness. This was where her father had died. How happy he'd been, she remembered bitterly, to be sent here. His eyes had shone when he explained how important was the defense of Vicksburg. The Yankees, he had declared, would want it desperately.

He had been right.

Finally, her mother declared happily, ''That's Abby's house.''

Holly reined the horses in and looked up at the large white frame house set back from the tree-lined street. There was a wide, sweeping porch with narrow, ornate posts. The lawn was neatly kept, dotted here and there with crepe myrtles trimmed to shrubs. There were a few dogwood trees and several magnolias.

A plump woman wearing a dress of pale blue muslin was sweeping the brick steps, and as she saw them she smiled and waved. Hurrying down the sidewalk, she called out gaily, "Claudia! You found Holly and brought her back with you. Oh, I'm so glad."

She reached the carriage as the two women alighted, and she embraced first Claudia, then Holly. "I'm Abby Pearson, and you don't know how pleased I am that you're going to be staying with us. I've got lots of room, and it'll be like having another daughter. Your mother already seems like a sister."

Holly smiled and responded politely, "It's nice to meet you, Mrs. Pearson." Then she decided to get things straight from the start and added, "But I'll only be here for a couple of nights. I promised Mother I'd go to the party with her. After that, I've got to go home. I've a lot to do there."

Claudia and Abby exchanged glances, Abby puzzled and Claudia weary.

They turned toward the house, but just then a man's voice called to Claudia. They waited as he approached.

He was not very tall, and of medium build. He was very well dressed. A carpetbagger, Holly decided. He directed a smile at her, which she acknowledged with a polite, cold nod. With dark, waving hair and a thin mustache, he was not unattractive, but there was something about his eyes that Holly found distinctly unappealing. "Holly," her mother was saying, "I'd like you to meet Jarvis's son, Roger."

Roger Bonham bowed and murmured, "You are almost as beautiful as your mother, Holly."

Claudia laughed. "And you are almost as charming as your father, Roger." Then she hastened to add, "I was going to send the carriage over. You didn't have to make a trip to get it."

He waved away her apology. "I thought you might be tired, and I wanted to save you the trouble."

Claudia clasped his hand. "You're so kind to me, Roger, and so is your father. I hope you both know how much I appreciate your friendship."

"We do," he assured her. To Holly, he said, "Will you be at Father's party tomorrow night? I would consider it an honor if you would save me a dance."

Before she could reply, Claudia interjected, "Of course she will, but"—she winked teasingly— "aren't you afraid Lisa Lou will be jealous?"

He stiffened slightly, his eyes even colder as he remarked that he could surely not be expected to refrain from mingling with guests at his father's party.

Claudia laughed good-naturedly. "Well, I've known Lisa Lou since she was a baby. She's always been spoiled and had her own way. I can't imagine her taking your flirting with other girls gracefully, Roger, but that's your business. Holly would love to dance with you."

Holly did not speak, did not smile. She had no intention of dancing with Roger Bonham or anybody else. She would go to the party and be polite, but that was all. Her mother would have to realize sooner or later how useless it was to push men at her.

Roger bade them good-bye and hurried to the carriage. Hoisting himself up onto the seat, he watched as Holly went into the house. Despite her baggy, worn clothes, he could tell that she had a lovely body. Young, innocent, probably naive . . . he would have no trouble getting what he wanted, her land, and that delectable body as well.

He popped the reins to start the horse moving, and he frowned. The girl was stubborn. He had seen that in her determination to hang on to her little parcel of land. He might not have an easy time with her, but it was going to be a challenge he'd enjoy.

❧ Chapter Five ❧

AS she bathed and washed her hair, doing every-thing desultorily because she wasn't looking forward to any of this, Holly's memory tormented her with scenes from parties before the war, when her life was charmed and everyone she loved lived within her charmed circle . . . her mother, faintly silly at times but kind and beautiful; her strong, wonderful father who seemed to know everything; and her beloved Grandpa, who taught her all the things her parents simply weren't interested in, things about the swamps and the woods, about hunt-ing and respect for the myriad wildlife abounding in Mississippi.

Holly hadn't been badgered into parties then, no indeed, there'd been no need. She'd loved being fitted for dresses and, when she turned fifteen, real grown-up gowns. While her appearance didn't mat-ter to her at other times, she frankly cared to be pretty for parties and she allowed Claudia to fuss over her.

Once she'd gone to a birthday party for her friend Anna Spencer, who was turning fifteen, and been astounded to encounter a boy who wanted to kiss her. John Williams, also fifteen, had been solemn about it, courting her hurriedly under a huge maple tree where the refreshments were laid out. She'd been unable to match his serious mood, assuming he was joking. She would always remember the hurt look on John's face when he realized she thought he wasn't serious.

John was the second boy from the Vicksburg area to die in the war, shot off his horse in a battle the Confederate soldiers won, decisively, that same afternoon.

Holly wondered whether any girl had kissed him good-bye when he marched off to war. Then she shoved the memories away and finished rinsing her hair. *I'm doing this for Mother. I have to attend this party for her sake. . . .*

A couple of hours later, Abby stepped back from the dressing table, smiling at Holly's image in the mirror. "You're beautiful, child, a sight to behold. Your mother was so right when she said you'd turn the head of every man at that party."

Holly gazed at herself in the mirror. The young woman staring back at her was anything but plain. She was a beauty.

What would Scott Colter think if he could see her now? Could he walk away so easily now? That ragamuffin of the swampland hadn't resembled this other self.

It was best, she told herself firmly, to forget Scott Colter, best to realize he wasn't for her. His kind didn't really care about anybody.

Abby touched her bare shoulder. "Are you all right? You're shivering. I'd better give you my lace shawl."

"No thank you," Holly said quickly. "I'm fine. I just want the evening to begin and end so I can go home."

"Holly, I want you to think of this as your home. Nothing would make me happier than having you stay here with your mother and me."

Holly smiled, appreciating Abby's generosity. There was no reason to be unkind to this nice woman.

Abby had styled Holly's hair, pulling the long tresses up to her crown. Ringlets of curls cascaded from a garland of fresh gardenia blossoms. Her dress was white lace over emerald satin. It had a dipping bodice, but a modest one. Holly liked the small puffed sleeves that dropped to her elbows. The skirt was not as bouffant as skirts had been before the war because no one wore hoops now. Ladies looked better without hoops, Holly decided as she looked at her reflection.

She was touching her neck with the sweet lilac perfume Abby had given her when Claudia breezed into the room, her eyes sparkling with excitement. She was delighted with Holly's appearance, and she whirled for them several times to show off her own gown of tangerine satin, the neckline most provocative.

Holly gave her mother many compliments, stiffening a little as she endured her mother's instructions for the evening. "Keep your political views to yourself. It isn't ladylike to expound. Be nice to everyone, including Yankees. The war is over, everyone believes that. And don't, for heaven's sake, talk about your plans for living in the swamps! Smile, dear, and be as lovely as you are.

"And remember," she went on solemnly, "it's an honor for us to be invited to Jarvis's party. There will be a lot of Union officers there. I want you to be civil to them."

Holly nodded, all the while praying silently, Please, just let the hours pass quickly. . . .

Jarvis Bonham sent a carriage and driver for them, and Claudia and Holly left; Abby standing on her porch waving and calling good wishes. Holly asked why she had not been invited, and her mother explained that Abby had, but declined. "Her husband died less than a year ago, so she doesn't want to be seen at such a grand party. Not yet."

Claudia chattered constantly, nervously, during the ride. Jarvis, she explained, hated having to host his party in the hotel ballroom, but until he had his own home, there was no choice. The hotel was old and run down, not the kind of place Jarvis was accustomed to. He had traveled, Claudia said, all over Europe. And he'd found exquisite pieces of furniture in Europe and bought them in preparation for the time when he would build a mansion. He had a shipping business, a factory in Illinois, and Claudia wasn't even sure what–all else.

Holly asked whether Mr. Bonham had completed the transaction for the purchase of Magnolia Hall, and her mother fidgeted, mumbled that he had, then quickly changed the subject. "He's had chefs busy for days preparing all the food for tonight! Goodness, I'm going to be so fat! And there's an orchestra, all the way from Boston. Maybe I can dance all the food away." She giggled nervously, eyes pleading with her daughter not to say anything further about Magnolia Hall, not to be hurtful. *Please, Holly, I am doing what I must.*

Holly remarked, ''He went to a lot of trouble for this party. He must want to show off his wealth.''

Claudia was quick to defend Jarvis. ''No, he doesn't. Jarvis isn't like that. And this isn't just an ordinary party. I told you, he's giving this party to welcome the new commander of the troops.'' Holly sniffed, and her mother watched her eyes darken and hurried on. ''The new commander is a hero. Jarvis wanted to give him the respect he's earned.''

''Hero?'' Holly laughed, incredulous. ''Hero to whom? Did he collect more Southern scalps than the average Yankee?''

Claudia would not apologize. ''No more! You are going to put your personal feelings aside and behave as a lady should. Do you understand me, Holly?'' She turned away and they rode the rest of the way in silence.

When they arrived at the hotel, a doorman helped them alight. They were barely inside the lobby when a man rushed toward them, all smiles as he embraced Claudia and kissed both cheeks. Then he stood back to look at Holly. ''You are every bit as lovely as your mother said you were, my dear.'' He bowed and kissed the hand she coolly extended.

Claudia flushed, terribly pleased with her daughter as she introduced Holly to Jarvis Bonham.

Holly's gaze raked him, scrutinizing closely, suspicious. He wore an expensive maroon velvet coat with white satin lapels and a dark red cravat. His trousers were black, and she saw the tips of expensive, shiny leather boots. He was, she decided grudgingly, not displeasing to look at. His dark hair was flecked with silver, and his narrow mustache was neatly trimmed. She noted, however, that while his eyes were blue and twinkled amiably, there was the glimmer of shrewdness there.

He led them inside to where he had managed to turn the plain ballroom into a world of enchantment. Bunting of silver and blue overshadowed the drab wallpaper. Hundreds of candles flickered in delicate crystal globes. Large nets, filled with fragrant gardenias, roses, and lilacs, hung from the ceiling. Their scent filled the room.

The orchestra was playing soft music from a flower-bedecked stand in the corner. The musicians wore red satin coats and white trousers.

"You must have some punch," Jarvis was saying as he walked between Holly and Claudia. Gently he took their arms in his, linking the three of them. "Champagne imported from the best region in France, where the grapes are the sweetest. And fresh strawberries, sweet and cold."

Holly took the crystal cup from him. Taking a sip, she told him politely how delicious it was. There were platters of fried chicken smothered in pineapple; sliced ham basted in a honey and brown sugar glaze; colorful salads; fancy pastries adorned with candy flowers. There were even silver dishes filled with delectable chocolates, which Jarvis had imported all the way from Switzerland.

"Perhaps one day you'll go there with me," he said amiably to Holly.

Had she heard him correctly? "You are inviting me to go to Switzerland with you?"

He nodded, pleased with himself. "You and your mother. I have a chalet near Zurich. Such a beautiful country. The snows make the mountains look like giant clouds. And in the summer, the wildflowers are glorious.'' She had no idea what to say. ''I have a house in Jamaica, also, near Ocho Rios,'' he went on. ''The house isn't all that luxurious, but the view of the bay is breathtaking. I own a large banana plantation there.''

''Jamaica?'' Claudia interjected brightly. ''Oh, I've always wanted to go there. I've heard the water is like glass.''

Jarvis gave her his full attention. ''When the sun is high, the water looks like blue silk from horizon to horizon. It's always warm there, too. I'm sure you'd love it.''

Claudia smiled demurely and fluttered her eyelashes. ''You plan to export bananas?'' she pressed him, hanging on his every word, every nod.

''That isn't the only promising crop, either. I expect to get involved in coffee, sugarcane, and coconuts, as well.''

Claudia laughed. ''Well, when you decide to visit Jamaica again, Holly and I would love to be invited.''

Holly could restrain herself no longer. ''Mother!''

Claudia giggled. ''You didn't inherit my adventurous spirit, I guess.''

''Come along.'' Jarvis escorted them toward the other guests. ''I want to speak to everyone and introduce you to anyone you don't already know.''

It was mostly the renewal of old acquaintances. Most of the guests were people who had attended lavish balls at Magnolia Hall before the war. Encountering them at a social event hosted by a Yan-

kee was ironic and sad, and she found herself becoming incensed again and again. She told herself
sternly that it would all be over in a few more hours,
and she could leave Vicksburg.

She was well aware of the admiring glances she
received from the many young Union officers, but
she did nothing to encourage any of them. Main-
taining a cool demeanor, she managed to maneuver
away from them without appearing rude.

She was standing alone to the side, having es-
caped her mother and Jarvis, when Roger Bonham
suddenly appeared. He did, she acknowledged,
look quite handsome in his white suit.

He bowed, kissed her hand, and said truthfully,
"I've been looking for you. Will you honor me with
a dance?"

Holly shook her head. "I believe you brought
someone with you, and I doubt she would like me
taking any of your time."

He laughed and leaned over to whisper, "May I
be honest with you, Holly?"

"Of course," she said.

"It wasn't my idea to escort her. Her father asked
me."

Holly shrugged. "Well, she considers herself
yours for the evening." She couldn't resist adding,
"It wasn't *my* idea to come this evening at all. My
mother asked *me*."

Roger roared with laughter and she laughed along
with him. "You are a delight, Holly. I would like so
much to get to know you better. May I call on you?
Please?"

Holly was about to tell him no when Lisa Lou
Pollock sailed into view. Her bright blue silk gown

set off her golden hair, which hung about her face in ringlets. There was an angry fire in her eyes. "So this is where you are being detained, Roger. Did you forget that you are my escort?"

She whirled on Holly. "My dear, when one comes alone to a party, she should be dignified enough not to throw herself at other girls' escorts."

A spoiled girl, used to having her own way, Lisa Lou never cared who she hurt. The urge to angrily respond was strong, but Holly held herself in check. "Excuse me. I'll leave you two to enjoy yourselves," she said, knowing Roger would understand the gentle irony.

Roger protested quickly, "No, don't go. I'd like to dance with you."

Lisa Lou stomped a foot in exasperation. "Roger Bonham, how dare you humiliate me this way? How dare you ask this"—her eyes flicked over Holly contemptuously—"*swamp rat,* to dance!"

Holly stood her ground and eyed Lisa Lou for a moment. Enough was enough. Then she turned and walked away, leaving the two of them to argue without her.

Jarvis found her moments later. He had in tow an anxiously smiling young man wearing the full-dress uniform of a Union officer. Tall, slender, with dark blond hair and happy blue eyes, he might have been attractive had he been dressed in Confederate gray. A single row of brass buttons ran down the front of his coat. Gold epaulets adorned his broad shoulders. His collar was high, and his wide shiny belt was trimmed with red cording. A red-fringed sash hung at his waist beneath an ornate scabbard and gold sword. The trousers were a shade of blue lighter than the coat. He looked handsome, professional—and Northern.

When Jarvis introduced her to Captain Neil Davis, the officer held out a white-gloved hand, clasping hers and bestowing the obligatory kiss on her fingertips.

With unsuppressed enthusiasm, he admitted, "Like every man here, I'm captivated by your beauty. I insisted Mr. Bonham introduce us. You'd make me very happy if you would honor me with a dance."

"Captain Davis has been in charge, pending the arrival of the new commander," Jarvis explained. "I must say, he has been quite effective."

"And most anxious to relinquish command," Captain Davis promptly informed him. Then he addressed Holly again, his eyes pleading. "If you refuse me, I will hound you all evening. You won't be able to get rid of me."

Holly laughed. "Very well, Captain Davis, but if I step on your toes, remember that you forced me into dancing with you."

He rolled his eyes in mock surprise. "I don't believe it. The goddess has consented to dance with me, though she turned down every other man. I am truly blessed tonight."

Enjoying his foolishness, Holly was led onto the dance floor. They began to waltz, and immediately he began to talk. "Were you born in Mississippi?"

She nodded, aware of the envious stares of the other young women. "And you, sir?"

"Pennsylvania."

He went on, "I must admit I came to this assignment with trepidation. Being part of the Reconstruction Army makes me uneasy. I feel as though I'm surrounded by the enemy."

"You are," Holly said flatly.

So, she thought, not all of her neighbors were welcoming the Yankees with open arms. "A defeated people don't welcome the presence of the conquerors," he informed her. "The war's over. We're one nation now, and everyone has to work together to rebuild. We must put resentments aside. Don't you agree?"

Why did we have to start a conversation like this one? "No," she said, "I don't. I'll never see that war as anything but a war of Northern aggression. I'll always be bitter."

He gave a low whistle. "The lady has spirit. I like that. You have a right to your opinion." A moment later, he asked, "May I call you by your first name? I'd like to be your friend. You'll see that not all of us Union soldiers are monsters."

Smiling, Holly said, "Showing me that would take more time than either of us has, Captain Davis. Yes, you may call me Holly."

"And you call me Neil. But," he said with a frown, "what's this about time? Don't tell me you're leaving Vicksburg."

He was so easy to be with that Holly found herself telling him her plans.

Frankly amazed, he exclaimed, "That's admirable. I'm afraid I've suffered under the delusion that Southern women are raised to be delicate fluff, and here you are talking of farming, starting your own small fishing fleet. I'm impressed. You're quite a woman, Holly. Perhaps you'd allow me to call on you. I'm fascinated with the river and the land around it. Is it far from here?''

"An hour by carriage. Less on horseback, if you know the shortcuts through the woods.''

"You'll allow me to call on you?" he persisted.

Attempting to make her voice gentle, so as not to hurt him, she began, "I really see no purpose—''

"I honestly just want you to show me around,'' he interrupted. "I don't have any ulterior motives.'' He winked mischievously. "At least, not right now. Can you refuse to be hospitable to a lonely soldier far from home?''

"Perhaps when I'm more settled,'' Holly hedged. "I've got a lot to do. I have no free time just yet.''

"All right then, I'll make a pest out of myself. I'll keep after you, I promise.''

He led her from the dance floor and offered, "I'll get some champagne. You wait right here for me. I don't intend to let you out of my sight. I can see there's not a minute to lose if I'm to convince you I'm irresistible.''

He disappeared in the crowd. Yankee or not, he was enjoyable company, a very nice man. She liked his sense of humor. She had probably smiled more in the past five minutes than in the past year.

Roger found her. "I really hated that scene, Holly. The young lady is . . . difficult. Please tell me you aren't angry with me.''

Holly shook her head. "I've no reason to be upset with you, Roger, and you can't tell me anything about Lisa Lou's disposition that I don't already know. Don't worry about it.''

Captain Davis returned, and the two men regarded each other warily until, after a moment had passed uncomfortably, Roger gave him a curt nod, bowed to Holly, and left.

"Can't leave you alone for a minute, can I?" Neil teased as he handed her a cup of champagne. "I better take you into my protective custody. I'll start by escorting you home when the party is over."

Holly stared at him. "I really don't know about that."

"By the time the evening is over, you'll be so smitten by me that you won't be able to refuse." He glanced around. "I wonder where our new commander is. Probably waiting to make a grand entrance."

Holly couldn't resist a barb. "I really don't care if he doesn't come at all. I hear he's quite a war hero, and I don't think I'll be impressed by the heroics of a Union officer," she said dryly.

Neil could not hold back a sudden wave of defensiveness. "He may have been fighting with what you consider the wrong side, Holly, but he won the respect of both Union *and* Confederate commands. His bravery is legendary. General Lee was heard to say he wished he'd fought on the Confederate side."

"I don't wish to be rude," Holly sighed, "but do we have to keep discussing the war? It's not a good idea."

Neil agreed. The uniform he wore was already a major barrier between them, and dwelling on the subject added bricks to that barrier. "The champagne is delicious, isn't it?" he asked. "Mr. Bonham is a man of taste. Being a simple farm boy from

Pennsylvania, I don't know the first thing about champagnes and wines.''

Holly was watching her mother dancing with Jarvis. "Yes, I agree he has good taste.''

Neil followed her gaze. "I've only been here a few weeks, but it's obvious he's taken a fancy to your mother. She's a lucky woman. He's very wealthy.''

"He got his money bleeding Southerners,'' she declared flatly. "He's a carpetbagger.''

His voice took on an edge for the first time. "That isn't fair, and I'd be doing you an injustice to allow it to pass. He's a businessman, with many interests that he had *before* the war. He came to Vicksburg to help the rebuilding here. He's provided scores of jobs already.''

Holly wouldn't argue and wouldn't give in, so she remained silent. He got the idea.

Suddenly a murmur went through the ballroom, and all heads turned toward the entrance. A crowd gathered there, and Holly saw Jarvis pushing through the throng, pulling Claudia along with him.

"That can only be our new commander.'' Neil extended his arm. "Come along. I'd like you to meet him.''

Holly resisted, but Neil chided, "Now don't be stubborn. He's the guest of honor.'' He tucked her hand in the crook of his arm, pressed it tightly against his side, and guided her through the throng.

"Holly, come meet our guest of honor,'' Jarvis called.

Neil drew her through the crowd and she kept her gaze on his face until she heard Jarvis say, "I'm pleased to present the new commander of the United States Army in Vicksburg.''

She turned from Neil to Jarvis, and then to the stranger.

Dear God, it couldn't be.

She was gazing up into dark eyes mysteriously framed by sleepy lids and thick, sweeping lashes. A powerful hand caressed her trembling fingers. The voice that penetrated the fog surrounding her was confident, husky, and warm.

''Colonel Scott Colter, at your service, Miss Maxwell.''

✤ Chapter Six ✤

A WEEK had passed, but hot waves of humiliation still shot through her whenever she
thought of that horrible evening. She tried to blank
it out, but the memories came at night, to keep her
from sleeping, and all during the day, too. How
could he have made such a fool of her? To let her
believe he'd fought for the South! Damn him, she
whispered to herself a hundred, no, a thousand
times a day.

At least, she recalled proudly, she'd kept her
aplomb that evening. Scott had bowed to her and
kissed her hand, and she managed to compose a stiff
courteous manner in time to acknowledge his compliments. Anyone watching would have thought she
was merely a resentful Southerner forced to endure
a Yankee. She could barely remember the pleasant-
ries exchanged among Scott, her mother, Jarvis,
and Neil.

Somehow, she had gotten through the agony and
stayed at the party a respectable length of time before telling Neil she had a headache and wanted to
leave, and, with a vague promise that he might visit
her soon, she bade him good night.

After a sleepless night, she wrote a note to her mother, telling her she was going home. Then she had gone to the bank, where a friend of her father's arranged a small loan. She bought a horse, a buckboard wagon, a few supplies, and went back to the shack in the swamps.

Here, protected by the tranquil waterways and woodlands, she vowed to make her future. She wouldn't look back. She had made a mistake, but there was no need to be ashamed. She would go on, stronger now, never allowing herself to be weak again.

She sat on the porch, working as fast as she could in the sweltering summer heat, repairing Grandpa's old nets. Last night's crayfish catch had been good. She had taken it to old Mr. Lucas Purdy, whom she'd known all her life, and he'd taken her catch, with his, to sell in Vicksburg. She would have to save every cent because, to make a profit, she needed a boat. Grandpa's boat had been lost to scavenging Yankees.

Her fingers were cut and bleeding from the net, but she couldn't stop. It had to be ready by sundown. A dozen crayfish had been lost through one small hole, and their escape represented money she desperately needed.

She sighed wearily, wiping the sweat from her eyes with the back of her hand. Yesterday she had chopped up the parched, red earth of Grandpa's garden plot. Thunderclouds in the east had promised rain late in the day, and she hurried to get the turnips and collards in. Mr. Purdy had said he'd use a little of her money to buy a rooster and a few hens for her, so she could have eggs.

Oh, there was so much to be done! She was so weary, and the day not half over. At night, she could fall across the bed, grateful as exhaustion dimmed the pain of her shame over that horrible night.

The sound of hoofbeats on the dry earth brought her to her feet instantly. It wouldn't be Mr. Purdy, not at this time of day and not on horseback. Dropping the net, she ran into the cabin and scrambled up on a stool to take Grandpa's gun down from its resting place above the mantel. Hurrying to the rear window, she peered out. Her blood ran hot with fury.

Pointing the weapon, she cried, "You stop right there or I'll blow you back up North, you no-good Yankee!"

Scott Colter reined his horse in. His voice was soft as he called, "Holly, we need to talk. Put the gun down."

Her gaze took in the despised uniform. "You just get out of here, *Colonel*," she spat the word. "You've nothing to say that would interest me. Why'd you come here? To taunt me because you made a fool of me? Made me think you were a Southerner? I *was* a fool, wasn't I?"

He dismounted.

She pulled the hammer back, the ominous click sounding in the stillness. "I'm not going to warn you again, Colter."

"It seems you're always threatening me with firearms," he said, moving toward the cabin. "Now, if you want to hang for murdering me, go ahead, but make sure you don't miss."

Undaunted, she called, "I never shoot unless I plan to hit what I'm aiming at."

If he felt any fear, it wasn't evident. He continued to walk confidently toward her. He took another step, and another, and she fired, the bullet hitting squarely between his boots, kicking up a cloud of red dust.

"Goddamnit, Holly, you're going to kill somebody," he yelled, but he stopped walking. "Hate me if you must. I can't do anything about that now. I came to warn you that you may be in danger. You'll have to hear me out."

"I'm listening," she said.

"I've got informants in town. There's a rumor going around that there are people who want to run you off this land."

He had her attention. She moved the gun ever so slightly so it was not aimed directly at him. "Who would want to run me off? I haven't done anything, and it's my land."

"I haven't been able to find out who they are, only that they resent a woman turning up her nose at the Union the way you're doing. Did you tell Lucas Purdy to let your fish catches rot before selling to Yankees?" he asked accusingly.

Holly nodded. "I meant it, too. I won't do business with you bastards and nobody can make me."

"For your information, Mr. Locklear almost lost his job at the bank for giving you that loan."

She laid the gun aside and scrambled up to sit in the window. "It was a legitimate loan. He knows I'll pay it back. Why should anyone care about that?"

"The bank's board of directors felt he gave you charity. After all, you didn't have any collateral, and you *won't* be able to pay it back."

"But he didn't lose his job?"

"No, Jarvis Bonham signed for your loan."

Holly gasped. "Damn him! I don't need him interfering in my business. I can make it on my own, and you and everyone else in Vicksburg will find that out if you'll just *leave me alone*. Now will you get out of here, please?"

He snapped, "You should thank Jarvis for saving Locklear's job, you inconsiderate little brat." His nostrils flared. "Damn it, woman, who in hell do you think you are, always with a chip on your shoulder? The goddamn war is over. Now listen to me."

He moved closer. "It isn't safe for you to be out here alone. A lot of people resent your attitude. Like it or not, there are those who just want peace. They don't take kindly to the way you're acting."

She pushed a strand of burnished copper hair back from her face. "Look, I mind my own business, and I'd appreciate everybody giving me the same courtesy. That includes you."

She twisted about in the window to reach for the gun, but Scott knew what she was up to and he was faster. Grasping her, pinning her arms at her side, he used his other hand to cup her face tightly. "You listen to me, you little spitfire. This is no place for a woman, especially a woman who's raised the dander of redneck radicals who believe every Rebel sympathizer should be tarred and feathered. I want you to come back to town with me and move in with your mother. Stop courting danger, Holly.''

She twisted futilely in his grasp, raging, ''You lying Yankee bastard, I'll blow your head off! You can't come here and tell me what to do. If my daddy and granddaddy were alive, they'd kill you for what you did to me.''

''Did to you?'' He raised his eyebrows. ''Oh, Holly, don't play the scorned woman. You wanted it every bit as much as I did—and you probably enjoyed it more,'' he added, goading.

How she ached to slap the arrogant smile from his face. ''You took advantage of me, and you know it! I'd never been with a man before.''

He shook his head, laughing softly. ''You were ready to find out what it would be like. I just happened to come along. It could have been anybody, maybe Neil Davis. He's sweet on you, you know. He wanted to come out here with me today, but I wouldn't let him.''

Holly continued to struggle. ''Will you just get the hell out of here?''

''Not until I make you realize you have no right to blame me entirely for what happened between us. Listen to me, damn it,'' he shook her roughly. ''I wanted to tell you who I was, but I knew once you found out, you'd react just as you are now.''

Between clenched teeth, she said, ''You got what you were after. And you knew I'd never let you put your filthy hands on me if I'd known you were a goddamn Yankee.'' His fingertips began to move gently across her face. ''Get your hands off me, Scott Colter, or I'll kill you, I swear I will.''

''So much fire,'' he murmured, lips brushing her

cheek, then moving to her neck. "Wasted in anger. This much fire should burn only in bed. . . ."

Holly fought him with all the strength she could muster. "You goddamn Yankee son of a bitch, I'd rather couple with a billy goat than have you touch me!"

He jerked his head back, and she saw raw, naked fury. "That does it. I warned you about that filthy mouth. If you were a man, I'd beat the hell out of you." As easily as though she were a sack of potatoes, he tucked her under his arm.

Oblivious to her struggles, he carried her around to the front of the cabin, then paused to look around. "Ah, there's what I'm looking for—good, strong lye soap." He found a pail of water, then dropped her roughly to the ground. Lowering himself to straddle her, he twisted her long, thick mane of hair around his fingers to hold her in place, then proceeded to wash out her mouth with the soap and water.

When he was satisfied that she'd had enough, he got to his feet. "Next time, a good, sound spanking will go along with it."

Holly gagged, spat, and scrambled to her feet. Hoarsely, eyes blazing, her whole body trembling with rage, she gasped, "You, you . . ."

Scott raised an eyebrow.

She bit back the words, and oh, they were some of the choicest. Tears sprang to her eyes, and she hated herself for the weakness. "Will you please just go? Get out of my life. Why do you go on tormenting me? Haven't you done enough?" She turned away, not wanting him to see the tears spilling.

Scott was instantly contrite. Damn it, he hadn't wanted to crush the girl's spirit. "I'm sorry. Hell, I came out here to warn you there might be trouble, not to hurt you. But you had to let go with that temper of yours, and I just wanted to teach you a lesson." He grabbed her and spun her around, and she wilted against his chest. He nuzzled her hair with his chin. "Holly, little sprite." He gently wrapped his fingers in her long hair and tilted her head back. Crushing her against him, his lips found hers, warm, seeking. He tasted the soap and laughed. "Your kisses should never taste like soap, Holly, only like warm, sweet wine."

Suddenly, Holly found herself laughing despite herself. "I have no wine, sir, only a mouthful of lye soap."

Their eyes met, and for the flash of a single moment, the curtain of animosity was drawn aside. They were a man and a woman, aware of the intimacy they had shared. The teasing flames of passion ignited once more.

Their smiles faded simultaneously. Holly stiffened in his arms, but he did not release her. "How I wish we'd met another time, another place," he said.

The curtain closed.

Holly shook her head. "I want to forget it. Go, please, and don't come back."

With a deep sigh, he moved away. "All right. If that's the way you want it. If you need me, let me know."

He walked away. Holly watched, a maelstrom of emotions spinning as she struggled to keep from calling out to him. There could not, she told herself, be anything between them except bitterness.

He mounted his horse, then looked at her. "Your mother knew I was coming out here and sends her love. Says she'll get Jarvis to bring her out for a visit soon. Neil will be by to check on you. I won't be back unless you send for me, Holly. I'll leave you alone because you asked me to."

With one last, searching gaze, he reined his horse about and rode away.

She watched him go, then returned to her net, working furiously. Danger? She could handle that. She had a gun and knew how to use it. She would not be frightened away from her home. To hell with Scott Colter. To hell with anyone and anything that stood in her way.

She lifted her face to the warm, gentle wind blowing in from the Mississippi River. She'd made Grandpa a promise, and she would keep it. She would live here in peace.

Besides, she reminded herself, there was nowhere else for her to go.

Scott rode on to Vicksburg, lost in thought. Would the devils ever leave him? Even before the war, before the treacherous Marlena, he'd harbored a deep, gut-wrenching suspicion of all women. Thanks to his mother.

Kate Colter had been beautiful, with coal-black hair and sultry brown eyes. Even as a boy, Scott had been all too aware of the way men in their small village on the Texas Gulf coast looked at her. His father had worshiped her. She could do no wrong.

Ben Colter put Kate on a pedestal and knelt at her feet.

A bitter smile twisted Scott's lips as he thought about the expression "crazy about" someone. His father had been crazy about his mother, all right—to the point where he really went crazy, when he caught her in bed with Wendell Polter. He had blown both of them to hell, then killed himself.

Scott had walked in on the carnage.

For a time, he'd been in a stupor, lost to the world around him. When his sister died suddenly from a fever, the local do-gooders wanted to send him to an orphanage and close the book on what they, by then, considered the trashy Colter family. Scott had run away.

The next fifteen years had been spent drifting, working at any job he could find to keep from starving, stealing when he had to. If the war hadn't come along, he'd probably have wound up in jail. But being a soldier had given him purpose, for the first time. Climbing up the ranks to officer had been his salvation. For the first time in so long he couldn't remember, Scott was at peace with himself.

Then Marlena Renfroe had burst into his life with the force of an exploding Parrott gun. Damn, she was beautiful. Tight, firm buttocks aching to be squeezed. Big, firm breasts yearning to be sucked and fondled. Hair the color of corn silk and eyes like fiery diamonds. She'd taught him ways to enjoy their bodies he'd never dreamed of and drove him crazy while she was doing it.

Yes, hell, he'd fallen in love with the bitch,

started thinking about settling down, a home, family. Marlena, making the rounds of the Federal camps as a singer, pretended he'd awakened the same longings within her, and so they made plans to get married.

He sucked in his breath and let it out slowly. Goddamn, would he ever forget finding out the truth about her? They'd made love that night, in his tent, and it had been the best ever. She'd enjoyed it so much he'd had to press his hand over her lips to keep her shrieks from waking the whole damn camp. Then they'd fallen asleep, and he'd awakened to find her gone. Worried, he went to look for her.

She had gone to meet a Reb scout in the woods.

There hadn't been time for anger. He was an officer and soldier first, a fool in love second.

He had slashed the throat of the scout, not using his gun for fear of alerting any Reb troops nearby. Then he'd clipped Marlena with his fist to get her out of the way, throwing her over his shoulder and returning to arouse his men. A good thing, for there had indeed been Rebs waiting nearby.

When the skirmish was over, he'd dispatched someone to take Marlena to a Federal prison. He hadn't seen her again, had admitted to himself sometime later that he'd been afraid to, afraid he might go berserk like his father and kill her.

Maybe she was still in prison. He didn't know. He'd learned a lesson. Never again would he allow a woman to have such a hold on him.

Then along came Holly. And there was just something about her that got to him. She was one hell of a woman, and he could easily become involved if he let himself. But he wasn't going to let himself. He would keep his vow to know women only for the glory of the flesh and nothing more.

Love could not play a part.

Love made men weak.

🎀 Chapter Seven 🎀

HOLLY awoke with a start, peering into the dark cabin. A half-moon lit the swamps, casting an eerie glow through the windows. Silver shadows danced across the split log walls. What had awakened her? Not the screech of a bobcat or the call of an owl or anything she was used to.

Fighting the urge to go back to sleep, she forced herself up and tiptoed across the rough floor to Grandpa's gun. It wasn't fear, she told herself, but caution.

She went softly to the door and was groping for the handle when she heard a horse whinny. A deep breath helped choke down the bubbling fear. She eased open the door just enough to get her foot through. Then, pulling the gun hammer back, jerked the door open with her foot, keeping her body out of sight. "All right, who's out there?" she called. "I've got a gun and I know how to use it."

Silence. But there was something there. She could feel it. She moved very slowly toward the opening in the door, allowing herself to look out.

Ringed by a halo of moonlight, a man sat on a horse, a black hood over his head.

"Hey, lil' Reb," his voice rang out. "War's over. Put down your gun."

Her finger tightened on the trigger. "I'll shoot," she warned in a clear voice. "What do you want?"

"Can't shoot all of us, lil' Reb."

There was a sound to her left. Two more men, also on horseback, also wearing that ominous black hood, were facing her.

The first man called, "We don't want no trouble, lil' Reb. We just want to talk. Put that gun down so nobody'll get hurt."

Rage was overtaking fear. "I don't talk to people who won't show their faces. Get off my land this minute or I start shooting."

"No need for that, Miss Maxwell."

A fourth man rode slowly out of the shadows. He, too, was masked. He walked his horse straight toward the cabin and she swung around, pointing her rifle at him.

"Stop right where you are! I've had enough of this. All of you, get out of here!"

He said softly, "We only want to talk to you, Miss Maxwell. We don't think it's safe for a young woman to be living alone out here. You should be with your mother."

Indignation made her sputter. "It's none of your business where I live!"

"We think it is!" His amiable manner disappeared. "The war's over. It's time everyone learned to live in peace. You can't go around snubbing Northerners, refusing to sell your fish catches to them. We won't put up with that kind of attitude. A fair price for your land has been deposited at the

bank with Mr. Locklear. You take it and start living
like decent folk, or we'll burn you out.''

"Yeah,'' the first hooded rider called to her.
"And we'll strip you naked and show you what happens to people like you. We'll make you pledge al-
legiance to the Union and march through Vicksburg
singing our glory songs.''

Burn her out would they? Strip her naked? "To
hell with all of you,'' she cried, enraged by the rider
who kept moving toward her. She fired.

The man screamed and toppled from his horse.
The others ran for cover, but Holly's cry rode over
the din. "I'll blow every one of you bastards
straight to hell. Get off my land!''

The wounded man writhed and twisted in the dirt,
calling to his friends. "Don't leave me . . . don't
leave me . . .''

The leader hesitated briefly. He reined his horse
about, looking from his fallen comrade to Holly's
rifle. Deciding not to chance it, he turned his mount
and took off after the others.

Holly walked onto the porch, down the steps, and
across the clearing to stand over the wounded man.

His face twisted in pain, he stared up at her and
begged, "Don't kill me. We weren't gonna harm
you, I swear. All we was gonna do was scare you.
Nobody would'a hurt you. That's the truth.''

She was afraid, but just mad enough not to show
her fear. "Where are you hit?''

"Shoulder.''

"That's where I aimed, but it's easy to miss at
night.'' She nudged him with her toe. "Get up.''

He clutched at his shoulder, blood trickling

through his fingers. "Can't. Hurts so bad. Gonna bleed to death."

Matter-of-factly she told him he wouldn't. "Now get up. We're going inside. I don't intend to be a sitting duck out here if your friends decide to come back for you."

He shook his head. "Can't. Hurts too bad."

She jabbed him again, harder. "You want me to finish you off?" She wouldn't have done it, of course, but he didn't know that.

He pulled himself to his knees, gasping, and she stayed right behind him as he stumbled into the cabin.

Inside, he slumped to the floor. Holly touched a match to a lantern and the room filled with mellow light. She kicked the door shut and bolted it, then moved swiftly to close and lock all the wooden shutters from the inside. Satisfied that no one could take a shot at her, she returned to the wounded man. He was still wearing his hood. "What's your name?"

"None o' your business."

"Do you want to bleed to death?" she asked simply, and he shook his head. "Then don't be smart, because it doesn't matter a damn to me whether you die or not."

"Alex Wellman," he said gruffly.

She told him to get up and sit at the table. "And don't try anything. I've still got the gun, and I think you found out I know how to use it."

He watched her warily as she moved around the cabin, getting water, bandages. She sat down next to him, placing the gun out of his reach but close to hers. Ripping open his blood-soaked shirt, she examined the wound. "The bullet went clean through. That's good. I won't have to dig it out."

She wrapped a bandage tightly around the wound, then sat back to look at him with narrowed eyes. "Talk, mister. What did you come here for tonight?"

He scowled. "I ain't gotta tell you nothin', girl, and you ain't gonna shoot me like a dog. You might as well let me get on out of here."

She reached out and yanked off his hood. Her eyes flicked over him. She had never seen him before. She knew instinctively that she'd remember if she had. He had beady little eyes, like a chicken snake, and his beard was scraggy. His hair was dirty and matted. An altogether unsavory looking character.

"Get something straight," she said slowly, so he would grasp every word. "I won't bat an eye at shooting you again. You may start talking now. Why did you and your friends come here?"

He watched uneasily as she again picked up the gun.

"We're the Night Hawks," he said, trying for a rebellious tone. "We were hired to do what the Federal occupation troops can't do. It's our job to keep peace and take care of uppity Rebs—like you," he sneered.

"Who hired you, Mr. Wellman?"

He laughed, showing yellowed, chipped teeth. "You ain't that stupid, are you? Ain't no way you can make me tell you that."

If he did tell, then whoever had hired them might kill him. "Why am I considered an uppity Reb?" she asked, though she knew well enough.

He shrugged. "Won't sell your fish to Yankees. Livin' out here thinkin' you're too good to live in town. Things like that. You were lucky tonight. We didn't realize what a feisty bitch you are."

She let that pass. Grandpa said insults from scalawags weren't to get upset over.

She moved away from the table, holding the gun. "We'll see what you have to say to the authorities when I take you in at daylight." She positioned herself on the bed. "You might as well get some sleep. We'll leave at first light. And don't try anything. I won't be dozing off."

He continued to glare at her for a while, then finally lowered his head to the table and fell asleep.

Exhausted, she spent the next few hours trying to put everything together.

When Mr. Purdy had returned with her chickens and money late the day before, she had told him of Colonel Colter's visit, that Colter knew she'd said not to sell to Yankees. There had, Mr. Purdy explained, been an incident when a Yankee got very angry when he was told this. He'd become so incensed that he began shouting, loud enough for everyone at the market to hear, about "that smart-alecky Reb woman" who thought she was too good to do business with him. People had muttered over it for some time, Mr. Purdy said.

But it didn't make sense. Why would that one incident provoke someone deeply enough that he'd hire men to frighten her? And what about the money they had said was deposited with Mr. Locklear? Something strange was going on.

With the first gray shadows of dawn, Holly shook her captive awake.

"Stiff," he protested groggily, rubbing at his bandaged shoulder. "Can't ride."

She jammed the gun into his back, and he yelped. "Outside, Wellman."

She guided him to the small shed behind the cabin. She'd decided against using the wagon, which would require both of her hands on the reins. She had to hold the gun. She made Wellman ready two horses, then mounted one and nodded for him to get on the other.

They set out for Vicksburg, Wellman riding directly in front of Holly. All the while, she scanned the bushes and brush along the road, alert for sign of ambush. "I doubt your friends will come looking for you," she remarked to him once. "Their kind only slithers out at night."

He remained silent, too sore to argue.

She spied the first soldiers on the outskirts of Vicksburg and realized she was actually grateful to see Yankees. There were four of them, and when they saw her, holding a gun on a wounded man riding in front of her, they charged forward with their own weapons drawn.

Before Holly could explain, Alex Wellman suddenly came out of his stupor and screamed, "She's crazy! The woman is tee-totally crazy. I won't doin' nothin' but huntin' last night down by the river, and she came up out of nowhere and shot me for no reason. Kept callin' me a Yankee spy."

The officer in charge eyed Holly and snapped, "Throw that gun down, miss. We'll take over now."

Holly gave her hair a toss, reading the stripes on

the man's shoulder. "Sergeant, you haven't heard my side of the story."

"Throw down your gun," he barked.

Holly reluctantly obeyed and one of the other soldiers dismounted and retrieved it. "Will you hear me out?" she asked quietly.

He motioned her to ride on. "You can talk on the way to the post."

The sergeant and Holly and Wellman rode side by side in silence for a few moments. Then Wellman addressed the officer. "You and me know the war's over," he murmured amiably. "But there's too many of these Rebs that don't. I was with the Twelfth New York Rifles," he added proudly.

"Good outfit," the sergeant acknowledged gruffly.

"Lying bastard," Holly said under her breath.

They reached the post and Holly dismounted. The sergeant's tight grip held her arm, and she was guided into a wooden building. Wellman was ushered toward the infirmary by one of the post soldiers.

A young soldier was seated behind a desk just outside a door at the rear of the room Holly was led to. As Holly and the sergeant entered, he jumped to his feet and saluted. "Sergeant Pearson. You got a prisoner?" He nodded toward Holly with interest.

"Maybe," Pearson responded gruffly. "The colonel in?"

"Not at the moment, sir, he—"

The soldier was interrupted by a startled cry of recognition as another officer entered the room. "Holly! What are you doing here?" Neil Davis rushed to her side. "Pearson? What is going on?"

he asked. The sergeant began to speak, but Neil interrupted immediately. "Let Miss Maxwell tell me."

She told him all of it, aware all the while that he was gazing at her with more than friendly concern.

"I'll be damned," Neil said when she'd finished.

The sergeant had been quiet long enough. "Sir, a man has been shot, and this woman should be charged with the shooting. Shall I lock her up now?"

"I accept full responsibility for her," Neil said firmly. "Miss Maxwell is not going into the stockade."

The two men locked eyes. Just then hard footsteps echoed in the hallway and in a moment the outer door opened. Holly found herself looking into the dark eyes of Colonel Scott Colter.

He strode briskly into the room, his presence quietly but overwhelmingly commanding. Looking right at Holly, he said, "It seems the trouble I anticipated has begun." His gaze was warm. "And it seems you are right in the middle of it, Miss Maxwell—which I *also* anticipated."

❦ Chapter Eight ❦

SCOTT took Holly into his private office. He didn't have to tell Sergeant Pearson or Captain Davis that he would take the situation from there. They knew it and stepped aside, aware, as always, that Colter preferred to conduct his own investigations without being bored by others' opinions.

He sat down behind a large desk and motioned to Holly to take one of the two remaining chairs. His gaze flicked over her, the warmth gone now. "Let's hear it, Holly," he said brusquely. Taking a deep breath, she let it out slowly. She told him everything, and Scott scrawled notes as she talked.

The whole time she talked, her stomach fluttered and her voice went from low to high and then back to low. Why, she accused herself furiously, couldn't she manage a little control? Scott Colter was just another man. Well . . . perhaps not. She looked away from him. Would he always have this effect on her? Did he know how she felt? Did she look as overwrought as she was feeling? She guessed she probably did. When she fell silent, he glanced up sharply. "Is that all of it?" She nodded. He stood. "Wait."

He left her. After a few moments, she got up and began to pace. The room was sparsely furnished. There was a desk and there were two chairs. A black-draped portrait of President Lincoln was on one wall, a portrait of General Grant on the opposite wall.

Walking to the curtainless window, she peered out into the inner compound and saw soldiers drilling. They looked as bored as she felt.

She took her seat once more. She should have been fishing, repairing nets, anything but sitting there wasting her time over something that wasn't her fault.

A sound at the door caused her to jump. She frowned, disappointed, to see it wasn't Scott, but Roger Bonham.

He knelt down in front of her, concern etched on his face. "It's all over town. Your mother is so upset. My father wanted to come, but I told him that you and I were friends, so I'd come and see what I could do to help you out of this mess."

She made a careless gesture and looked out the window. "Everything will be fine. I didn't do anything wrong. I was just protecting myself and my property. I hated to shoot anyone, but I had no choice."

He reached for her fingertips and held them tightly, through she tried to pull away. "Please, Holly. Tell me what happened."

She didn't want him there, but there he was. It was rude to keep staring out the window, so she steeled herself and faced him, noting his impeccable light blue cravat, his white shirt and dark blue coat. His boots would, she knew, be polished to a fine

sheen and his trousers would have a knife crease.
Why did all of this irritate her? Was it only because
she looked like a ragpicker or was it something beyond that?

He was talking so earnestly. She made herself be
attentive. Why make another enemy?

With a weary sigh, she told her story for the third
time. He listened quietly, then declared, "It won't
happen again. By God, I won't stand for this.
You've a right to live where you want to live."

She laughed wearily. "That's what *I* thought. But
this isn't *my* land here any more. It's being taken
over by outsiders, vultures!" she flared.

"Holly, no, my dear. You're mistaken." He
moved back to sit in the chair next to her. "We
Northerners who've come South are, for the most
part, aspiring men who've moved here in an attempt
to make new lives—"

"Picking the carcasses of the beaten South," she
cut him off abruptly.

"Not all of us," he said gently. "I agree there are
a few troublemakers, but some have been sent as
missionaries to minister to the needs of former
slaves. Some of them, true, resent Southerners, like
you, who stand in their way. They're trying to unite
our country in peace, Holly." He went on before
she could stop him. "It's quite unusual for a young
woman to take over land, in her name. And to be so
rudely independent. Your attitude has angered
many people. You must understand that."

She stiffened. "I do not have to trade with Yankees, if you happen to be referring to the incident in
the market yesterday."

He gave her a sad smile. "Do you expect that kind of attitude to be warmly received?"

She jerked her hands from his. "You speak of peace. I find that hypocritical. You Yankees are the ones who came down here to tell us how to live. You caused the trouble in the first place."

Roger shook his head. "Do you condone slavery?"

"I never went along with that. My father was good to our servants. They weren't mistreated. And it's none of your business anyway."

Roger touched her shoulder gently. "Holly, historians will probably spend the next century studying the reasons for the war, but I'm concerned only with your welfare."

She turned her face away. "I only want to be left alone. Is that asking too much?"

"The way you handled the situation last night isn't going to solve anything," Roger said.

Holly clenched her fists together. "No one is going to come on my land and threaten me, Roger, and the next time it happens, someone is going to get killed."

He smiled gently. "Then we'll just have to make certain there isn't a next time." He cupped her chin in his hand, forcing her to meet his reassuring gaze. "I'm not only going to offer you a tidy sum for your land, my dear, I'm going to give you back your original investment! You can move into Vicksburg and be with your mother, and I promise you'll be the belle of every social function. I intend to make a pest of myself, vying for your company."

He slipped his hand inside his expensive coat, then smoothly placed her grandmother's brooch in her lap. "Where did you get this?" she gasped, looking from the brooch to him and back again.

He smiled, enjoying the moment, and told her about buying it back from the jeweler. "I know it meant a great deal to you. Accept it, please, as a gesture of friendship."

"But . . ." she sputtered, staring at the brooch, shaking her head. "I'm sorry. I can't accept it. I'd be in your debt, and I could never repay you."

"No, my dear, you don't owe me anything. Consider it evidence of my goodwill and friendship. I'll be insulted if you don't accept it. It would hurt me, Holly."

She stared at him. If it weren't for those cold eyes, he would be attractive. Oh, what difference did that make? What was she thinking of? "You want that land, don't you?" she asked simply. "Or you'd never have gone to the trouble to find out where I got the money to pay the taxes."

He glanced away, with a hangdog look on his face as he shook his head and said in a confidential tone, "Not me, Holly. My father. I won't be held accountable for him. My interest is in lumber and building. I really don't need your land, but Father fancies himself a land baron. He wants the site of Magnolia Hall so he can build a mansion for himself, and he wants to own all the connecting property, particularly the river frontage. Something about developing a port there for riverboats. When I heard what lengths you went to in order to keep your land, I bought the brooch back."

She blinked, confused. "You mean you don't agree with your father?"

He shook his head. "No, Holly. If you want the

land, then you should have it. It's yours by right. Believe me, my only concern is for your well-being. If you won't let me take that piece of land off your hands so you can move to Vicksburg where you'll be safe, then I have no choice but to accept your decision. But at least take the brooch. Don't insult my good intentions, please."

There was no time to wonder at all this, for at that moment, Scott Colter entered. After glancing from Holly to Roger Bonham, seeing the brooch in her lap, Scott took his seat. He nodded curtly to Roger. "Mrs. Maxwell seemed quite upset when I talked with her a short while ago. She said you were disturbed, too." There was a hint of mockery in his voice and Roger did not mistake the tone.

"It was nice of you to go by there, Colonel. I'm afraid the gossips wasted little time in letting her know that her daughter had shot a man. How is he, by the way?"

Scott looked at Holly as he said, "He isn't hurt badly. Did you mean to kill him?"

Holly grinned. "If I had, he'd be dead."

"He sticks to his story. He says you meant to kill him," Scott said quietly.

Holly shook her head. "I could see him clearly. I aimed off his shoulder, so it would be a flesh wound. And that's what it was. If he cares to pay me another visit, I'll be glad to make a truthful man out of him, instead of a liar," she added. Scott sighed at her unrepentant attitude. "Look, Colonel Colter. I don't care what Wellman says. I told you the truth. Now may I leave? I've other things to be doing besides sitting here being treated like a criminal."

Scott went on as though she had not spoken. "It's easy for people to believe his story because you're getting a reputation as a hotheaded, rebellious wildcat."

"And I imagine he has a reputation as a no-good, lying son of a bitch," she said smoothly.

Scott raised an eyebrow. "Maybe I should have used stronger soap."

Roger looked from her face to the colonel's in confusion. "Is there some part of this I don't know about?" he snapped.

"Not that it's any of your business," Scott said lazily. "Wait outside, please. I'll speak to Holly alone now."

Roger did not like being dismissed. "What do you want me to do, my dear?" he asked. "I'll stay if you like."

"I'll be leaving soon, too, Roger. This isn't getting anywhere." She stood up.

"You will sit down," Scott said so fiercely that she nearly fell back into her chair. "You will leave when I say you can go. Not before." He shot a look at Roger. "You have been dismissed, Bonham."

Roger stood. "I'll wait outside, Holly. Then I'll take you to your mother." He went out, shooting an angry look at Scott before slamming the door behind him.

When they were alone, Scott informed her he had been to the bank to talk to Mr. Locklear. "He doesn't know anything about any money being held for you."

She stared at him. "So? Does that prove anything except that the Night Hawks told him there'd been trouble and to forget the deal? Now he's scared to admit the truth.''

He nodded imperceptibly.

''Does that mean you believe me?'' she asked, exasperated.

''I do. I've told Wellman to get out of town and tell his friends to do the same. I won't tolerate vigilantes in my territory.''

''Then I won't have to worry about them again! Thank God!''

Candidly, he informed her, ''They aren't going to turn tail and run just because they've been warned. They'll hang around as long as they're getting paid.''

''Well, what are you going to do about it? *You're* being paid, I believe, to keep peace in this area.''

Suddenly, his expression changed. ''Let me worry about that. You just watch yourself. I won't tolerate vigilantes, but neither will I put up with citizens taking the law into their own hands. That includes you.'' He got up and escorted her to the door. ''I'll have some patrols around your property from time to time. You'd be wise to watch who you're shooting at. Now, if you'll excuse me, I have other matters to tend to.'' He got to his feet and went to the door.

Holly was baffled by his coolness. She was being abruptly dismissed. She walked to the door slowly, then turned to face him. Standing there, so close, the passionate memories rushed back to her. He touched his tongue to the sensuous fullness of his lower lip, as though tasting a kiss and she felt a tremor move through her. The spark of awareness crackled silently between them.

"The dress you were wearing the other night was lovely," he said lightly. "At the party I realized you're a real beauty when you want to be."

Holly felt wholly vulnerable. Mustering confidence, she gave Scott a mock curtsy and smiled. "I thank you, kind sir, and it seems *you* can be a real gentleman . . . when *you* want to be."

He reached out and touched her face gently with his fingertips, trailing downward till he was cupping her chin. For an instant, Holly stood frozen, then she shook free and quickly jerked open the door.

She bumped right into Roger, who gripped her arms to steady her. "Are you all right? You look . . . upset." He gave Scott an accusing glare. Scott smoothly closed the door on them.

Holly shook her head. "I'm fine, Roger. I just want to get out of here." He guided her to the outer door.

"They took your horse to the post stables, because they didn't know whether or not you would be detained. I have my carriage outside. I'll take you to your mother's."

Neil Davis had been standing to one side, shuffling some papers, obviously listening. He moved to block their path. "If you'd like me to, I can get your horse and ride with you to your mother's, Holly. Or I'll take you back to your place, if that's what you want."

"I'm taking care of her," Roger countered curtly, "but thank you for your concern, Captain."

She looked from one to the other. Damn, why did Scott affect her this way? She wanted time alone, to think. The last thing she wanted was the company of another man right now. "Thank you both," she told them, "but I prefer to walk." With a polite nod, she left the building before either could think what to say to stop her.

The day was lovely, a warm, gentle breeze blowing in from the south. She winced at the grotesque skeletons of burned trees along the way. Once, their limbs had been lush and green, with magnolia blossoms or the popcorn glory of white dogwood flowers. Now everything was drab, dead, thanks to the Yankees and their siege of Vicksburg. Here and there, piles of rubble lay where great houses had once been.

Devastation and poverty—these were the gifts the war had bestowed upon Mississippi. To those who had survived, the present seemed intolerable; the future, hopeless. The war had destroyed the South's physical assets and its whole way of life. The entire Confederacy was bitter and exhausted.

Farmers lacked tools, stock, seeds. Plantations fell to carpetbaggers who hovered like vultures. Mills, mines, and factories were shut. Many country roads were impassable. Bridges that had not been burned were in desperate need of repair. Most river steamboats had been captured or destroyed, and the rest were worn out. The few southern railroads left were currently being used by the Federal government.

Passing the burned remains of the old slave market, she recalled her family's horror of slavery. Not all Southerners had been slavers.

There were some Negro men standing by the remains of the market, and they watched her with angry, hostile eyes. It mattered not that they didn't know her, didn't know her hatred of slavery. To them, she was just a white Southerner. That made her responsible for their bondage. She saw their ragged clothing, skinny bodies. They were starving. They had paid a terrible price for freedom.

"They don't know what to do with themselves, do they, Miss Maxwell?"

Holly whirled around and saw a man leaning against a blackened tree trunk. He was older—in his early fifties, she thought—and he had a lean, craggy face and a bushy, graying beard. He wore the tattered trousers of a Confederate uniform, and a worn dark muslin shirt.

Alarmed, Holly asked, "How do you know me? I don't think I've ever seen you before."

He grinned. "I knew your daddy. Fought with him. A fine man, he was."

"But how do you know me?"

He shrugged casually. "Oh, everybody knows you, Miss Maxwell. It's all over town that you shot one of them Night Hawks last night. I watched you going into the post, and I hung around, waitin' for you to come out."

He nodded toward the group standing by the slave market. "Saw you starin' at them niggers," he drawled. "Sad, ain't it? They just don't know what to do with themselves, now they're free. 'Course, the government's promisin' 'em forty acres and a mule, but some of 'em don't want to go back to the fields, so they'll steal and murder to keep from goin' hungry. That's why we got to teach 'em their place."

Holly felt her cheeks growing warm. "We don't need more trouble. Please leave me alone. I don't want to talk any more."

She nodded politely and began walking away, but he fell into step alongside her.

He snorted. "Funny hearin' you talk like that. Folks are callin' you the loudest Reb around here."

"If I'm a Rebel because I only want to be left alone, then I'm a Rebel."

She picked up her step, but he darted ahead of her, blocking her path, ignoring her angry look. "We're gonna talk, lady, 'cause me and my men got something *you* need, and you got something *we* need. You'd better listen. Whether you know it or not, you got big troubles."

Holly was agitated but she refused to show fear. "Will you get out of my way? I can take care of myself. I proved that last night."

He laughed. "Girlie, you were just lucky last night. Now that the Night Hawks know you got some guts, they'll be ready next time. And there will be a next time. That's why you need me and my men. We'll make sure you can stay on your land."

She cried, "I don't need help! Now get out of my way!"

He grabbed her and pushed her up against a nearby tree. "I ain't messin' around. I hear things, and you can believe me when I say the word's out them Night Hawks are gonna get you. I don't mean you no harm, I swear it. Me and my men want to make a deal. You got a good place to hide out in them woods, and you know the swamps. You help us out by lettin' us meet there, where we won't be spied on, and if times get bad and one of us has to run from the law, you can hide us in the swamps. In return, we'll see to it you're protected from the Night Hawks."

"What are you and your men up to?"

He jerked his head back toward the slave market. "Like I said. They're gonna cause trouble. They're uppity, and smart-alecky, and they gloat because we lost the war. We gotta keep 'em in line. Yankees ain't gonna protect Southern whites, you know. Me and my men are bandin' together to look after ourselves and our families. We ain't takin' no guff off niggers—or Yankees."

Holly nodded. "You're going to become vigilantes, just like the Night Hawks. But you'll be on the side of the South while they're on the side of the North. The war will continue."

He grinned. "You got it. Help us. Remember, you need us," he added.

She shook her head slowly, sadly. "You're only going to cause more problems for yourself and everyone. This isn't the answer. I don't know what the answer is, but there has to be a way that won't cause any more grief."

"You ain't got a better solution, have you?" he bellowed. "Tell you one thing," he jabbed at the air, "if we Southerners don't stick together, we're gonna be grovelin' in the dirt, eatin' worms to keep from starvin'!"

Holly could feel enough pity to dissipate her anger. Sincerely, she told him, "I wish I could help you, but I can't. I don't want more trouble, I just want to be left alone. I'm afraid I'm not a crusader."

She turned away, and this time he didn't try to stop her. "You'll change your mind," he called after her. "They ain't gonna leave you alone. And you'll come crawlin' to us for help. You'll see. We all got to stick together, else they'll trample us into the ground.''

She quickened her pace, lifting her skirt above her ankles, relieved when his voice faded away. She nearly ran when she got within sight of Abby's home.

❧ Chapter Nine ❧

CLAUDIA had been keeping an anxious vigil, and she threw her arms around Holly. "Oh, thank God! I was afraid something like this was going to happen." She stepped back to study her. "Ever since I heard, I've been a nervous wreck. What *did* happen? I want to hear everything."

Holly had dreaded this moment. "Whatever you heard, believe me, it wasn't that bad. I just had some prowlers, and I wounded one of them. It's over, so let's forget it and have a nice visit."

Claudia knew by that set look on her daughter's face that she was in one of her stubborn moods. Nothing would make her talk until she was ready. Forcing herself not to press the point, she motioned Holly to follow her upstairs. "Come along, then. I've got something to show you, something you're going to love."

Holly dutifully tagged behind her mother. Entering her room, she was stunned to see the creation her mother gently lifted from the bed.

The dress was made of delicate spun silk, the bodice a soft shade of lavender. The neckline was cut quite low, with tiny satin ribbons to serve as straps that would drape gently off the shoulders. A sash of darkest purple hugged the waist, while the skirt began its cascading drop in the same shade, blending to softer and softer hues of lavender to the hem. Small, crocheted rosebuds dotted the layers of netting overlaying the skirt, each rosebud framed in delicate dark green leaves.

Holly's reaction made Claudia very happy. "It was made especially for you in New Orleans by a real French designer from Paris. With your hair and eyes and these colors, you'll look like a fairy princess." She clapped her hands in childish delight.

Abby came in just then and cried, "I know just how to style your hair, too. High rolls of curls swept up off your neck to show off the jewels Claudia borrowed for you."

At that, Holly knew something was going on. "All right, you two, what's the secret? Where on earth did you borrow jewels?"

Claudia busied herself arranging the dress on the bed. Without looking up she began, "It was Jarvis's idea—about the jewels. When he saw the dress, he remembered he had an exquisite sapphire necklace with matching earrings in Mr. Garrington's safe at the jewelry store. He said they'd be stunning with the dress."

Holly folded her arms across her bosom and nodded thoughtfully. "And the dress? Who paid for it? And what's the occasion?"

Claudia and Abby looked at each other and broke into giggles. They threw their arms around each other, and Abby cried, "You might as well tell her, Claudia. You can't keep it a secret. That isn't fair."

Claudia stepped back and shook her head. "Not

now." To Holly, she apologized, "I'm sorry, dear, but I can't tell you anything now. There's a very special party tonight. Jarvis and I were planning to surprise you by going to see you today and insisting you come back to town with us so you could attend. That's the reason for the dress and the jewels."

Holly's spirits fell. It didn't take much imagination to figure out that Jarvis Bonham had asked her mother to marry him. But she would let her mother play her little game if that made her happy. She did not have to fake a yawn as she said, "I didn't get much sleep last night. If I'm expected to go to a party tonight, I'd better get a nap."

Claudia agreed, and she and Abby left the room, whispering together.

Holly fell asleep immediately and it seemed only a few minutes before Abby shook her awake, but it was actually two hours later.

"I brought you some hot tea." Abby placed a small tray on the dressing table. Her eyes twinkled. She was enjoying the mystery. "Mr. Bonham's having the party in the Allison house, where he's staying till his new home is completed."

Holly said bitterly, "You mean the new house he's building around the shell of Magnolia Hall."

"Now, dear," Abby soothed her, "you must look at it like this. Magnolia Hall is just a crumbling shell of something that was once magnificent. Be glad that it will rise from the ashes. I've seen Jarvis's sketches, and the mansion he's building will be beautiful. Wouldn't you like to see a tribute to that fine land? Believe me, dear, it's much better than memories."

Abby talked on, incessantly singing Jarvis Bonham's praises, while Holly had a bath and washed her hair. She tried not to be rude about Jarvis. Abby meant well. She turned her thoughts to other things—Scott Colter being foremost in her mind. Dear Lord, why couldn't she just forget him? Why did he have to come back into her mind all the time, sneaking like a thief. Those mysterious, brooding eyes held her in thrall. He had seduced her. A *Yankee* had seduced her. But she did care for him, and she wouldn't lie to herself about it.

Yet there had to be a way to remove him from her heart and her blood. The only way to do that, she told herself, was to fill her life with hard work, leaving no time for dreaming. . . .

An hour later Holly stared at her reflection in wonder. Abby beamed, proudly basking in her success. Holly's auburn-gold hair was layered in cascades of curls, entwined with dark purple ribbons. Soft wisps draped dramatically around her slender throat and hung softly to her smooth white shoulders. "You are so beautiful, child. So very beautiful," Abby said.

Holly grinned in disbelief. Where was the ragamuffin? Who was this sophisticated creature? She was positively warmed by the vision, and anxious to get to know this dazzling new being that was herself.

A light supper of fruit and cheese was all any of the ladies wanted. Soon it was time to dress, and Holly stood before the mirror once more. In the delicately shaded dress of lavender silk with its yards and yards of net overlay, her hair a cinnamon crown of glory, she was stunned by herself all over again.

The glittering sapphires at her throat and dangling from her ears set it all off to perfection.

Claudia appeared in the doorway and exclaimed, "I can't believe I gave birth to a child so beautiful!"

Holly smiled at her. "Why should that come as a shock, Mother? You're a beauty."

In truth, Claudia had never been lovelier. Her gown was cream satin, the skirt one long, flowing sheath to the floor. Simple, but elegant. The diamond and emerald choker at her throat was her only adornment.

Rushing across the room to embrace Holly, Claudia pronounced, "We're both beautiful tonight, and we're both going to be very, very happy. You'll see, dear. The sad times are behind us."

Claudia was so proud, so happy. They made their way down the stairs, Abby chattering excitedly. Holly was surprised to see both Roger and Jarvis in the foyer. She might have known Roger would be her escort. Her mother would have engineered it. He was resplendent in a coat of scarlet velvet, accented by a white ruffled shirt, black cravat, and black trousers. He gave her a sweeping bow before coming toward her to stand at the bottom of the stairs, waiting. He wore white gloves, which he removed, and held out his hands to her.

"I must be dreaming," he called boldly. "Fairy princesses don't come in pairs, do they?"

Claudia laughed and hurried down the stairs to meet Jarvis. Holly took her time, thanking Roger for his compliment as she stepped down into the foyer.

His eyes devoured her as he took her arm and

said, "I confess that I demanded to be your escort tonight. I hope you don't mind."

Before she could reply, Jarvis interjected, frowning, "I just want you to know that what happened last night is an outrage, Holly. I've told Colonel Colter to get to the bottom of it, fast. We won't tolerate things like this around here."

Holly regarded him coolly. He sounded sincere, but she could not help wondering just how genuine his concern was. Roger had said that his father wanted her land, after all. Suddenly she found herself hoping that her mother's engagement would be a long one. She wanted time to find out all there was to know about Mr. Jarvis Bonham.

In the silence that followed Jarvis's pronouncement, an air of subtle tension settled about them, and Claudia hastened to retrieve the festive atmosphere. "She doesn't want to talk about it, Jarvis. She just wants to forget it, don't you, dear?"

Holly shrugged. "I won't forget it, of course. And I'll be ready if they come back. I just don't see why we should talk about it. We are on our way to a party, remember?"

Roger flashed his father a look. "Of course. Now isn't the time to discuss it. I'm sure Colonel Colter will handle it, and I intend to look after Holly, myself, from now on."

Holly allowed that to pass. There would be time later to set him straight.

Roger led her to his carriage, Jarvis escorted Claudia to another.

"Forgive my father and his hypocrisy," Roger sneered when they were on their way. "He'd be tickled to death to see you off your land. Then he could own more property. Don't worry.'' He patted her hand. ''If you do decide to sell, I'll give you a good price. You won't have to sell to him.''

Holly regarded him curiously. Why was he being so nice to her, and so openly condemning of his father? ''You don't seem to like your father very much, Roger.''

He snorted, popping the reins across the horses' backs impatiently. ''That's too complicated to go into right now, Holly. When we know each other better, I'll bore you with all the details. Let me just say that *I* am not what you think I am—a bloodsucking carpetbagger preying on the South. I'm a businessman. I get what I want by hard work. *Honest* hard work,'' he added with a meaningful look.

''So how do you feel about him marrying my mother?'' Holly asked bluntly.

He allowed himself a smile. ''Not much gets by you, does it? The reason for tonight's party was supposed to be a big surprise.''

''Really, it didn't take much to figure out what was going on. Mother and Abby were giggling like schoolgirls all day. And the way she and your father look at each other . . . well.'' She shrugged.

He nodded. ''I know. As to how I feel, well, to be honest, at first I thought your mother was after his money.''

Holly bristled. ''She isn't like that.''

''Wait a minute,'' he laughed and held up a hand to silence her. ''I said at first. What else was I to think? The woman who marries him will live like a queen. It was only natural I'd be suspicious. Then, after I got to know Claudia better, I saw her for the warm, lovely person she is. I've grown quite fond of her. I think she really loves him.''

Silently, Holly admitted that she admired Roger's honesty. "Do you think he'll make her happy?"

He shrugged. "Depends on what she wants. If she can be happy with a ruthless, money-mad and power-crazed husband, fine. If she expects warmth, sincerity . . ." He shook his head. "There's not much in my father to like." Holly was too shocked to speak. "I do hope we're going to be friends, Holly," he went on. "I know you've been through a lot and that you've got a lot of painful memories. I won't rush you. But I do want to warn you that I find you a very beautiful and appealing woman. I intend to pursue my deep interest in you. I hope you won't mind."

The last thing she needed was this. "I think," she said quickly, anxious to make him understand, "you should know I'm not interested in a man courting me, Roger."

He smiled confidently. "Courtship will come later. First, I just want to be your friend. You can't have any objection to that, can you?"

What could she say? They rode the rest of the way in silence, Holly wondering just how stiff-necked she was being.

The Allison house was ablaze with lights. Roger pulled up in front and a servant took the reins from him. As they reached the wide, white-columned porch at the top of the marble steps, a Negro in a red velvet coat and white knee-length trousers bowed, then held the door open for them.

Holly stepped inside, her heart suddenly heavy with memories of happier times. The Allisons had been close friends of her family for as long as she could remember. Now Robert Allison lay in a grave in the Vicksburg cemetery, killed in the siege as he fought to defend this very home. Myrtle, his wife, lay beside him, having died of a broken heart, unable to overcome the loss of her husband and all three of her sons.

With a rush of bitterness, Holly wondered whether the Allisons were turning over in their graves right at that moment. She assumed that many Southerners tossed in their coffins, the way things had turned out.

Roger led Holly through the crowd. She was aware of the admiring glances of the men, the envious looks of the women. She knew she looked lovely, but she acknowledged that she was also probably somewhat of an oddity. She was the "little Rebel" everyone was gossiping about, the one who'd been so outspoken about despising Yankees. Yet there she was on the arm of a carpetbagger.

Roger offered her punch, made from fresh peaches. "Father sent a wagon all the way to Georgia to get the first crop," Roger commented. "Nothing's too good for Father."

Holly noted the impressive refreshment table, laden with exotic fruits and lavish pastries. She wished she could take some back to Grandpa's cabin.

"A small gathering, compared to Father's other parties. But there's so little space here. He invited only a select few tonight. The invitation list for the wedding will be something very different. Anyone of importance will be there, rest assured—politicians, government officials from all over the country. It will be the biggest social event of the year in Mississippi, maybe in the entire South.''

He sounded resentful. ''You don't approve of the marriage, Roger, I know.''

''My dear, I never approve of anything my father does, because he always winds up hurting someone. But he didn't ask my permission.'' She tensed. ''Believe me, Holly, it is nothing to do with Claudia. She's a charming lady, and I've grown quite fond of her, as I told you. The truth is, I just don't *like* my father, and that makes me dislike anything he does.''

Could he truly hate his father so much? Suddenly she felt a need to be alone for a while. ''Excuse me. I need to freshen myself.''

She hurried away from him. She didn't, however, turn toward the stairs and the ladies room she knew would be provided on the second floor. Instead, she moved through the foyer and out the doors into the warm night, wanting to escape the sense of oppression that had suddenly descended around her.

She was almost through the door when she came to an abrupt halt. A whirlwind of emotions attacked her at the sight before her. Anger, jealousy, humiliation, all warred with one another, and she commanded herself to control the storm inside her.

There was Colonel Scott Colter, devastatingly handsome in his full dress uniform. Lisa Lou Pollock clung possessively to his arm. She turned slowly and saw Holly staring. Their eyes met and held, Lisa Lou sending a silent message of defiance.

Holly turned away, biting back tears. She ran

blindly for the stairs. Oh, damn, why did she care? Why did she allow herself to care? She hurried up the stairs as fast as she could, praying that no one would see her tears.

🦋 Chapter Ten 🦋

NO one saw her mad rush up the stairs. Grateful to find the ladies room empty, she reached for the white porcelain pitcher and poured water into the bowl beside it. She dipped into the cool water and gently patted her flushed face.

She stared at her stricken expression in the mirror above the table. This is ridiculous, she told herself adamantly. She took several deep breaths, felt her heart return to a smooth rhythm.

Facing her reflection once more, she was able to smile. No man, no Yankee, was going to affect her this way. She would return to the party, hold her head high, and enjoy herself. Roger was pleasant company, after all. Still, she found something unsettling about the man. . . . Shaking the thought away, she smoothed her hair a little, careful not to dislodge the ribbons, and told herself to look happy.

The door opened, and Holly stiffened as Lisa Lou Pollock breezed in. Holly nodded coolly.

Lisa Lou was lovely, dressed in a pale blue satin gown that complemented her carefully coiffed golden hair. The pleasing image was ruined, however, by the anger twisting her face. "You're just like your mother," she hissed.

Holly was stunned. "I beg your pardon?"

Lisa Lou gave her head an arrogant toss. "Just like her," she said contemptuously. "You see a man you want, and you go chasing after him. Everyone in Vicksburg knows Roger Bonham has been courting *me*. My friends couldn't wait to tell me how you've been hanging on to him. You wheedled and begged him to bring you tonight, didn't you? You really don't have any pride." Holly tried to move on by, but Lisa Lou planted herself in her way. "You're going to listen to me. Just who do you think you are, Holly Maxwell? You live in the woods like white trash, you shoot a man, then you have the nerve to show up here and try to mingle with decent folk. You think a fancy outfit makes you a lady? You think you can hang on to a gentleman like Roger Bonham with bedroom tricks, I suppose. You're nothing but a trampy, little slut!"

"That's enough," Holly cried. There was a limit. "You've no right to talk to me like that, Lisa Lou," she warned, eyes flashing dangerously.

"You think I'm afraid?" Lisa Lou screeched. "What are you going to do, shoot me? Or maybe you want to tear my hair out."

"What I want"—Holly drew in a long breath, let it out slowly—"is for you to get the hell out of my way before you make me do something. Move." Her voice rasped harshly.

But Lisa Lou's tirade had gotten the best of her. "You won't get Roger. I'll see to that. And don't think I haven't noticed the way Colonel Colter looks at you—the same way my daddy's hound dog looks at a bitch in heat. Why, look at your mother," she rushed on, eyes dancing wildly. "She used every trick she knew to get Jarvis Bonham to propose— because he's rich."

Holly reached out and grabbed Lisa Lou by the shoulders, catching her off-guard. She flung her to the side, and Lisa Lou stumbled. Holly walked out and slammed the door behind her before Lisa Lou could recover.

Awash with fury, Holly was trembling from head to toe. But she was proud that she'd been able to leave without giving that vicious girl a beating.

She was walking so fast, head down, that she didn't see Scott. She bumped squarely into him, and he grabbed her shoulders to steady her. "What the hell is wrong with you?" he demanded.

"None of your damn business, Colonel. Just get out of my way," she lashed back.

Momentarily taken aback, he let her go. She took a few steps, then turned. "You'd best go find Lisa Lou, Colonel. If she finds both of us missing at the same time, she'll think I'm a bitch and you're a hound dog."

He called after her, but she kept on going down the stairs, across the foyer. She was almost out the front door when Jarvis Bonham saw her and rushed over.

"Whatever is the matter, Holly?"

"I have a terrible headache. I'm leaving."

"You can't do that. It would upset your mother. We're about to make an announcement—"

"Yes, I know," she interrupted gently. She lowered her voice. "I know you're going to announce your engagement to my mother, and—"

"And you don't want to be around to hear it," he cut in. "I suspected you would object, Holly, but out of respect for your mother, you could at least put up a courteous front."

She was shocked. Shaking her head firmly, she hastened to reassure him. "Believe me, Mr. Bonham, my mother's happiness is all that matters to me. If she wants to marry you, that's fine. You've been very kind to her, so I'm sure you care for her. Why would I have any objection?"

He cocked his head to one side, looking at her sharply. "Then what's wrong? You're upset. Did someone do something to upset you?" Oh, how could she explain herself to this man? When she said nothing, he took command. "Your mother would be upset if you left now. I won't allow you to spoil this evening for her." He steered her back inside, and Holly allowed him to have his way. What would it be like to have such a domineering man for a stepfather?

Roger saw them and rushed over to take Holly's arm. "Is anything wrong?" he asked.

Jarvis regarded his son coolly. "Would you mind behaving like a gentleman and staying with your lady? Something upset her. She won't tell me what it was, but I found her ready to leave."

"Holly?" Roger looked at her sharply.

She waited until Jarvis had walked away. "It's nothing, really. Your father's a bit nervous. I'm fine."

"Are you sure?" he asked, and she nodded.

Jarvis signaled to the musicians to stop playing. Then he escorted Claudia up to the platform.

They took their places, and Jarvis exchanged an

adoring gaze with Claudia before giving his attention to his guests. Everyone was silent in respectful anticipation. Taking a deep breath, Jarvis began, "I've a wonderful announcement to make to you tonight, and I hope you will all share my happiness. But first, let me tell you how much moving to Vicksburg has meant to me.

"I'm well aware," he continued, grinning broadly, "that some of you didn't welcome us Yankees with open arms. But you've made me feel at home here, and I want you to know I appreciate that."

Someone called out jovially, "The war's over!"

A ripple of applause bolstered the sentiment.

To each his own, Holly thought, exasperated with the display. Let them welcome the Yankees.

"So," Jarvis went on, his chest swelling, and his face glowing. "It makes me very happy to share my wonderful news with you, my new friends. Claudia Maxwell has done me the honor of consenting to be my wife."

The crowd exploded with real applause, everyone surging forward to offer congratulations. Claudia was much loved by the old guard, and a symbol of happier times in Mississippi.

Holly went to her mother, gave her a hug, and stiffly shook Jarvis's hand.

Out of the corner of her eye, she saw Scott, and when the orchestra had begun playing again, she said to Roger, "You promised me a dance."

But he had promised that dance, so after giving Holly a look of apology, he led Lisa Lou onto the floor.

For Holly, the evening was over right then. She

was not going to tolerate Lisa Lou's smirks from the dance floor as Roger held her in his arms. Nor was she going to continue to pretend she didn't notice Scott Colter. She had stayed for the announcement, she had said and done the proper things, and that was all she would do. The next time she saw Roger, she'd apologize to him, but she told herself it didn't matter whether he was angry or not.

She was halfway down the front steps when someone called her name. Turning, she frowned at the sight of Captain Davis hurrying down the stairs. "Holly, where are you going?" he asked anxiously. "You can't leave without your escort."

She sighed. Why did so many people concern themselves with her welfare? "I have a headache, Neil. I want some air. I'm going home."

He shook his head. "You can't walk home alone. It isn't that safe during the day, much less at night."

"I really want to be alone, Neil," she said firmly.

"I'll be glad to walk with you, Holly. I'd feel better about you."

She shook her head. "I know the way to Abby's quite well, thank you. It's a pleasant walk. Good night, Neil." She went quickly, disappearing into the shadows. Dejected, he returned to the party. . . .

There was a quarter-moon and the velvet night was lovely, but Holly hurried through the shadows. No need to be afraid, she told her pounding heart as she eyed the swaying branches overhead. Hadn't she lived alone, night after night, in the swamps? She'd lived with bobcats, wolves. But this was unknown territory. She knew what to expect from the wilds of nature.

The streets were deserted. It was late, and there were no lights inside the houses. She could hear the gentle chirping of crickets, but it was still awfully quiet. A dog barked somewhere, and a night bird trilled high above, as if letting her know she was not truly alone in God's kingdom.

Only a little way more, she thought as she rounded a corner. Abby would be asleep, thank heaven. She didn't want to answer any questions. She hurried on, clutching her shawl around her shoulders.

Suddenly, Holly froze. Was that a scream?

The sound died as quickly as it had been born, and Holly turned toward the thicket to her left. There was, she recalled, an old cemetery there, just up on the knoll. A church had stood there, destroyed during the war. Only the graves remained. Had the scream come from there?

She continued to stand there. What to do? Continue on her way, or find out if anything was wrong?

Taking a deep breath, she stepped cautiously into the thicket. Fear burned in the pit of her stomach. That scream had come from someone in trouble, of that she was sure. To continue on her way would be turning her back on a person in need. Grandpa had always said it was wrong to deny help to anyone if help could be given—even if that meant danger to yourself. ''You gotta live with yourself,'' he'd told her so many times. ''How can you do that if you turn your back on a fellow human being? It'll come home to you, too. One day you'll want help, and somebody will turn away from you.''

Holly made her way carefully through the bushes, sorry that her elegant dress was being damaged. Nothing to be done about that. Instinct was driving her onward. She paused, listening.

There was a sound like scuffling, struggling. Very carefully, so as not to make any noise, she crept forward until she reached the top of the knoll. Very faintly, she could see the dark outlines of tombstones.

Then, horrified, she saw several men grappling with something on the ground. There were three, no, four men. Their voices, low and guttural, floated to her on the night wind.

"I say kill the bitch and be done with it. She 'bout clawed my eye out."

"Hell, don't kill her till I have my turn. I got my yen up, and I ain't stickin' it in no dead nigger."

"Barney, you shit, hurry up. It's my turn."

Raw, savage rage overrode Holly's fright. They were raping the woman on the ground. She leaped from the brush and ran toward them, screaming.

The attackers sprang to their feet, startled, and their victim began to crawl toward Holly.

All but one of the men fled right then. The remaining man glared at Holly in the moonlight. How ridiculous he looked, his trousers down around his ankles.

He yanked up his trousers, his burning eyes never leaving her face. "Holly Maxwell, you're gonna get yourself killed one day."

Her hand flew to her throat just as the girl reached her. *He knew her name*. But how? She squinted, finally recognizing him as the man who had approached her earlier that day.

Was this, she asked herself sickly, the kind of person who considered himself kindred spirit to Holly Maxwell? Dear God, no! "You!" she hissed. "You disgusting . . ."

"Yeah, it's me, girlie, and I promise you on the grave of whoever the bastard is that's under my feet here, you're gonna pay for this. We gave you a chance to be one of us, but you turned up your nose. Now you signed your death warrant by buttin' in where things don't concern you."

The girl was climbing to her feet, Holly holding her hand to steady her.

Holly called out to the man, "Someone heard me scream and they're coming—"

"Yeah, yeah," he called as he turned to run into the woods beyond. "I ain't goin' to jail over no nigger. But I'll take care of you later, bitch."

"Are you all right? Can you walk?" Holly asked the girl. "We've got to get out of here now. I was lying. Nobody's coming. We're on our own."

"Yes, yes, let's go," the young Negro girl moaned. "I'll make it."

Holly led the way back the way she had come as the girl continued to sob quietly, choking out her words. "I ain't hurt too bad, missy. I's bleedin', but them devils ain't got the best of Sally."

But, Holly thought dizzily, the girl was naked, and at least one of them had had his way with her.

"Just a little ways," Holly told her. "If they do come back now, we can run into the street and scream and surely to God someone will hear us."

Just as they crashed through the last remaining

bushes of the thicket, the sound of hoofbeats reached them. Dragging Sally, Holly stumbled into the street, waving her arms and yelling.

Scott Colter reined in his horse and swung out of the saddle in an instant. "Holly, what in hell—?"

She told him, the words tumbling forth, and his face tightened to a grim mask as he drew his side arm and moved away from her toward the knoll.

"No need," she said. "They ran. They're gone." Suddenly, she gave way to the bubbling hysteria she'd been fighting. Hot tears of rage spilled as she cried. "What has happened to this town? My God, can't you do anything? It's your *job* to keep peace! Young girls are being raped in cemeteries while you go traipsing after your women!"

Scott might have laughed over this sudden admission of jealousy. "Let's go," he said tightly to Sally.

Holly followed close behind Scott and Sally as the three of them walked the short distance to Abby's house. Scott knew better than to ask the injured girl if she could ride. She couldn't. When she stumbled, he picked her up and carried her, giving his horse's reins to Holly. She led the horse, her eyes on Scott all the way.

🐾 Chapter Eleven 🐾

SALLY stirred restlessly in her sleep, now and then moaning softly in her nightmares.

Holly had given in to weariness and dozed in the chair next to the bed. Suddenly she awakened, alert to the horror of the night before. She leaned over and gently touched Sally. "You're safe . . . safe now. No one's going to hurt you."

Sally's lashes fluttered open. Large, brown eyes mirrored stark terror. Holly had seen that same expression so many times in the eyes of a deer in that last second before a bullet killed it. She hated that look, always had, refusing to kill an animal if any other source of food could be found.

"Please believe me," Holly said softly. "You're safe, and no one is going to hurt you. I'm your friend."

Sally glanced warily around the room, the panic slowly disappearing. Her stare fixed on Holly as she asked tremulously, "Who are you? Where am I?"

Holly smiled and tucked the sheet closely under the girl's chin. She explained about Abby's house and told her, "My name is Holly Maxwell. If you don't remember everything, it's just as well."

Sally struggled to sit up, but Holly gently pushed

her back. "I do remember what happened," Sally
declared, "most of it, anyway. I got to get out of
here. They'll come back for me and they'll kill
me!" Her voice broke, and she pressed her fists to
her mouth to keep from screaming.

Holly quickly reached for the glass of brandy she
had placed on the bedside table. "Drink this," she
urged, "and you aren't going anywhere. I told you,
you're safe. Those men wouldn't dare come after
you. And you're going to be fine. A doctor examined you and said all you need is rest." She did not
tell her about the torn flesh the doctor had discovered. She would recall everything soon enough.

Sally downed the brandy, then flashed Holly a
guilty look. "I was tryin' to steal from 'em, and
they caught me, and that's why they was doin' what
they was doin'."

Holly was aghast, not at the girl's confession, but
that she could rationalize so easily. "Stealing or
not, they had no right to hurt you, Sally."

Sally was quick to inform her matter-of-factly,
"Their kind does that, 'specially since the war.
They say us freed slaves are gettin' uppity, that
there's only one way to handle us—hang the men
and rape the women."

Holly was furious. "What could you possibly
have been stealing from trash like that?"

Sally glanced away. "Food. I ain't had nothin' to
eat in three days. I been travelin' all around, lookin'
for work, but there ain't no work for freed slaves,
'specially women. I just got so hungry that when I
smelled somethin' cookin', I followed my nose. I
saw them men campin' up by the ruins of the old
church. Some taters were lyin' to one side, and

since they was busy drinkin', I figured they wouldn't see me when I sneaked out from the bushes to grab me some. But they did see me.'' She winced. ''You know what happened then. Now I gotta get out of here, 'cause they'll be after me.''

Holly stared at her in wonder. Sally was a pretty girl, with skin the color of rich, brown coffee, and dark eyes framed by thick lashes. She could see that the sheets framed a bony body. Holly shook her head. ''Don't worry, they won't be back. And we're going to get something to eat. I'll tell Abby you're awake. She's very nice.''

Suspiciously, Sally asked, ''Why you doin' this for me, missy? I'm a nigra.''

Holly took a deep breath. ''It doesn't make any difference to me, Sally. You're a human being, and you need help. What other reason do you suppose I need?''

She found Abby in the parlor with Claudia, and immediately they began firing questions at her.

''What do you plan to do with that girl?'' Abby wanted to know. ''I know you mean well, Holly, but really, dear, a Negro in my house. In one of my beds. I just don't know. . . .''

''Whatever made you do such a thing?'' Claudia cried. ''Why, God forbid, it could have been *you* those men attacked. Whyever did you leave the party without an escort?''

Holly was not about to defend herself at that moment. Addressing Abby, she said, ''Please, would you fix her something to eat? She hasn't eaten in three days. She's starving.''

''Well, of course, I'll feed her,'' Abby sighed, ''but then what? I'm sorry, but she can't stay here.

Dr. Grant didn't like being called out in the middle of the night to look after a Negro.''

Holly didn't care about Dr. Grant's feelings. "He'll get paid. I'll pay him myself.''

"Holly," Claudia began, hoping she was using her most patient voice. "The girl can't remain here. You can understand that. There are ruffians who continue to cause trouble, and you don't want to bring any trouble down on Abby, not after she's been so good to us. This is an imposition on her hospitality.''

Holly was anxious to return to Sally. "I do understand, and she won't be staying long. As soon as she's able, she'll be on her way. I promise.''

On her way where? Holly asked herself as she ran back upstairs. No telling what she'd been through even before last night's horror. No home, most likely. What was to become of her?

She found Sally just as she had left her, propped up on the pillows, looking very frightened. Holly drew her chair closer and sat down. "Abby will be up with something soon. She's a very good cook. Now tell me about yourself, Sally. Do you have family?''

Sally began to pick nervously at the sheet covering her. "I did once, but we got separated when we was sold to different folks. I guess I was seven, maybe eight, the last time I saw my mama. I don't know, 'cause I don't even know how old I am now." She squeezed her eyes tightly shut in an attempt to hold back the tears, but they spilled down her dark, sunken cheeks anyhow. She recounted her painful story. She had been torn from her mother's clutching arms because the plantation owner who bought Sally had no need of an old, pregnant "nigger wench," as he'd called her mother. Sally was young and would eventually, the man thought, make a good breeder for "good, strong buckstock" the man already owned.

Sally had become pregnant twice, giving birth to stillborn babies both times. Her master had decided she was worthless and sold her to someone else, who used her in the cotton fields. He mistreated all his slaves. Just before the war ended, Sally, along with all the others the man owned, ran away to hide. None of them had any real place to live.

"You're free now," Holly reminded her. "Listen to me. You can stay with me. I want to look after you—and I can certainly use the company." Quickly she told her about her home in the swamplands, her plans for herself.

Sally's eyes widened. "You want me to stay with you? But you're white. What would folks think?"

Holly laughed. "When you come to know me better, you'll realize how little I care for folks' opinions." Sally kept staring at her, disbelieving what she was hearing. "You can work with me, help me fish and raise vegetables in the garden. We'll share what I have. We'll make out."

Sally continued to look doubtful. "I don't know."

"But," Holly prodded, "I'm offering you a home, Sally. And I'll be grateful for your help."

Sally's eyes narrowed. "Tell the truth, missy, I just don't know what to make of what you offerin'."

Holly assured her it was not going to be a life of luxury for either of them.

"Bein' free is the most precious treasure God can give one of his children, missy," Sally said passionately.

"I ain't askin' for an easy life. I'm willin' to work hard."

"Then it's settled? You'll come home with me?"

A smile spread across Sally's face for the first time. "Yes'm, I will. Maybe I can be of some help to you. Sounds like you need a hand, and I figure it's the least I can do fo' you. Thank you, missy."

Holly assured Sally she was not in her debt. "Just eat, rest, and as soon as you feel up to the ride, we'll be on our way," she said, excited by the prospect of having a friend to live with. The cabin got awfully lonely. "Oh, and, Sally," she finished. "Call me Holly, please, not 'missy.' "

When Abby arrived with food, she told Holly that Colonel Colter was waiting for her in the back parlor.

The room, at the rear of the house, with a view of a nearby woods, was charming. The walls were bright yellow, and all the furniture was white wicker covered with green cushions. An abundance of windows allowed the morning light to spill into the room, making it cheerful and gay. Dozens of clay pots held healthy-looking plants.

Scott rose when Holly entered. She sat in a chair, eyeing him carefully. "Get to the point, Colonel," she said without the usual social amenities. "I've got a busy day ahead of me, and you're taking up my time."

He regarded her coldly. "I don't give a damn about your time, Holly. You've sure taken enough of mine lately. I want to know about last night. Tell me everything.''

Holly rolled her eyes. ''Really, Colonel Colter, must you force me to repeat the sordid details again? I told you everything last night.''

Leaning close to her, placing his hands on the side of her chair, he said, ''You were upset. Your concern was for the girl. Fine. I understand that. But now tell me all of it. I've got a job to do, and you're making it difficult. I don't like that.''

She sat up straight in the chair and pushed her hands against his chest in an effort to make him move away. It was like trying to move a boulder. Indignant, she retorted, ''I don't care what you like and don't like.''

He smiled slowly, maddeningly. ''Talk. I'm losing patience.''

She shook her head, baffled. ''Why are you so angry? What have I done?''

For an instant, his eyes opened wide, then narrowed again. He was very angry, more so than she had known.

''I'll tell you, Holly,'' he said harshly. ''I'm fed up. You walked out on your mother's party like a spoiled child, never mind if you ruined the evening for her. You were mad because I was with another woman when I ought to be grieving to death because you're too good to be courted by a Yankee soldier. Not that I want to court you, mind you. I'd wind up beating the hell out of you, you little brat.'' Holly was too aghast to speak. ''But I don't care about all that now,'' he said tightly. ''What I do care about is that girl. You said you saw the men and I want to know what they looked like. Tell me anything that might help, because I'm going to bring law to this town if it's the last thing I do.''

He straightened and sat down on the sofa, waiting.

She was furious. The nerve of him, thinking she was jealous. ''I hate to disappoint you, Colonel, but my leaving had nothing to do with you. What vanity!''

He waved impatiently. ''Forget that, damn it! It's not important. Tell me what happened last night. I don't have all day.''

She told him, bluntly, angrily, all she remembered, and when she finished he asked her to repeat the part about the man recognizing her. She obliged reluctantly.

''And you're sure he's the one who spoke to you earlier about helping him and his men?''

''Yes. I think I heard one of them call him 'Barney.' '' She stood. ''I can't remember anything else, and I do have things to do. I would like to go to your post and collect my belongings,'' she added sarcastically.

Suddenly, he grinned, warmly. ''I'll have one of my men bring your horse and gun, Holly. I wouldn't want to cause you any difficulty.''

''How thoughtful,'' she snapped. ''Now please go, Colonel.'' She walked to the door and stood there waiting while he, with insolent slowness, adjusted his scabbard, dusted at an imaginary spot on his dark blue coat, then made his way toward her. He paused and gave her a taunting smile. ''Don't fret too much over Lisa Lou, Holly. I'm just marking time with her until you grow up.'' He patted her cheek.

She slapped his hand away. "Don't you dare touch me, Scott Colter, ever again."

He grabbed her, pulling her against him as he kissed her. He released her after a long kiss and chuckled, "When are you going to grow up and admit this is what you want, little spitfire?"

"How . . . how dare you?" she sputtered.

He gave her a mischievous wink. "I dare, Holly—that and much more. It was good, wasn't it? *All* of it."

He turned and left, and she fought back the impulse to run after him and tell him a few harsh truths. Damn the man! He was arrogant and conceited and thought every woman in the world swooned over him. But she was not like other women. She was proud of that.

And someday, she vowed furiously, she would make him sorry he'd treated her so casually. Pride demanded she make him pay.

❧ Chapter Twelve ❧

HOLLY scattered corn, watching the clucking chickens as they fluttered and fought over their food.

She wiped sweat from her face with the back of her hand, glad she always took the time to braid her hair so it wouldn't be clinging to her. It was the time of dog days, so-called, and the weather was terribly humid. She recalled learning long ago in school that these hot days were named after Sirius, the Dog Star, which rose and set with the sun in July and early August. Well, she thought wearily, the middle of August was almost here, so it was time for that star to go somewhere else.

Mosquitoes hovered above the sleepy waters of the slough, and a bullfrog jumped up onto a rotting stump as Holly watched. Frogs and turtles abounded there. How she hated eating them for supper, but she'd learned to make do. She had no choice.

Things had not been going well for her. Money was scarce. Rain was scarce. The late garden of snap beans and sweet potatoes was parching. The fish had quit biting. Even night shrimping was bad.

Too many times the fishermen who took her nets to the Gulf in exchange for half the catch returned to say her nets had been pulled up empty, as had theirs.

No matter, she admonished herself, she was living the way she wanted to live, as a free spirit. She'd kept her promise to herself and her promise to Grandpa.

Things were going well for her mother, and Holly was glad about that. Every Sunday afternoon, Claudia and Jarvis visited her, bringing fried chicken, potato salad, and usually a cake or pie. Always there were fresh vegetables. Holly protested, but they insisted.

She was amazed to know how quickly Magnolia Hall was being rebuilt. She had to give Jarvis credit, too. Hiring nearly fifty people to get the place built fast meant lots of Negroes and whites were employed who otherwise would not have been.

Holly had not returned to Vicksburg since that last trip, but her mother was only too eager to keep her well informed. Her favorite topic was Lisa Lou Pollock. "That girl always did have her way about everything," she'd said on her most recent visit. "She chases after Roger because he's rich, and she chases after Colonel Colter because he's handsome."

Holly hadn't responded, so her mother prodded. "Don't you agree? He *is* handsome. Those eyes, why, a woman could drown in them."

"Mother, really! I wish you could hear yourself, prattling on about the man like . . . a giddy schoolgirl."

Her mother smiled knowingly. "Why, Holly, you're angry. Perhaps you're jealous, too."

Holly kept a rein on her tongue. She hadn't seen Scott and she was glad. Neil Davis had been out several times on patrol, always happy to see her. Holly liked him. He was nothing like Scott. Far too nice for comparison.

One Sunday Claudia and Jarvis arrived in a new, large carriage. The driver was a young Negro named Norman Grady. He and Sally had met that day, and now they spent every possible moment together. Norman was working at Magnolia Hall as a groomsman, preparing the newly built stables for the fine stock of horses Jarvis was buying. It seemed Sally was over there all the time now. Oh, Sally still made time to do her share of chores, but Holly was a little sad to see her moving closer to Norman, because she knew Sally would leave her soon.

It was funny, but she and Sally talked easily about slavery, about the plight of the freed Negroes, about the Night Hawks. But they shied away from discussing their early lives. It was as though neither was willing to part with the only precious thing she had left—memories, personal memories. All had shared equally in the horrors of the war just recently over, and all shared equally in poverty and exhaustion. But a person's life before the war was his own to keep, and since it was all he had left, most chose not to talk about it. Talking might loosen the boundaries people had constructed around their pasts. Better to leave the past intact by leaving it alone.

On the whole, Holly was glad to have Sally there. She was good company. She worked hard. And when she sensed that Holly wanted to be alone, she let her be.

The sound of a horse approaching brought Holly out of her reverie, and she went around the cabin, smiling, ready to see Sally and Norman. She had caught a big catfish that morning and planned to make a delicious stew, with hand-rolled dumplings. There was plenty if Norman wanted to stay. Holly knew he wanted to.

But it was Roger Bonham, dismounting from a magnificent black stallion. Impeccable, as always, he was wearing red riding breeches and a white, ruffled shirt. He smiled confidently, and began walking briskly toward her, his black knee-boots gleaming.

"Roger, whatever brings you out here?" she asked in a lusterless tone.

He grasped her hand and kissed her fingertips, then pretended to glower at her. "I didn't trust myself to come out before this. I've been so angry with you for running out on me, I'd have turned you over my knee and spanked you." He smiled. "I *was* hurt. But I've also had a lot of business to tend to." He glanced around, then looked back at her. "I came out to ask if you're going to allow me to escort you this weekend."

Holly pursed her lips. The wedding. She hadn't let herself think about it very much. "Are there many parties planned? I should remember, but I don't. Mother talks about it, but I must admit she goes on so that my mind wanders." It was true. Claudia was excited all the time, and she made Holly nervous.

Roger assured her that many activities were being

planned. "I stopped by to see Claudia before I left, and she said to tell you she's expecting you this week for final fittings on your gowns. She also said to tell you she was ordering you to let me escort you this weekend," he added, grinning confidently. "So why don't you make me a happy man and say yes?"

Holly stared down at her hands, blistered and callused. She looked a sight, but there was Roger, asking her anyway. A myriad of parties to face . . . . "I don't know. I—to be honest, I thought I'd just go to the wedding. I haven't given any thought to anything else."

"Your mother would be so hurt, Holly. She wants her happiness to include you." He rushed on to another subject. "Have you been to see Magnolia Hall lately? It's magnificent. Father's calling it the palace Claudia was meant to live in."

"I've been too busy, Roger. I still am. I don't see how I can get away for more than a day, really." He frowned, and because she knew she was being cruel to her mother, she gave in. "I'll go with you, Roger. Thank you."

"Wonderful!" he cried. "We'll have a marvelous time, I promise. Now then," he suddenly became serious. "How have things been going for you here? I haven't heard of any more trouble. Is everything all right?"

She shrugged, uncomfortable. She didn't like the way he was looking at her, so . . . so intensely. "It's hard work, but I'm managing. There hasn't been any more trouble. The army comes out on patrol now and then, but lately they haven't been here as often. I think everything has calmed down."

He stared at her in silence awhile. "You haven't forgotten my offer, have you? I'll give you a fair price for your land, Holly. A beautiful woman like you shouldn't be out here living like this, worrying constantly and—"

"Enough!" She forced a smile, trying to be jovial. Oh, how she hated to discuss her personal life. "I am doing fine, Roger, and if we're to enjoy ourselves this weekend, I must ask that there be no more talk like this. I don't like it."

Something flickered in his eyes and, in a moment, was gone. She stepped away.

"Very well, Holly. Just remember I'm here if you need me, all right?"

"I'm grateful," she responded, feeling guilty because she wasn't at all grateful.

They turned at the sound of hoofbeats, and Holly was delighted to see Norman. Sally was behind him, on the horse's rump, her arms tight about his waist, face pressed dreamily against Norman's shoulders.

"Does he hang around here very much?" Roger asked quietly.

Holly told him the story, finishing, "Sally's making a pest of herself at Magnolia Hall, I'm afraid. She's over there constantly. She says she's helping Mother, and I'm sure she is, but it's Norman she goes there for. Isn't it wonderful? They make such a nice couple." She hurried over to greet them. "Norman, can you stay for supper? I'm making catfish stew."

Norman gave her a happy grin of acceptance, but the expression disappeared the moment he saw

Roger Bonham glaring at him. "I . . . I don't know," he said hesitantly.

Roger nodded to him curtly. "I think you better get back now, Norman. I'm on my way there, and I want to talk to you about a horse coming in this week." He turned to Holly, suddenly brusque. "I'll be in touch. Your mother will be delighted to hear she can count on you sharing her happiness this weekend."

He mounted his horse and, without a backward glance, rode away.

"I better go," Norman said, twisting around to help Sally alight. He looked apologetically at Holly. "Thanks, ma'am. Another time, I'd be delighted."

After he'd gone, Holly echoed her disappointment to Sally. "I wanted him to stay."

Sally shrugged. "Well, the way Mastah Roger was lookin' at us, it's probably best Norman just went on and did what he was told. You know"—she shot her a meaningful glance—"there are folks who don't approve of me livin' here with you. Mastah Roger is probably one of 'em. Me and Norman was talkin' about it on the way over here. It's not a good thing."

"Is there something you're trying to tell me?" Holly asked.

Sally looked down at the ground. "Yes'm. I guess. Your mama asked me today if I'd go to work for her. I think I should." She lifted pleading eyes. "Don't you be mad with me now and think I ain't grateful for what you've done for me. I am. But I been thinkin' how I might bring trouble down on you by stayin' here. Besides, you ain't got a whole lot. You share your food with me times when you ain't got enough for yourself.''

Holly snapped, "Really, Sally, if it's Norman, if you're wanting to move over there to be close to him, then say so. Don't make excuses.''

Sally followed her inside, her brown cheeks glowing with a pinkish hue. She understood Holly's pride. Holly didn't want to give in to "trouble."

"He's gonna ask me to marry him, I know he is. Maybe I feel stronger about him than he does me, right now, but I want to be around so's he won't forget me.''

Holly picked up a long-handled cooking spoon and stirred the bubbling stew. "I won't try to talk you out of it, Sally,'' she told her, "but just remember, you are not a burden to me here. I'm glad to have your company, and I'll share with you whatever I have.''

"I know that, I know that,'' Sally said quickly. "I just want to be closer to Norman. And I am worried you might have trouble on account of me. A nigra livin' with a white woman—oh, that ain't looked on well by lots of folks.''

Suddenly Holly slammed her palms down on the table with a resounding smack. "Don't do this to me, Sally,'' she told her firmly. "Don't tell me you're afraid to stay here. It sickens me to hear such a thing. I can live as I choose and so can you. There is nothing to fear!''

Sally dropped her head. "I'm sorry.''

Holly plunged on. "I might suggest, too, that it pays to keep a man guessing. You're making your feelings too obvious by going over there to be close to him.''

Sally lifted her gaze challengingly. "Is that why you ain't got a man? 'Cause you don't know much about it?" There was good humor in her eyes. "You're so pretty," Sally was quick to tell her. "What I mean is, I know you ain't in love with no-body. Like that soldier, the one with the pretty blue eyes? He comes by here and you can tell he's just waitin' for you to act like you're interested, but you don't. You ain't even wantin' Mastah Roger to come callin'."

"Sally, really!" Holly faced her, hands on her hips. Despite her agitation, however, she couldn't help but be amused by the girl's concern. "When I decide I need a man in my life, I promise you'll be the first to know. So can we change the subject now?"

Sally turned away, a little sorry she had intruded. There was, she knew, a deep secret her friend was harboring. Maybe when she discovered what it was, then she would understand why Holly closed her heart to love.

It was late, and Holly tossed and turned restlessly on the fragrant, but lumpy, pine-straw mattress. "What is wrong with me," she whispered out loud, hearing Sally's gentle breathing from the other side of the room. She couldn't sleep, though she'd spent the day working hard. The moon was high, casting silver light across the room, and still she was wide awake.

She remembered, for some strange reason, whole evenings from the past, evenings of parties at their house or a neighbor's house, maybe the John Tollitson place, which was four miles away from

Magnolia Hall and older by a generation. In some lovely setting or other her mother would dance with her father, and Holly would be so proud of them, the handsomest couple in Mississippi. She would spend most of the evening with her friends, her girlfriends, talking about schools they might be going to or places they might soon visit with their parents. Later in the evening, she would dance with a boy, hesitantly, feeling just plain silly, and then go back to the group of girls by the piano.

What was strange, Holly thought, lying under her grandfather's comforters and looking out the window into the dark skies, was that whole evenings from a past she'd never see again should come flooding back to her without her wanting them to, whole evenings of happy times gone for good. It was an extra piece of torture, unfair and astonishingly cruel.

She got up and padded across the floor, quietly unlocking and opening the door, stepping outside into the gentle night. Lifting her face to the sweeping canopy of stars, she wondered what it was she felt eluding her. What, precisely, did she long for?

As quietly as the night wind, dark eyes beckoned. Smiling, teasing lips called to her. Strong arms folded her against a naked chest. Memories. She had only to close her eyes to see Scott Colter as clearly as though he was there.

Her fingertips instinctively touched her lips, and, for an instant, she could feel the warmth of his seeking mouth against hers. Damn, why couldn't she let her heart go? Why couldn't she give in to the restless spirit stirring within? Aching to break free? Why couldn't she run to him?

Lost in sweet memories that would not be denied, she failed to hear the stirring in the woods beyond, to see the man stealthily making his way across the yard.

He moved to the end of the porch and stepped silently over the railing. Only when he was right behind her, did she sense him.

His hands closed around her throat, stifling her scream. He leaned forward, so close she could feel his sour breath coming from the slit in his white hood. "No need to struggle. This time, bitch, you ain't got no gun."

He lifted her from the porch, dragging her across the yard. She struggled futilely, her feet kicking up dust. She felt herself slipping away as the pressure on her throat increased. Then, just as she was about to pass out, he released her, quickly stuffing a rag in her mouth.

He flung her to the ground and she lay there, fighting to breathe around the gag as he roughly jerked her hands behind her back and tied her wrists.

She saw the others then, all wearing the ominous-looking white robe and white hood. They formed a ring around her, and one spoke. "We ain't puttin' up with what you're doin' out here, Holly Maxwell, lettin' a nigger wench live with you like she was white. We're gonna show you what we do to trash like you and that nigger."

Tied, she watched in helpless horror as two of them ran to the woods, emerging with a large, wooden cross. One of them quickly dug a hole, and when he was done, the cross was set upright.

The sky exploded in a brilliant blaze of golds,

reds, blues, and greens as they set a torch to the cross. The fire against the black Mississippi night sky was awesome.

She struggled frantically to maneuver herself back, away from the wildly leaping flames, but she froze when a scream tore through the night. Sally was being dragged from the cabin, her own shrieking muffled against a gag.

One of the men dragging Sally shouted, "See what happens, nigger? See what happens when you think you're white? We ain't puttin' up with shit-skins!"

Sally was thrown toward the fiery spectacle, landing only a few feet from the flames. The heat seared her skin and scorched her nightgown, and she scrambled in the dirt, desperate to get away. The men allowed her to go only so far, then circled her, preventing escape.

"This is just a warning," one man roared, kicking Sally in her side. She drew herself into a knot, writhing.

A man near Holly yelled to her, "You listening to all this, nigger-lover? You seein' it good? 'Cause if the wench don't get out, we'll come back. And next time we'll hang her black ass and burn down your goddamn shack."

"Like this!" another called, racing to the cabin. He tossed the blazing torch and it landed squarely on the porch.

Laughing, shrieking like demons, the ghostly figures ran into the woods and disappeared. A few seconds later, rapid hoofbeats reverberated against the ground.

The porch caught fire. Oblivious to the scraping

of her body against the dirt, Holly struggled forward, looking at Sally, pleading silently, trying to shout despite the gag, but Sally was writhing on the ground, hysterical.

At last Holly reached Sally, throwing herself against her. That snapped Sally out of it, and she began untying Holly's ropes.

Freed, Holly yanked the gag from her mouth. "Water! From the well, Sally. Hurry or the whole place will go."

Holly grabbed a straw broom near the door and began beating wildly at the flames. The straw caught fire. Cursing, she tossed the broom away and ran inside. Grabbing the remainder of the catfish stew from the fireplace, she ran back to the porch and flung it on the flames as Sally reached the porch with a pail of water.

They stood and watched as the last sizzling flames died out.

Only then did Sally's hysteria return. Holly made sure Sally was not really injured from the kick, then helped her into bed. She found an old jug of muscadine wine Grandpa had made long ago. Pulling the cork free, she winced at the rank smell but urged Sally to drink. "You've got to get hold of yourself."

Holly was blinking back tears of her own—but not tears of fright. No. She was beyond fear. She was mad. Spitting mad. Fighting mad. "Drink," she commanded harshly, and Sally coughed and choked on the burning wine. "Drink and then try to sleep, Sally. It's over."

Sally gasped and swallowed, shaking her head.

"Ain't over," she choked. "Ain't gonna be over till I get out of here."

Holly shushed her. "Nonsense. They're only using you as an excuse. Don't worry. They won't catch me off-guard again."

Sally cried herself to sleep, and after she was quiet, Holly placed the gun within easy reach, then looked out the window. The burning cross was almost out, only a mass of charred timbers now. She stared at it until the sight sickened her. She finally fell asleep, the gun beside her.

❧ Chapter Thirteen ❧

SCOTT Colter lay on his back, arms behind his head, staring at the ceiling of room number 7, the Delta Hotel. The mattress sagged and the sheets were gray. What was left of the wallpaper was a ridiculous pattern of horses and cactus plants. Besides the iron-poster bed, there was a rickety table, a chair with splintered rungs, and a rusting spittoon. From the saloon below, the sounds of a tinny piano and raucous laughter drifted upward.

It was a goddamn depressing place, but it was perfect for meeting a woman without being seen. Directly outside the door was a narrow, dimly lit hallway running straight to the stairs, and the stairs led down to a back door that opened into an alley. It had to be that way. Damned if he could afford for anyone to know he was taking Lisa Lou Pollock to bed.

He swung his legs down onto the floor and walked to the window overlooking the alley. It was pitch dark. Good. Maybe she wouldn't come. That'd be fine.

He had brooded about this all day. He didn't like using women, and ever since Marlena had used

him, he knew firsthand how it felt. But, well, this
was different—a little different anyhow. Lisa Lou
was the kind who always had to have a man. If it
weren't him, it'd be somebody else. So it might as
well be him, because he had a job to do.

Oh, Lisa Lou had let him know it was Roger Bonham and his money she really wanted. Scott was
just someone to take her pleasure with, and damned
if she didn't seem to love it. A real wildcat. Nothing
shy about that one. She swore he was the best she'd
ever had, and, without conceit, he figured she was
telling the truth. He'd always had a belief where
women were concerned, that if a man took a woman
to bed, he owed it to her to make sure she was properly pleasured. He enjoyed knowing a woman left
his arms satisfied. Most came back to him as fast as
they could.

Holly was the only exception.

He slammed the palm of his hand against the
wall. He wished he didn't care. He'd tried so hard
not to. But something about her had gotten to him
and wouldn't go away. She hated Yankees. Well,
time would take care of that. But what did he want
from her? Hell, he didn't know.

She despised him. He could live with that. She
never wanted to see him again. He could fix that.
But there was something about her he couldn't
fathom, something that drew him. What?

The irony was, she was right in the middle of his
real reason for being in Vicksburg. She didn't know
that, of course. No one must know, or his secret
mission would be destroyed.

He rubbed his eyes. Everything was so almighty
complicated.

Meanwhile, there was Lisa Lou. That had worked out well because her father, Talton Pollock, was probably a member of the Night Hawks. In fact, Scott was confident he knew the identity of all the Night Hawks. Oh, but there was more, much more. And thanks to Lisa Lou, he now knew that Roger Bonham was paying visits to her father. That was just fine, since Roger Bonham was Scott's primary interest.

The doorknob turned. By the time the door opened, Scott had grabbed his holster from the back of the chair and was pointing his gun.

Lisa Lou stepped inside, a flurry of pink skirts and lace petticoats. Her golden hair hung loose about her glowing face. She smiled seductively. "Oh, my, Colonel," she cooed. "You aren't going to shoot a woman just because she wants your body, are you?"

He replaced his weapon and turned to face her as she scurried across the room to him. He was bare-chested, wearing only dark blue trousers, and she danced her fingers through the thick, dark mat of hair, provocatively kissing his nipples. "I've counted the hours till this moment, Scott. It's all I think about—being with you."

He wrapped one strong hand around her neck and laughed. "When you aren't thinking about getting Roger Bonham to marry you."

She made a face, pressing closer. Her breasts were spilling from the bodice of her dress, and she knew it. "Now, Scott. Don't you be jealous. A girl has to look out for herself, and you did say you're not the marrying kind."

He raised an eyebrow. "And if I were? Would

you marry a poor soldier who's lucky if he makes forty dollars a month?''

She fluttered her long lashes, a look she had practiced many hours before a mirror. ''Of course I would, if I loved him and he loved me. That's all that *really* matters. Besides, you're a colonel, so you make more than that. You're just teasing me.''

''And if Roger Bonham were to ask you to marry him, and you didn't love him,'' he goaded, ''don't you think his wealth would compensate for the lack of affection?''

She laughed, shoving her breasts against his chest. She moved her hands to his narrow waist, pulling him even closer. ''Why, Scott, darling, you're jealous. And I thought I was just someone to take your pleasure with. And what pleasure it is!''

Good, Scott decided, let her think he was jealous. She wouldn't suspect the real reason for his probing questions. ''Have you seen Roger lately?''

She shrugged. ''Not socially. He did come to see Papa this evening, though. I thought maybe he was coming by to ask to escort me to his father's wedding this weekend, but he was there to see Papa. He seemed mad about something.''

''Did you leave before he got through talking to your father? He might have been planning to speak with you when they were finished.''

She moved her fingers down his stomach to the front of his trousers, probing teasingly. ''He didn't stay long. He and Papa went into the study, and after ten minutes or so he walked out of the house without even looking at me. It was strange, because he'd been by earlier, then left to go home, and then he came all the way back again. It was already dark.

I didn't ask any questions, though, because Papa gets very upset if I'm nosy."

Scott was having trouble concentrating. Her cool fingers were probing deeper into his trousers, and she was tickling him expertly.

"Maybe Roger'll ask you tomrrow," he murmured, pressing his hands against her buttocks.

She shook her head. "I'd rather go with you this weekend. He'll be too busy to pay any attention to me." She gave an exaggerated sigh. "If I were as cunning and conniving as the Maxwell women, I wouldn't have any problems. That Claudia certainly knew what she was doing when she set her sights on Jarvis Bonham. I reckon he's the richest man in Mississippi, and she'll be the richest woman."

Scott decided now was not the time to tell her he had no plans to escort her to the wedding. He was properly aroused, and he said in a husky voice, "Unfasten my trousers. See if you find anything you want."

"Oh, yes," she laughed, delighted, nimbly undoing the buttons. "I'll find something I want . . . and then I'll *get* what I want."

She freed his erect organ and began to slide her hand expertly up and down it, gently but urgently. She knew exactly what she was doing. "Suppose you get undressed and into bed," he whispered.

"No." Her voice was so firm, so sharp. He stared at her, and suddenly she dropped to her knees before him, placing her hands firmly on his hips. Her eyes were feverish as she whispered, "I want to make you happy, Scott. I want to please you till you beg to be my slave forever."

He started to protest, but her lips closed around him and he was, for the moment, lost. . . .

When she had taken him to glory, he reached down and lifted her to her feet. He dropped her on the bed and, without bothering to undress her, lifted her skirts and removed her underthings and plunged in. She gasped, moaned, whispered, "I can't believe you're still ready. Oh, Scott, oh—" Her words were lost in cries of ecstasy. . . .

Later, when they lay side by side, Lisa Lou once again brought up the subject of the weekend. "Even though Holly hates me, my parents received invitations to everything. Jarvis is determined to make his silly old wedding the biggest thing that ever happened around here. At least, with you escorting me, Holly will see that she can't have every man around here. It's obvious she's got eyes for you."

Scott was bored. If there was one thing he hated, it was pillow talk. He'd pleased her several times, and she'd taken care of him. What did they have to talk about?

It was different when there was real caring. Hell, he'd wanted to stay with Holly, talk to her, just be with her. With Lisa Lou, it was a waste of time. "Don't you think you should be getting home?" he asked. "Your father might find you gone. I don't need him looking for me with a shotgun."

She hadn't bothered to pull her skirts down and she continued to lie there with her legs spread. She liked the way she looked. Absently, she answered, "Oh, Papa won't check on me. He rode out right after Roger left. Mama went to bed with one of her headaches."

Scott tensed. If Talton Pollock left after a visit

from Roger Bonham, that probably meant the two were in cahoots, as he'd suspected. "No need to take any chances. It's late. You should get back," he said abruptly, jumping off the bed to dress.

Irritably, Lisa Lou pushed her skirt down and sat on the edge of the bed. "Why are you always like this?" She glared at him. "You never want to stay with me. It might interest you to know that a woman doesn't like to be dismissed . . . like"—she sputtered with anger—"like a prostitute who's finished her job!"

Scott suppressed a smile. He was well aware of a woman's needs. "I'm sorry. All right?" he said softly. "I've got things I have to do. Forgive me?"

She pouted, folding her arms stiffly across her bosom. "Are you going to escort me this weekend."

He took a deep breath. Time to get it over with. "Sorry. I'm not sure I'll even be going."

He braced for the storm. It came.

Lisa Lou exploded in fury, leaping to her feet to call him a selfish bastard. Screaming that she would never speak to him again, she flounced out of the room and slammed the door.

Scott reached for his holster and buckled it on. He'd give her two days before she came to the post to whisper what room she'd be waiting in. She'd thrown fits before when she didn't get her way, and it never bothered him. Make a slave of him? Hardly. Only as long as the passion lasted.

He left the hotel and made his way back to the post. All was quiet. A good sign. He exchanged salutes with the sentry outside the door to the main building, then went to his office. Taking a bottle of whiskey from the bottom drawer of his desk, he poured a drink, then sat down and propped his feet up.

Holly came to mind. But then, Holly always came into his mind. She could be devastatingly beautiful at a formal party, or little-girl, pixie-cute in the woods.

It was no accident that he'd been in the swamps the day they met. He'd been there to look around, learn the land, try to figure out just where the gold had been brought ashore and buried.

The gold. The goddamn gold.

That was why he'd been sent to Vicksburg in the first place—to look for Union gold that no one was even supposed to know was missing.

It had happened in the final weeks of the war. A shipment of gold worth over a million dollars had disappeared somewhere in Missouri while being secretly transported from California to Washington. The general responsible for the unauthorized transfer, now a recently appointed undersecretary of state, had been ordered to leave the gold where it was, in California, in a fort. But the general didn't share his colleagues' optimism over a Union victory. What if the South won? So, on his own initiative, the general moved it secretly, planning to get it safely to Washington. He expected to be rewarded handsomely for taking initiative and saving the fortune.

The Federal government had not known of the plans, but thieves had. The gold was stolen. The security lapse had to have occurred inside, and Colonel Scott Colter was given orders to find the shipment and do so quietly. The entire operation had to be conducted discreetly. If word got out that the gold was missing, a great many people would suffer, not the least of whom would be the undersecretary of state who had caused the mess.

The gold had been part of a wagon train, accompanied by a handful of guards. The raid occurred just as the wagons were crossing the Missouri River. The guards had been left for dead, but one had lived and reported overhearing the thieves talking about plans to head down the Mississippi River. Miraculously, the man had heard the name "Bonham" spoken twice, during the raid.

Scott took that information to the general, now undersecretary, responsible for illegally removing the gold in the first place, and he had stared incredulously at Scott. "Bonham! Jarvis Bonham could have leaked the information. I trusted him. I had to. I had to get his permission to cross his land in a stretch not normally traveled along the Missouri River. A long stretch in Illinois. Hell, we couldn't risk a public crossing. But . . . but Bonham's a respectable man. I've known him a long time. I'd never suspect he couldn't be trusted, not in a million years. Not Jarvis Bonham."

"We're not talking about a million years," Scott quipped. "We're talking about a million *dollars.* That kind of money can sell a lot of trust, General."

Scott investigated Jarvis Bonham's background and found himself sharing the general's surprise. There was no shadow on his past. He had great wealth, too, but Scott supposed even a wealthy man might be tempted by a million dollars in gold.

His gut feeling was that Bonham was not responsible, but he continued the investigation according to the little he knew. A break had come with the bribing of a river rat, Sol Hinky, who knew something worth knowing. Hinky had been drinking and dozing in the bushes along the bank, in Illinois, when he heard a commotion. Waking, he watched in the moonlight as crates were loaded onto a boat. The crates were heavy, he knew, because it took several men to carry each one.

He'd not overheard anything, he told Scott, because not long after he woke up, he developed a bad case of the hiccups and someone heard him, knew he was there. He took off running, and they'd come after him, shooting at him. Frightened, he had never told anyone what he'd seen. He'd also never told anyone that he'd recognized one of the men helping load the ship. A ne'er-do-well named Wiley Olmstead who lived in nearby Cairo.

Scott took another swallow of the whiskey as he recalled that next crucial juncture. He couldn't let anyone know he was looking for the shipment of gold. He'd told Hinky only what the old drunk needed to know and no more. If Olmstead knew that the boxes he loaded had contained gold, then he wasn't going to talk about it. Further, he could tip off the thieves that someone was on their trail.

Scott found Olmstead and followed him around awhile until he learned what an unscrupulous man he was. Not liking the method, but knowing it was the only route open to him, he accosted Olmstead one night as he left a saloon, held a gun to his neck, and took him to the very dock where the gold had been loaded. "You helped load something here a few weeks back. Tell me everything you know about it. Everything, Olmstead, 'cause I know everything about you.''

"I ain't tellin' you a goddamn thing!" his prisoner screamed.

Scott gagged him easily and dragged him into the murky river, tying him neck-deep to one of the pier pilings. When Olmstead's eyes were bulging with fear of the water moccasins that abounded, Scott yanked him out of the water and tossed him on the muddy bank. He loosened the gag, and Olmstead babbled, begging to be believed. He didn't know what was in the crates. "They gimme ten dollars to help get the boat in here and out, 'cause I know the tricky currents. That's all I did—helped 'em in and out. I don't know nothing."

Scott was not satisfied. "You're bound to have heard something. I want to know every goddamn thing you heard . . . every word, name, anything."

Thrashing in the mud, Olmstead tried with all his might to remember. Someone, he recalled, said something about having a cousin in Vicksburg he was looking forward to seeing once the job was finished. That was about all Scott got out of the encounter—that Vicksburg was probably where the gold had gone. And he got a few names from Olmstead. One of the names was Bonham. Curiously, the description didn't fit a fifty-three-year-old man. The fellow Olmstead thought was called Bonham was in his late twenties. It had been dark, of course, but still. . . .

Scott took Olmstead with him to Washington rather than leave him behind to talk, and he trumped up a charge that would keep Olmstead out of the way until the gold was found.

Realizing he needed help in the investigation, Scott set out for Vicksburg with Captain Neil Davis. It hadn't taken long to learn that Jarvis Bonham, at the urging of his son Roger, had purchased a large tract of land on the banks of the Mississippi. Now Scott was sure. It was Roger who was behind the theft, not Jarvis. He'd probably found out about the gold coming through by reading correspondence between his father and the general.

All Scott had to do at that point was find out where in the Vicksburg area the gold was hidden. Slowly, the pieces of the puzzle had begun to fit together. Had Holly not found a way to keep her land from being sold, the Bonhams would have purchased it along with the larger tract. The Night Hawks were determined to scare her off that very parcel of land. Therefore, the gold had to be on, or close to, Holly's property. It made perfect sense. The terrain around the swamp was so full of hollows and rises that anything could be buried there.

There were still a lot of questions. Were the Night Hawks actually the gold thieves? Not all of them. From what he'd been able to learn about Talton Pollock, the man had been in Vicksburg when the theft took place. Still, Pollock had dealings with Roger, and Scott was planning to learn whatever he could about Pollock.

Time was important. Scott had to solve the mystery of the theft before it became publicly known that the gold was missing. His own military record would surely be blighted if it came out that he'd helped keep the lid on things. And now, with Holly, he had a personal stake in the whole, rotten mess.

Scott shifted in his chair, reaching for the whiskey, then deciding not to drink any more. What were the Night Hawks up to? Were they riding that night, or not? How much could he afford to worry about Holly without driving himself into a frenzy?

He had put together enough about the gold and Roger Bonham to know that Holly wasn't in any real danger. They might burn down her grandfather's shack to scare her off, true, but there was no way a clever manipulator like Roger would bring trouble down on himself by letting someone get badly hurt or killed. No, Holly was safe. If he believed otherwise, Scott would not have allowed her to stay where she was. He'd have found some way of getting her back to Vicksburg.

Of course, she didn't know that. She had every reason to be terrified. Damn the girl, why did she have to be so all-fired set on having her own way? She wouldn't budge and nothing could make her. He smiled wryly. Holly and Lisa Lou had more in common than they thought.

He stretched. He needed sleep, but he knew he'd lie awake awhile, as always, staring at the ceiling and wishing he could forget Holly.

It would, he surmised with a slow smile, be much easier to solve the riddle of the stolen gold than to fathom the mystery of Holly Maxwell.

$\text{\textcolor{black}{≈}}$ Chapter Fourteen $\text{\textcolor{black}{≈}}$

HOLLY awoke in a sweat of terror as the world exploded in a rolling thunder of hoofbeats. It all came back—the angry men in hoods, the cross flaming crimson against the black sky. Grabbing her gun, she had it cocked by the time she opened the door.

"Holly, don't shoot!"

She squinted in the sudden glare of early morning sunshine. It was Roger, reining in his horse and leaping from the saddle.

He held out his arms to her. "Put the gun away. It's all right." He approached slowly, in case she was hysterical and might shoot. "Sally came at first light and told us what happened."

"It's an outrage!" Jarvis Bonham arrived then, face tight with anger as he swung down from his horse. "Now put that gun away and tell us what went on here last night."

Six or seven men, all armed, rode up and dismounted, taking in the blackened, charred remains of the cross and exchanging looks.

Holly laid the gun aside, since it seemed to be

making everyone so nervous. "What about Sally?" she demanded. "Is she all right?"

Roger nodded. "She was naturally hysterical. Said she wouldn't stay here another minute knowing what she'd caused to happen."

"She didn't cause a damn thing to happen," Holly snapped, going back inside the cabin. "Those bastards were trying to scare me off my land again, that's all. I suppose I'm going to have to kill somebody before they'll leave me alone," she said.

Jarvis followed Holly and Roger inside, shaking his head. "There's no need for all this trouble, no need at all," he said irritably. "Holly, you know you have a home with me and your mother. Leave this place. You're just causing everyone a lot of worry and grief by being so stubborn."

She turned on him, glaring. "Mr. Bonham, I resent your interference. Your marrying my mother doesn't give you any rights over me. I think"—she drew in her breath, let it out slowly—"that I would like for you to take your men and go."

Good grief, was there no end to the girl's obstinance? "Can't you see we're trying to help you?" he roared. "Enough's enough. Now get your things and come back with me. I have to tell Claudia about this, and she'll take it easier if you're there when I do. She'll know you're all right if she can see you."

Holly shook her head, and Roger said, "Father, maybe you'd better do as she asks. I'll stay with her till the soldiers get here." He stood between them, looking from one to the other.

Holly blinked. "Soldiers?" she asked.

Roger sighed, feeling his own patience waning. He was determined to be the peacemaker, but she was so difficult. "Did you think the army wouldn't have to be notified about something like this? Now, I know you're upset, Holly, but be reasonable. I'll stay here with you till you finish answering their questions, and then I'll take you to Magnolia Hall.

"You know you want to go there," he rushed on before she could say anything, "to see how Sally is. And you need to prepare for the wedding."

He was right. She also admitted to being upset about Jarvis. She wanted to like the man, but he was not helping matters by trying to take over. She knew he wanted to buy her land to add to his empire. Maybe, she dared to wonder, he was behind the scheme to frighten her away.

Roger snapped at Jarvis, "Will you do as she asks and get out of here? It's obvious she resents your presence."

"It's obvious," Jarvis responded indignantly, "that my efforts at friendship have been in vain." He turned and strode angrily out of the cabin, calling to his men to mount up.

Holly was at once contrite. After all, he was going to be her stepfather. She had been rude. She'd let her emotions and her imagination run wild. She started after him, but Roger caught her arm.

"Don't."

She looked up, stunned. "Why not? I should apologize. I was rude."

"So was he." He held her arm, but gently, and his voice was soft. "It isn't important that you get along with him, Holly. It's best you keep your distance. Believe me, I have reasons for telling you this. Just let him go. I'm here, and you can count on me.''

She was so confused by all this. Why was Roger so hostile toward his father? And what was he alluding to? Why should she keep her distance? There was no time, however, to ponder these things, for Jarvis had no more than led his men away, than riders approached from the opposite direction. She walked to the window and peered out, chiding herself for the sudden wave of disappointment at seeing Neil Davis leading the patrol. It might have been Scott.

Roger went out to meet the soldiers. ''Captain Davis, when is the army going to put a stop to these blasted night riders!'' he yelled without preliminary. He pointed to the remains of the cross. ''Look at this. Blasphemy! How long is this going to go on?''

Neil chose not to respond. He looked beyond him to Holly, standing in the doorway. ''Are you all right? Did they hurt you?'' he called. There was real kindness in his voice.

She shook her head.

He dismounted and walked toward the door, ignoring Roger, who watched, eyes narrowing.

Neil took her hand, eyes searching hers. ''Are you sure you're all right? Can you talk about what happened? I need to know all you can tell me.''

Roger came alive then, storming, ''Hell, no, she won't talk about it. You'll just upset her. I'll take her inside and get her settled, and then I'll let you know whatever she tells me.''

Neil looked at him stonily. ''I'll ask the questions, Mr. Bonham. I really don't know what your interest is in this incident," he added.

"Incident!" Roger snorted. "You call it an 'incident' when hoodlums ride on helpless women? I might say I've shown more interest in Miss Maxwell's welfare than the damned, inefficient army ever has!"

"That's enough out of you!" Neil's voice cracked like a whip. "Go away before I lose my temper."

"Why, I'll have you court-martialed—" Roger shouted.

Holly quickly stepped between them. "It's all right," she said to Roger. "I'm sure the captain needs to question me. Just wait for me, and when he's finished, I'll go with you to see about Sally."

Roger nodded stiffly, all the while meeting Davis's burning gaze, letting him know he was not afraid, and was acquiescing only out of respect for Holly.

Holly motioned Neil to follow her inside. "I'm sorry about all that. I'll be glad to tell you what I know."

She sat down at the table, and Neil took a seat next to her. His blue eyes shone with affectionate concern, and he placed a gentle hand over hers, squeezing. "Start at the beginning, and leave nothing out."

She did. He listened intently, then said, "I'll relay what you've told me to the colonel. You go now and check on the girl, then get some rest. I'll try to get by later in the day to ask her some questions."

Holly dared to yield to her overwhelming curiosity. "Might I ask why the colonel didn't come?"

She tried to sound only mildly annoyed, nothing else.

Neil couldn't tell her that Scott had indeed come along but, seeing Roger, had gone into the woods to avoid a confrontation. Scott's prime suspect in the gold theft mustn't be allowed to think Scott was interested in whatever went on there. Let Roger think, Scott had explained to Neil, that Scott hardly even knew who Roger Bonham was. An occasional social meeting, all right, that couldn't be avoided. But nothing should make Roger wary of Scott.

"He's busy in town," Neil told her. "But he'll want a full report. Whether you think so or not, he manages to keep abreast of everything that goes on within his command."

She shrugged. "It's not important. I'm sure you'll do a good job, Neil." She gave him a sincere smile of appreciation.

Neil looked at her thoughtfully, arguing with himself. He should mind his own business, he told himself. Maybe he was just jealous, but damn it . . . "I can't help but be curious, Holly. You and the colonel don't seem to bring out the best in each other. I fought with him in the war, and we were together for almost four years. I know him, and I sense that something happened between you two that caused you to be enemies. Am I right? It's so strange." She kept her head lowered in what she hoped was a dignified, but resentful, silence. "I'm sorry," he said finally. "It's just that, he's a fine man, if you'd give him a chance. He makes a hell of a friend."

Holly smiled coolly. "It isn't important that we be friends, Neil. Please don't concern yourself."

Oh, Lord, he felt like a fool. "Okay, I'm sorry."
He plunged on. "I'd like to see you, Holly, even
think about courting you later on. And, well, I
wasn't sure if, you know, if you and Colter might be
seeing each other if you get things smoothed out."

She stood. "I think we both have things to do,
Neil," she said pointedly.

He nodded and left the cabin. Holly hurriedly
took a sponge bath from the water basin, then
dressed in a long beige cotton skirt and a green muslin blouse. Brushing her hair, she pulled it into a
neat bun at the nape of her neck. There would be
time later for a proper bath and shampoo at Magnolia Hall.

Roger was waiting for her outside. He'd saddled
her horse, and he helped her mount. They rode
away, leaving Captain Davis and his men to search
for whatever clues the Night Hawks might have left
behind.

They did not see Colonel Colter come out of the
woods as soon as they left. . . .

Riding along the riverbank, Roger offered, "I
can see why you love it here."

It was so peaceful. Like the old days, riding with
Grandpa. "It's so beautiful . . . and mysterious,"
Holly said. "The old-timers say the men of the river
country had to be tough and tricky to survive.
Grandpa used to say a man who made his living on
the river had to be part horse, part alligator, with
touches of snapping turtle and wildcat."

Roger laughed heartily. "All that? And you think
you can survive? A lovely fluff of a girl like you?"

She knew he wasn't making fun of her.
"Grandpa said he raised me to be what the old-

timers call a 'hoss,' so I don't worry about my-self.''

"A *'horse'*?''

"Not a 'horse,' Roger,'' she laughed. "A 'hoss,' pronounced just like I said it. That's a man who's known for strength and courage. You have to be strong to live here. It's big-fish-eat-little-fish.''

He smiled. She was warming to him. Good. Maybe his whole scheme was going to work out sooner than he'd thought. Fine, because time was precious. "It doesn't sound very pleasant,'' he said.

She ignored his remark, and went on wistfully, almost reverently, "There's a code of honor here, though. Like when the floods come. A fisherman will choose to die of hunger rather than eat fish trapped in a half-submerged shed. It wouldn't be fair to eat the fish, because the fish are fighting for their lives, same as they are.''

Roger sniffed. "Ridiculous. Honor for fish? Really, Holly, people around here are brought up on nonsense.''

He did not see the cryptic look she gave him. It was times like this, Holly realized, when the nag-ging suspicion returned. Something told her that Roger Bonham was a very complicated person . . . and not to be trusted. There was just something, something she couldn't define. Something dictated she be wary.

"Grandpa said the river was almost holy, that he got his strength from it, so it must have given him life. He wanted to be buried in it, but Mother wouldn't hear of such a thing, so she had him put in the family cemetery on our land . . . now your fa-

ther's land,'' she added tightly. ''He didn't tear it
up, did he?''

''Oh, of course not, Holly,'' he said airily. ''Father may be land-hungry and power-hungry, and I
may get quite disgusted with him from time to time,
but he's not the sort to destroy cemeteries.'' He
looked at her and laughed condescendingly.

Holly lapsed into silence, the peaceful moment
between them thoroughly shattered by her doubts.
He was polite enough, and he seemed to care for
her, but each time she tried to talk to him, she felt
further and further away from him. It seemed he
was making fun of her.

They rounded another sweeping curve of the
great river, and Holly rose higher in the saddle so as
to see better. The magnificent view never failed to
make her heart beat faster.

The house, two stories tall, stood high on the hill,
a lush carpet of grass rolling toward them. A low
stone wall was set at the base of the hill. There was
a wide veranda, and the view from the house was
spectacular, sweeping for a mile around and more.
The windows were in sets, two large sets on the
main floor, with four smaller, narrower windows
just above. The second-floor windows jutted out to
give the appearance of towers.

Roger's face twisted in a sarcastic grin. ''Father
said he's always wanted to have a house like this for
the woman who could make him happy.''

Something struck Holly then. Hadn't Jarvis built
a dream house for Roger's mother? Hadn't he been
happy with her? But Roger was talking and she
hardly felt she could ask him.

''He's had to get the grounds ready in time for the

wedding, and it's still not all done. In the spring, he's going to have the grass replanted in different shades of green, to look like a checkerboard! There'll be full-time gardeners tending the rose gardens, a large pond for goldfish, and he plans on gardenias and jasmine. Father said he wanted every breath your mother breathes to be sweet,'' he added with contempt. Did he hate his father for showing off? But Roger was quite a dandy himself, after all.

Holly was impressed with what Jarvis had accomplished. And he was providing employment for lots of people. ''It's certainly more lavish than our old house. Frankly, I'd be very resentful if it weren't my mother living there.''

Roger sniffed. He rambled on about the house. The upstairs had six large bedrooms, each with a private bath and dressing room. All flanked an upper gallery. Claudia's suite was to the rear, for a view of the gardens, and Jarvis's was beside hers, to the front. ''Yours and mine are on the opposite side, you know,'' Roger drawled.

''Mine?'' Holly said. ''I won't be living there. I have a home.''

He reached over to pat her hand. ''Nothing would please me more than to have you move here so we could be together more often. After last night,'' he grimaced, ''I'll be worried sick about you out there in the swamps by yourself.''

''I'll be fine. As for your wanting us to be together more often,'' she paused, trying so hard not to offend him, ''I don't want us to court, Roger, and I'm sorry if you've gotten the wrong impression.''

He stiffened, staring straight ahead. ''Your

mother didn't feel she was too good for a Yankee.
What makes you think you are?''

Holly gasped, ''Roger! That's not the point!''

''Yes, it is,'' he·whipped about to glare at her.
''Everyone knows how stubborn you are, not caring
that you worry the hell out of everybody by insisting
on living in the swamps. Don't you think the army
has better things to do than keep an eye on you?
Doesn't it bother you to cause so much trouble?''

Holly could not believe this. Always, Roger had
been polite, kind. And here he was, railing at her as
though he had only hatred for her. He was suddenly
a stranger, and suddenly she knew what it was about
him that caused her to be so apprehensive. He was a
stranger. She never knew when he was being his
true self and when he was acting.

''I offered to buy your land,'' he went on in a voice
thick with resentment. ''You don't have to sell to
my father. I'll take it off your hands, give you a fair
price, and you can move here. Or move to town. Or
go to New Orleans. Go anywhere you want to go.''

''I have to keep that land. I made a promise, and I
intend to keep it, no matter what.''

''Then keep the damn, worthless land,'' Roger
cried furiously. ''Just get off of it. Move. Quit worrying your mother and everybody else. I'll give you
money to live on. So will my father. Just get out,
Holly. Stop being such a problem.''

She bit back tears of humiliation. She dug her
heels into her horse's flanks and rode ahead.

Roger viciously popped his riding crop over his
horse, taking him into a fast gallop. As he flashed
past her, he yelled, ''Just go your own way, Holly.
I've no time for a pigheaded woman!''

She slowed down, watching him race ahead. Why had he reacted so violently? Whatever was the matter with him? Good Lord, he was a complex person—and she surely wanted nothing more to do with him if she could possibly avoid it.

A cloud passed and the dazzling sun disappeared as she reached the long entrance path to her mother's home.

❧ Chapter Fifteen ❧

ROGER Bonham was breathing almost as heavily as his horse as he rode into his father's new stable. He was furious with himself. Why had he lost control in front of Holly?

Never, he told himself as he leaped from the horse, had he encountered a woman so damnably stubborn. What was it going to take to get her off that goddamn land? Already he was being forced to slip out there and dig up a little of the gold once in a while, to give to his men. He thanked heaven for the rough terrain. The digging left no scars. His men were impatient. They wanted their full shares so they could be on their way. They were thoroughly discontented with being part of the Night Hawks, and they all wanted out. He had to get Holly out of there fast, at least long enough to make a massive dig and be done with it. Bringing out a million dollars in gold bars a few at the time might take a hundred years.

He glanced about in the shadows irritably. Where was that worthless Negro? The horse needed a rubdown, and Norman was probably coddling that wench of his. Hell, she'd been scared almost white.

Why hadn't Holly reacted the same way? She hadn't acted frightened—just mad as hell. Why?

Something moved in the shadows. "Norman," he yelled. "Take care of this horse. If you don't start earning your keep around here, I'll have my father run your sorry ass off this land." At least he didn't have to control himself in his father's stables, thank heaven.

Barney Phillips stepped noiselessly out of a stall.

Roger nodded, unsurprised. "At least you showed up here. You did something like I told you to," he said bitterly. "You idiots weren't too effective last night. Holly wasn't scared away. Just the wench—and she's not who we're after, you know," he reminded him sarcastically.

Barney picked at his teeth with a chipped fingernail, studying Roger. "Seemed scared at the time, she did. Don't know what else we could'a done except kill the nigger right in front of her, and you said not to kill nobody."

"You fool!" Roger wondered for the hundredth time how he could have picked such ignorant people to work for him. Well, there hadn't been a hell of a lot of time to be choosy. "Of course I don't want anyone killed. Not unless it's absolutely necessary. That will bring the law down on us, you moron. God, I wish we could get that gold so you and the rest of the idiots could get out of here."

Barney snorted. "You don't want that any more'n we do, Bonham. Don't know of one of us that ain't itchin' to go home. 'Specially when you expect us to take orders from that shit-brain, Pollock,'' he growled. Barney wasn't too bright, but he knew when he was mad.

Roger sighed. He didn't like Talton Pollock a bit better than his men did, but Pollock was the one who'd given him the idea of hiding the gold where it was. No one around Vicksburg knew, of course, that Pollock had been a traitor in the war, selling information to the Union. Roger, anxious to stay out of the fighting, had been only too happy to work for the government. His job had been seeing to it that spies and other undercover people got paid. That was how he'd met Pollock. Later, when he overheard Jarvis talking to that pompous general about allowing the gold to cross his property, he had seen a way at last to make a fortune and stop living off his father.

He'd realized he needed Pollock's knowledge of the river and the local terrain, and, sure enough, Pollock had decided where the gold should be hidden. Choosing the Maxwell property, he'd cited easy access from the river, isolation, and the fact that the old man who lived there was often away for a couple of days at a time. Roger would have no problem getting title by paying the taxes, and there wouldn't be anything the old man could do about it. The plan had been so simple.

"So what are we gonna do next?" Barney was riled. "How long can we keep ridin' on her land in the middle of the night without one of us gettin' killed? Look what happened to Wellman. That little gal knows how to shoot. You can't tell me she couldn't 'a killed him if she'd wanted to.''

"Wait a minute!" Roger cried, rubbing his hand

across his forehead. "Where is Wellman? Still hiding out?"

Barney nodded. Wellman had no intention of leaving till he got his share of the gold. "He said you told him you'd bring his gold out so he could be on his way, and I don't mind tellin' you he's gettin' real pissed. Says he's tired of sittin' on his ass doin' nothing while you're draggin' yours. Truth is," he added in warning, "I'm gettin' worried about him. You don't do somethin' soon to get him gone, he's liable to go to the law.

"The other night me and a couple of the boys went to take him food and liquor, like we do every couple of days, and he said he had a good mind to just go get the gold himself, then turn you in to the law to take the heat off him while he hightails it outta here. He even asked if any of us would be interested in joinin' him. Now I told you I was with you, Bonham, but I can't speak for the others. They're gettin' restless and you better do somethin'."

Roger smiled. The stupid bastard didn't know he'd just given him a great idea. This time, Holly would be so frightened she'd never return to her land. It meant she would have to get hurt, but she would mend in time. Besides, he smiled to himself, he'd be there to kiss away the hurt.

"You goin' crazy?" Barney demanded testily. Roger's smiles and laughter were always so ugly. "I just get through tellin' you we got big problems with Wellman, and you start laughin' like a loonie."

Roger dismissed him with a careless wave. "Go tell Wellman I've got one more job for him to do, and then his share of the gold will be waiting and he can be on his way. Tell him''—Roger's manner became deadly—''to slip in here and hide out and wait till he sees his chance. Then I want him to attack Holly, slap her around, hurt her. All the while, I want him threatening to kill her. I want her, damn it,'' he said fiercely, ''to think she *is* being killed. I'll rush in at the last minute and save her. I'll let him get away, she'll be properly scared, and I think our problems will be over.''

Barney's eyes bulged. He was going to let that girl be hurt? Like everyone else, Barney figured he was getting sweet on her. ''You sure you know what you're doin'? Wellman keeps sayin' if he ever gets a chance, he'll fix her good. He's liable to kill her for real . . . or make her wish he had, if you know what I mean,'' he added ominously.

Roger's face tightened in a mask of deadly rage. ''You tell that bastard if he rapes her, I'll cut his balls off myself. Tell him that. He's to slap her around, hurt her a little, but if I don't happen to be around at the time, he's to beat her *and leave her*. Nothing more. Make sure he understands exactly how far to go.''

Barney nodded. Yeah, he'd tell Wellman, all right, and hope he could impress on him just how Roger Bonham looked when he said it.

''You want him to come now?'' Barney asked.

''As soon as he can get here. If Wellman is making the dangerous threats you say he is, then I want him paid and out of here.''

''You'll have his share of the gold waiting when he's done? You want me to tell him that?''

Roger nodded. "Tell him he'll get everything that's coming to him," he said quietly.

Barney disappeared into the shadows and Roger left the stable a moment later.

Everything seemed to be going his way now. It was a shame Holly had to be hurt. She was beautiful and intelligent—qualities he would demand in a wife. He would surely require a wife in order to achieve social command. Who knew? He might even run for governor. With all his gold and a captivating wife like Holly, there would be no stopping him.

He frowned. He'd never be able to tolerate that high spirit of hers, though. A woman was supposed to be subservient to a man, obeying him without question. But there were ways of taming her, enjoyable ways. Once he gave her what a woman like her needed, she would be his slave. Oh, it might take a beating or two now and then, or tying her to the bed to teach her a few minor punishments he'd learned in that brothel in New Orleans he'd liked so much, but she'd come around. He'd break that wild spirit of hers, oh, yes, he would.

Jarvis admitted Holly to the house, stiff but cordial, saying he hoped they'd forget the unpleasantness of the morning. Holly murmured the proper responses, wondering whether she could ever be easy with Jarvis.

He gave her a tour of the downstairs rooms of the house, though she'd seen most of it when it was being put together. The furnishings were installed now, and she was impressed by the fragile formality. Dresden figurines decorated marble-topped tables, and Meissen vases were filled with fresh gardenia blossoms. The paneling was a shade of cream which Jarvis explained was popular in France just then. Her mother had chosen the lilac draperies, silk rather than velvet, because velvet, she felt, made a room oppressive.

Claudia joined them, radiant in a morning dress of orange and green taffeta that rustled with her every movement. Giving Holly a tight hug, she declared that the most wonderful weekend of her life was complete. "Because you're here, my darling," she beamed. "We'll forget last night, and if I have my way, you'll never go back to that dreadful place. Come along now, I'm going to show you *your* room. I decorated it myself, so I insist you fall in love with it!"

Holly glared at Jarvis, and he became defensive. "I didn't have to tell her about last night," he said. "Sally told her everything. She knew the whole story before I even got back here."

To her mother, she said, "I didn't want anything to spoil this weekend for you."

Claudia's radiant smile vanished. "The only thing that will spoil my happiness is for you and Jarvis to continue to wrangle with each other. I knew there was going to be more trouble. I wasn't surprised, I'm just thankful no one was hurt. Now we can just forget this for now?"

So, Holly realized as she glanced from one to the other, their love was putting her on the outside. So be it. Claudia's happiness came first. She would get through the wedding, then stay out of their lives.

Jarvis said he had work to do in his study and left

them. Claudia led the way upstairs. Reaching the upper gallery, they turned to the right, then stepped inside Holly's room. It was a marvel.

Sunlight poured through the beveled glass of the long, narrow windows, which were framed by pale blue satin draperies. A carved-stone fireplace ran the width of one wall. The ceiling was covered in ornate plasterwork, a pattern of huge magnolia blossoms.

Slowly turning around and around, Holly gazed upward, marveling at the crystal chandelier. Hundreds of tiny, delicate prisms caught the sunlight and shot it downward to dance merrily on the deep burgundy carpet.

The furniture was all dark, rich mahogany. The bed was four-postered and high, with a tiny stepping stool beside it. The bright yellow spread was crocheted in a lacy pattern, and the canopy above matched, even to the tiny green leaves and dark golden roses.

On each side of the bed was a small table covered with a crocheted doily to match the spread and canopy. On one table was an oil lamp, the base and globe rounded and covered in hand-painted dogwood blossoms. On the other table was a porcelain pitcher and bowl, also painted with dogwoods.

A dressing table sat against one wall, a fluffy skirt of white net overlaying satin of the same shade of blue as the draperies. An oval mirror in a gold frame hung above, and on the table lay an ornate silver-handled brush, a mirror, and a comb, all decorated with a scrolled "M," for Maxwell.

Claudia picked up the mirror and smiled at the initial. "Jarvis is so thoughtful. If you would only give him a chance, the two of you could be such good friends, and . . .'' Her voice trailed off wistfully, and Holly wished she were not perpetually hurting her mother.

There was a huge wardrobe covering nearly half of another wall, and when Holly opened the double doors, she was stunned by the dazzling array of ball gowns, day dresses, and riding costumes. Rows and rows of leather and satin slippers of all colors lined the bottom of the wardrobe.

Shaking her head in wonder, she moved on to the dressing room. What was she to say to all this? No thank you, I don't want it? How could she say no without seeming churlish and ungrateful?

Beyond the dressing room, in the bathroom, was a tub of porcelain, a tapestry dressing screen, and even a chamber pot disguised as a chair. Every comfort had been provided.

Another door led to a glassed-in terrace overlooking the gardens, the grounds, and the lush forest and fields beyond.

Helplessly, she turned to her mother. "I've never seen anything so lovely. I'm . . . very grateful.''

Claudia kissed her and smiled, tears shining. "You have a home here now, and nothing would make me happier than to find when I return from my honeymoon that you're living here.''

"Where is Sally?'' Holly quickly inquired. "I'd like to see her.''

Claudia assured her Sally was fine. "Jarvis had the old barn converted into rooms for the servants who don't live here, and there are rooms above the new stable, too. I told her to rest in her room all day. There's going to be so much to do this weekend.''

"I'd like to see her." Holly turned, anxious to leave this room that offered so much but asked so much of her.

The rest of the day passed quickly. The dressmaker arrived for the final fittings for both Holly and her mother. The florist called, needing to consult with Claudia. The orchestra leader stopped in to go over the musical selections for the last time. So many plans! Holly felt uncomfortably out of place.

She chose a modest beige lace dress from her wardrobe for dinner and brushed her hair to hang loosely past her shoulders. Jarvis had said that cocktails would be served in the parlor, and when she entered the room she was unhappily surprised to find Roger there, standing by the liquor cabinet. The last thing she wanted was another confrontation.

"Holly, how delightful." He smiled in greeting. "What can I fix you? Wine? Brandy? Champagne? How was your day? Busy, I suppose."

What was going on? He acted as though they hadn't parted in anger. "Wine, thank you." She forced a smile. "White wine."

Clinking glasses in a brief toast to the weekend's happiness, they eyed each other and he apologetically began, "I'm sorry about this morning, Holly. Believe me, the last thing I want is for us to be enemies, the last thing. Whether you like me or not, we can at least be cordial, don't you agree?" Without giving her a chance to say anything, he rushed on, "I wasn't myself this morning. To be honest, I was quite upset because of what happened to you last night, and I guess that's why I was so, uh, so unruly. You're beautiful, and I'd love for us to become close, but I had no right to make assumptions about that. Can you forgive me?''

Holly nodded. Anything was better than animosity, but she couldn't let him think this meant he could get close to her. ''The house is so lovely,'' she said, determined to focus his attention away from her. ''Jarvis has done a wonderful job.''

He laughed, a distinctly hollow sound. Why did he have to be that way? Wasn't it hard enough for her? ''His dream house. Here's to Jarvis!'' He lifted his glass.

''Why didn't he build his dream house for your mother?'' she bluntly asked.

Roger frowned.

''He and my mother didn't bring out the best in each other. If she hadn't died, they'd have grown old and miserable together. No need to lament over that now. Too many pleasant subjects to talk about.'' He downed his drink and poured another. ''Tell me, have you seen your Negro friend? Has she recovered?''

Holly told him she hadn't wanted to wake Sally, but would visit her after dinner. ''I won't go to bed until I've talked to her.''

He nodded, smiling secretively. Why was Roger so peculiar sometimes?

After a dinner of roasted capon with almond dressing, sweet potatoes, snap beans, and too much champagne, Holly declined the lemon pie and excused herself. "Tomorrow is going to be a long day, and I do want to see Sally."

Claudia reminded her, "We have the tea at ten, the luncheon with the ladies from church at noon, another tea at four, and the dinner party tomorrow night. So get a good night's sleep."

Holly was almost through the door leading to the rear hallway when Jarvis snapped at Roger. "Are you going to let her wander around in the dark by herself? Go with her, son."

Holly didn't notice Roger's hesitation. "I can find my way," she said. "After all, I grew up here." She smiled to soften the pointed remark. "I'll take the lantern from the kitchen. I won't be long."

Roger rose, sounding less than sincere as he offered, "I'll be glad to walk with you." He hesitated, glancing at his dinner plate. "I suppose I've had enough to eat."

She waved away his offer. "Stay. Finish your dinner. You're all treating me like a child."

Finding a lantern on a table in the kitchen and lighting it, she made her way outside into the warm night. Why, she fumed as she walked to the stable, couldn't they all leave her alone? She had enough to think about without everyone watching her every move.

She was almost to the stable, light spilling from the windows of the living quarters upstairs. Lost in thought, she didn't see the man leap from the shadows. He threw his arm around her neck, crooking his elbow under her throat, cutting off her scream. Yanking her against him, he dragged her toward the stables. "You better just come along quiet, girlie, 'cause if you piss me off any more'n I'm already pissed off, I might just go on and kill you instead of makin' you wish I would.''

Amidst the stabbing terror, Holly recognized the voice. She clawed at his arm, but he squeezed tighter. "Keep that up, and I'll kill you now, damn it." He pressed hard against her throat until she stopped struggling. Then he hurriedly dragged her through the shadows and into the stable.

Taking her to one of the stalls at the rear, he flung her to the ground, instantly landing on her and straddling her to hold her down. He slapped her, hard, twice. He did it again. Forward. Back. Again and again. Holly tasted blood. Pain stabbed her face and jaw like knives of fire. She was losing consciousness in the terror and agony, slipping fast.

"Gonna have a good time teachin' you a lesson, bitch," Alex Wellman cackled. This was fun. Bless Roger Bonham for arranging this, he thought wildly, happily. Not only was he getting revenge on her, but his share of the gold would be waiting when he was done, and he could leave there and head home and get on with his life—a rich man.

He hooked his fingers in the bodice of her dress and ripped it apart, exposing her breasts. Fondling brutally, he giggled. Holly lay in a stupor, unable to move, unable to cry out.

"Hell, you ain't out of it," Wellman snarled, digging his dirty fingernails into the soft flesh of her breast and twisting. She moaned, body jerking convulsively, and he laughed, delighted. "Shit, no, you ain't out of it, 'cause I ain't gonna beat you senseless. I want you to feel everything I'm doin' to you. I want you to remember me the next time you point a gun at a man." He ducked his head and sunk his teeth into her and this time she screamed, which only spurred him on. Bonham's orders were to punish her, but he wasn't allowed to rape her. Cut his balls off, that's what he'd threatened, Wellman recalled bitterly. Who'd Bonham think he was, anyhow? He'd die if he tried to cut Wellman's balls off. Die, that's what.

He yanked up her skirts and jerked her legs apart, tearing at her undergarments. He would have his fill, by damn, then slap her around some more. Pulling himself up to his knees, he fumbled with his pants. "Gonna be good, bitch, real good," he panted. "Alex Wellman knows how to please a woman, make her—"

A shot rang out and Alex grunted, eyes incredulous as he realized that a bullet had hit him in the back. There was no time to contemplate his fate, for his fate was upon him. He fell forward onto Holly, and was dead a moment later.

Pistol smoking, Roger stepped forward and kicked Alex to the side, then knelt beside Holly. She whimpered, barely conscious. "It's all right, Holly," he murmured in his most sympathetic voice. "I'm here. No one is going to hurt you any more."

Outside was the sound of feet running and then the sound of gunfire. Norman Grady came charging in, yelling into the darkness, "What's goin' on in there? Who's in there? I got a gun!"

"Put it away," Roger barked. Hell, he didn't need that blundering fool to charge in and shoot *him.* "Get a lantern. Holly's been hurt. I killed a man."

"Lawdy, Lawdy. . . ." Norman moaned, fumbling for the lanterns he kept hanging on nails just inside the door. Striking a match and touching it to the wick, he hurried over. Seeing the dead man, Holly's agonized face and torn clothes, he turned away, horrified.

Roger pulled Holly's dress around her, then lifted her and carried her out of the stable. Just outside, he met Jarvis and Claudia. "She was being attacked," he spoke in a rush, hurrying by them toward the house. "I had to kill the man. Don't know who he was. Don't know how bad she's hurt. Somebody send for a doctor."

Claudia screamed, close to fainting, but Jarvis held her steady. She commanded herself not to give way. Her child needed her.

Jarvis was snapping orders right and left. "Norman, ride for the doctor, ride like lightning. Bobo, you go for the law. Somebody, go in there and make sure that bastard's really dead. If he isn't, tie him up. If he is, stand guard. Make sure nobody messes with the body."

Holding Holly, Roger took the stairs two at a time and rushed her to her room. He laid her on the bed as gently as he could. Claudia and Jarvis dashed in and began fussing over her as he stood back to survey the results of her "lesson." It looked like only a few bruises. Wellman hadn't been able to rape her, so her injuries were nothing major. She would be fine.

Grinning, Roger turned away so no one could see his smile. He just couldn't help that satisfied grin.

Everything had gone so well. "I think I need a drink," he called over his shoulder.

Jarvis called out proudly, "You deserve one, son, you surely do."

Roger's grin stayed with him as he ran down the stairs. *"I surely do,"* he mimicked under his breath.

Chapter Sixteen

HOLLY was spittin' mad, as her grandfather would have said. Staring at herself in the mirror, she couldn't remember being angrier. The bastard. The cowardly, low-life worm. So what if he'd felt justified in revenge because she'd shot him first? She'd been facing him when she did, and she'd shot him in defense, for heaven's sake. The scum!

She touched the bruise beneath her right eye. Purple and red and green and yellow. On her left cheek were four red marks—the imprint of Wellman's hand. Perhaps that was what infuriated her the most, the fact that he'd left his mark on her flesh. How dared he?

She turned as the door opened. "Darling, darling, get back into bed," urged Claudia. "You haven't had any rest! You were awake all night."

"I'm too angry to sleep," Holly snapped, turning to look at herself again. Picking up her brush, she began to pull it through her hair, smoothing the long tresses about her face and shoulders.

Claudia shook her head. "You must rest. You'll have to miss the dinner party tonight, I know, but if you're up to it, you can attend the ball tomorrow night.''

"I'm going to the party tonight," Holly said flatly.

Claudia eyes widened. "But . . . but Holly, dear," she stammered, "your face. By tomorrow, some of the redness will be gone. I'm sure you aren't up to seeing people now anyhow."

"That's what *they* want, Mother. They want me to take to my bed and cry and moan and be frightened. I'll die before I give them my fear." Claudia stood there, staring at her. "The hoodlums responsible for this," she pointed to her bruises, "the bastards responsible for terrifying Sally—for everything that has happened to me lately—aren't going to make me yield to them. I refuse to cower and cry and be a sniveling little victim."

Claudia was all too aware of her daughter's high temper. Sighing, she told her, "Colonel Colter and Captain Davis are downstairs. They'd like to speak with you, if you feel up to it. They just finished talking to Roger."

"Tell them to come up," Holly said. Was there no way of avoiding Scott? At least Neil would be present, diffusing some of the tension.

She dressed in a mauve silk dressing coat, and applied a touch of color to her lips in hope of distracting from her bruises. Then she sat in a chair near the window. Almost at once there was a knock on the door. She called "Come in," and hated herself for the rush of disappointment at the sight of Neil alone. "I thought Colonel Colter was with you," she blurted, then wished she hadn't.

Neil hurried over, oblivious to her words because

the sight of her punished face had stunned him so. "If Roger hadn't killed the man who did this to you, Holly, I'd do it myself." He knelt before her, searching her eyes anxiously. "Are you truly all right? Is there anything I can do?"

She shook her head. "Thank you, Neil, no. It's over. The less said about it, the better." She wished she could love him. He was so kind.

He sat in the chair opposite her. "I know you get tired of hearing it, but the best thing you can do is move off that land and move in here. You aren't safe out there, and the army can't be around every minute to watch over you."

"I haven't asked them to," she said sharply. "I haven't asked anybody to watch over me." There was a pause. "I haven't told this to another soul, Neil, but I'd almost reached the point of doing just what you said. But leaving is out of the question now. They went too far last night. I'm going to stay on my land and show them they can't frighten people." She sighed. "It's all so ridiculous when you think about it. Who am I hurting by living there? You'd think that property was valuable or something."

Neil stiffened, hoped she didn't note his reaction.

"If it's any comfort, you aren't the only person being persecuted," he rushed on. "What's happening here is happening all over the South. Gangs taking the law into their own hands. There's even a rumor that Mississippi is going to do formally what all the Southern states have started doing informally—establish a 'black code' that will forbid Negroes to testify against whites, and have Negroes who aren't working arrested for vagrancy, then hired out to anyone who needs them.''

Holly was horrified and said so.

"It all sounds terrible," Neil said. "It *is* terrible. The die-hard Rebels are out to terrorize Negroes— anyone else who gets in their way. They want to get rid of Northern troops in what they consider *their* country and go back to the two-tiered system with the Negroes on the bottom. Sometimes I think there'll never be peace," he finished with a dismal sigh.

There was another knock on the door, and when Sally entered, Holly leaped to her feet and ran to embrace her. Behind her, looking most uncomfortable in a lady's bedroom, stood Norman.

"You's all right, missy?" Sally stopped, stunned. "Oh, Lawdy, the bruises—''

"I'm fine, Sally, really," Holly told her firmly. "You and I are much too strong to let those monsters do us any real damage. Aren't we?"

Sally didn't look at all convinced. Her nightmare was too fresh. "Holly," Neil said, "I've got to be going." Walking toward the door, he finished, "If I can do anything for you at all, let me know."

Holly gave him a grateful smile, and the door closed behind him.

The two women sat down, spontaneously clasping hands. Norman remained standing. Sally had an urgent manner that stopped Holly before she could speak.

"I told Norman he had to get your permission to do what he wants to do," Sally began, " 'cause you need to know what's going on."

Holly turned to Norman expectantly.

"It's like this, Miz Maxwell," he said nervously, shifting his weight from one foot to the other. "I got to thinkin' how all of a sudden them Night Hawks is actin' like they want to get through with you, be done with you. Right on top of burnin' the cross and scarin' Sally and you, they beat you up. They ain't about to let up. They's wantin' it over with. That's what I think."

He paused, breathing deeply to calm his racing heart. Holly nodded. She liked Norman. There was something about his manner that she trusted. "Please go on," she urged.

That eased Norman considerably. Most white folks would brush him aside. "Miz Holly, I don't think they're gonna back off now, even if Mastah Roger did kill one of 'em last night. I heard him talkin' to the army men this mornin' out at the stable, and he tol' them he didn't expect more trouble, 'cause he was certain you'd be smart enough now to see the danger. 'A man's dead because of her stubbornness,' that's what he said. But that ain't the way you see it, is it? You ain't gonna back off, are you?"

"Of course she is," Sally interjected. "She won't go back there now." She looked to Holly hopefully. "Will you?"

Holly decided not to answer until Norman was through.

"The way I got it figured," he went on, "they's gonna think you got so much spirit and fire that what happened last night is gonna make you just that much madder. You'll be more determined to show 'em they ain't gonna scare you off your land. That's what they'll think."

"Exactly," Holly informed him, ignoring Sally's horrified look.

Norman nodded, pleased he'd been understood so far. "They know you're here. I think they'll do somethin' else tonight—like maybe set fire to your cabin. So I'm goin' over there and keep an eye out, just in case. First sign of trouble, and I'll hightail it back here for help." His chest swelled with pride.

Holly eyed him worriedly. "I don't know, Norman. You could be right, but I don't like you putting yourself in danger on my account."

"But—"

"No, Norman," Holly declared firmly, having made up her mind. "It's too dangerous. I don't want you getting hurt. Let's just get through this weekend and then next week we'll talk about it some more, all right? But I'm ever so grateful for all the thought you've put into this."

Sally, much relieved, rose and began to steer Norman toward the door. "You heard her. She don't want you to do it. Now let's leave her alone and let her get some rest." It was plain that he had more to say, but he looked once at Holly, then reluctantly left the room.

Outside, having heard it all, Roger Bonham hurried down the hall and entered his room before he was seen. Chest heaving with fury, he paced up and down. Damn that Negro! He wasn't going to honor Holly's request, either. Hell, no. Roger knew Norman Grady was going to be nosing around the cabin tonight. That was going to mess things up just fine. What better time than tonight for his men to get in and dig up some of the gold? But if Norman came around and discovered what was going on, it would spoil everything.

Or would it? He stopped pacing and a slow, secretive smile spread across his face. . . .

He left his room a minute later and walked back down the hall to Holly's room. He mustered his most pleasant expression before knocking and entering. "May I come in and see how you're doing?"

Holly glanced up and greeted him warmly. "Roger. How nice of you to come by. I was hoping I'd get a chance to say thank you for looking out for me."

He hurried over to press his lips against her outstretched hand, then gingerly touched her bruised cheek. "I only wish I'd gotten there sooner. I don't ever want you hurt, Holly. And about yesterday morning," he rushed on, "I want to apologize. I had no right to blow up at you that way. It's just that you've come to mean so much to me, and it hurt to feel you were rejecting me."

With all candor, she assured him rejection was not what she had in mind. "I want you for a friend, Roger. At this point, that's all I want from you—or any other man. I didn't mean to hurt your feelings and I'm sorry if I did."

He nodded reluctantly, then grinned with the impishness of a small boy. "I warn you. I don't give up easily. I'm going to make a real pest of myself. I'll convince you I'm irresistible. I really *am* irresistible."

Holly laughed, delighted. "I already know that—just as I know I'm being stubborn. But will you be my friend?"

Roger assured her there was no problem there. Then, acquiring a solemn expression, he glanced around the room before confiding, "There's another reason I hope we can be close, Holly." He shook himself as though in mental anguish. "It's my father. I don't altogether trust his motives where your mother's concerned. I regret having to tell you this, but I fear for her happiness. I really do."

Clearly, he had struck a nerve. "Why, Roger?"

Roger went through his paces, reciting the speech he'd rehearsed. "My father is a hypocrite who presents a front of being kind, generous. I know him for what he is. Ruthless. He never cared anything about me or my mother. I watched him mistreat her till she was a cowering shadow."

Holly shook her head from side to side in denial.

Dropping his chin, Roger stared pensively at the floor. "I'm worried about how he's going to treat Claudia. I want you to watch out for her as much as you can. I'll do the same, of course. Not that there's much we can do," he finished mournfully.

Holly could only hope this was an exaggeration. Children sometimes saw their parents in a very harsh light. "Thank you. Thank you for being my friend . . . and my mother's." Had she misjudged Roger? She gave him a genuine smile of thanks, and he nodded.

"I'll be on my way. Claudia said you were insisting on going to the party tonight, stubborn wench that you are." He grinned fondly. "Get some sleep, my dear. You must be tired, and you've got a big weekend coming up."

He left, and Holly lay down, staring at the ceiling. She had a great deal to think about.

Roger hurriedly left Magnolia Hall. He had one last errand. Find Barney Phillips and explain that he'd had no choice but to shoot Alex Wellman for not following orders and attempting to go too far with hurting Holly.

In her room in the converted barn, Sally pleaded with Norman not to interfere, to do as Holly had asked.

Holly stirred restlessly in her sleep, as though already aware, somehow, of the way the four of them were about to come together.

🦋 Chapter Seventeen 🦋

WINE dimmed the pain, and Holly took another sip and stared at her reflection. She had managed to camouflage the bruises with several layers of powder. She looked pale, but the fresh bruises were invisible.

Her gown was of gold satin, the ruffled skirt dotted with blue sequins. Her mother's gift to her was a sheer hair covering studded with tiny diamond chips. When the light caught the net, it gave the illusion that her auburn tresses were studded with stardust.

Yes, she told herself, a bit woozy as she sipped the rich Burgundy, she looked very nice. But where was Sally? She hadn't been in since earlier in the afternoon. Even Claudia was complaining about her absence.

There was a soft rap on the door, and Holly frowned at the sight of Roger's beaming face. Where *was* Sally? "You're beautiful," he breathed. "I not only gain a lovely stepmother this weekend, but a gorgeous stepsister, as well."

Holly thanked him, said that he was outstandingly handsome in a waistcoat of red velvet, a white ruffled shirt, and black cord pants. And he was, too, she told herself. "Excuse me," she said bluntly. "I'm not quite ready. I was hoping Sally would come in and help me with the finishing touches."

His eyes were vaguely shadowed. "You don't need any finishing touches, my dear. One can't improve on perfection. I came to escort you downstairs."

Holly shook her head. "No, I'll wait awhile longer for Sally, Roger." She thought about the bottle of wine waiting on her dresser, wanting another glass to still the nervousness, knowing that gossip about her attack would have spread. People would be staring. She hated needing the crutch of alcohol, but forgave herself at once. "I'll be along in a moment."

"I'm saving every dance for you, Holly. I hope you're looking forward to it as much as I am."

She couldn't speak, warned herself against giving him false hope. Walking to the door and opening it, she managed a wan smile. "Thank you, Roger. I'll remember."

Alone once more, Holly paced up and down her room, drank another glass of Burgundy, and finally decided Sally was not going to arrive. She left and made her way down the stairs, holding tightly to the banister.

The great hall was decked in ivory magnolia blossoms and red, yellow, and white roses. The fragrance was divine. A string quartet filled the air with soft, romantic melodies, and along one wall in the parlor, pink linen-covered tables offered rare and tasty appetizers—smoked oysters, pickled clams, fish baked in a batter of meal and cheese, lemon and peach pastries, olives imported all the way from Greece. Jarvis had told her proudly that all of his ships were busy that week just unloading the specialties for the wedding.

Her mother was standing inside the foyer with Jarvis, greeting their guests. Radiantly lovely, she wore a gown of beige lace and satin. About her neck was her wedding gift from Jarvis, an elegant choker of diamonds, emeralds, and rubies. Holly grinned at her, then joined her for a while in the receiving line.

It was a lovely evening, and Holly began enjoying herself immensely, despite curious stares from some of the guests. People were scrutinizing her for evidence of violence. No matter. With Roger constantly refilling her champagne glass, she was far too happy to bother with nerves. She wasn't the least self-conscious, she found.

At one point, her mother touched her arm and said, "Dear, maybe you're drinking too much champagne. You seem a bit tipsy."

Holly giggled. Funny to hear her mother say such a thing. "I've never been 'tipsy,'" she responded saucily. "So I wouldn't know how it felt. How would you know, anyway, Mother? You can't know unless you've been that way, now can you?"

Just then Roger appeared with another glass, and Claudia snapped, "Please stop drowning her, Roger. She's practically reeling as it is."

Holly didn't hear. She was talking to a man who'd just entered. "Claudia, I will look after Holly," Roger said angrily. "You look after my father."

"I'll see that your father speaks to you about your behavior," she said, just as angry.

He faced her, so furious that she drew back. "Do that," he whispered, so quietly that no one heard except the two of them. "Make trouble, Claudia, and you'll have more trouble than you will believe."

In her happy stupor, Holly was oblivious to the fireworks between Roger and her mother. It was a wonderful feeling, being in her own world, not worrying about anything. When Roger approached and took her arm, handing her the glass of champagne, she was perfectly content to let him lead her around the room. She had dismissed all her worries, even dismissed the haunting memory of dark, tantalizing eyes, powerful arms, warm lips.

With a startling jolt, time ran together and she found herself staring right into those eyes, the eyes that tortured her dreams. She swayed. Beside her, Roger did not notice, engrossed in conversation with an acquaintance. He dropped his hold on her arm and moved a little away.

She continued to stare at Scott, who was smiling in a mocking sort of way. Did he know she was "tipsy"? Lord, she hoped not. How devastatingly handsome he was in his full-dress uniform—black coat with double rows of brass buttons, gold cord trimming the high collar and cuffs. Braided gold epaulets at the shoulders, light blue trousers with bright red stripes down the sides, a red-fringed sash at his waist.

Finally, he spoke, so low she had to strain to hear him. "You look good, Holly. Neil said you had a few bruises, but you seem to have concealed them.''

He started on by, but Holly grasped at his shoulder, bewildered by this casual demeanor. ''Is that all the concern you have for me?'' she challenged angrily.

He was expressionless. ''If Captain Davis isn't doing a good job with his investigation into your welfare, then I would certainly be interested in hearing any complaints you might have.''

''That's not what I mean, and you know it. Am I just an investigation? Someone to turn over to one of your officers? A pesky, bothersome assignment?''

He shook his head, still expressionless. ''That's not the way I would like to think of you, but you've left me little choice, don't you think?''

Suddenly, the room was spinning, the air stifling. Cigar smoke made her feel nauseated. The laughter of the others was deafening. ''Never mind, Scott,'' she said miserably. ''Just forget I said anything at all.'' She turned and made her way through the crowd, hurrying as fast as she dared through the kitchen, out the back door and into the cool night.

Lifting her billowing skirts, she ran through the side yard and down the gently sloping land, not stopping—she'd made her way often enough, Lord knew—until she reached a bank overlooking the river. Moonlight filtered down through the graceful, sweeping boughs of one of the few weeping willows Yankee fires hadn't destroyed. She sank to her knees, running her fingers through a thick bed of cool clover. A teardrop splashed on the back of her hand, then another. The happy, buzzing glow of the champagne had left her.

She'd made a mess of her life by making a promise she couldn't really have understood. She missed Grandpa unbearably. She cared far too much for Scott Colter, when it was too late to do anything about it. Everything that mattered was gone.

"You can't keep running away from life, Holly."

She gasped, jerking around to see Scott staring down at her in the moonlight. "Go . . . go away," she stammered. Oh, *why* had she said that?

He sat down beside her but made no move to touch her. "No. I'm not going away. And neither are the other things about your life that are worrying you. You've got to deal with them and with me."

She hiccuped, crying again. "I haven't got any worries. Everything is fine, thank you. And if you would stop bothering me, I'd be completely happy."

He tried to conceal his amusement, but he couldn't. "Are you happy out here on the ground, searching for four-leaf clovers, while a party's going on inside?"

She sniffed, nodding, still staring at the ground. "I was till you came along."

He laughed then, long and loud. "Why, you're drunk. *Really* drunk. I ought to throw you down and rip off your clothes and have my way with you. You probably wouldn't remember a thing about it tomorrow. Then you wouldn't accuse me of seducing you—like you did the last time."

She finally decided to face him. "You bastard," she declared, looking at him steadily. "You conniving, sneaky, *Yankee* bastard. I think I made it perfectly clear that I hate you and never want to see you again.''

He shook his head. ''You've made nothing clear except that you're the most stubborn female I've ever run up against. You're also a liar, and not a very good one. You care for me. You care a lot. You're just too pigheaded to admit it, even to yourself.''

She started to get up, to flee the words and him, but his hand snaked out to grab her arm. ''You aren't going anywhere. You're going to sit here till you sober up. I'm not going to waste my energy in trying to convince you you're wrong about me, us, but you're not going back inside and make a fool of yourself. So keep looking for four-leaf clovers like the little girl you truly are.''

She sighed, sitting back down again, and he released his hold. He was right. ''I guess I made a fool of myself,'' she admitted. ''I've been wrong about a lot of things . . . including that day in the woods,'' she said softly, praying he wouldn't make it harder for her. ''I shouldn't have blamed you. I wanted you to make love to me, but I didn't want to admit it, even to myself. I was always told it was wrong before marriage. And you turned out to be a Yankee, on top of everything else.''

Tenderly, he brushed a wisp of hair back from her face. She was the loveliest creature he'd ever seen. ''I'm not entirely blameless. I should have told you from the beginning who I was, but once I saw how fanatically you hated all Yankees, I didn't want reality to spoil a beautiful day.''

''Reality,'' she laughed bitterly. ''Reality? How

much nicer life would be if we could just drink champagne and stay warm and live in a dreamworld. No pain, just lots and lots of champagne. And dreams.''

"How would you know when real happiness came to you if you walked around in a stupor?'' he asked quietly, and she shrugged, wordless.

There was a silence while she thought, and then she blurted, "Reality is my father being killed by Yankees, my grandfather dying of a broken heart, having bastards try to run me off my land and beat me up.''

"Face it, Holly,'' he sighed. "You *must* move off the land—at least for now.''

She jerked her head up, moonlight illuminating red flashes in her cinnamon eyes. "Give in? Never!''

Scott sighed, stared pensively out at the gently rolling river, a wide black ribbon in the shadows. How he wished he could confide in her, tell her the truth, but he couldn't. Finally, he said, "Maybe it will be over soon.'' And maybe it would. A few more pieces of evidence, and he could make his move.

Holly stared at his perfect profile as he gazed at the river. Why did it have to be this way? How could it have been wrong when she'd been so happy with him? How could it?

With a sigh, he turned from the river, looked down at a patch of clover illuminated by moonlight. With a laugh, he reached and plucked a four-leaf clover and held it out to her. "Here. Maybe your luck will change. Maybe you'll have a life filled with champagne days.''

In that instant, Holly knew what she wanted, and throwing everything else to the winds, she took the clover, pressed it to her lips, then tossed it into the night. "I don't want champagne, Scott. I want you, your love. Now."

Startled, Scott hesitated, but only for an instant. He gathered her close to him and she yielded, her soft breasts thrusting against his chest. His kisses came down, warm, devouring with passion.

He carried her to a small grouping of trees off to the right of the riverbank, a perfect shelter, a safe place for star-crossed lovers who had, at last, found each other's arms. Gently, he placed her on the sweet-smelling grass and lay down beside her, kissing her neck, her shoulders. He moved the bodice of her gown down past her breasts, stopping to rain kisses on the firm, hungry flesh. "Be sure, sweetheart," he whispered fiercely. "Be sure this is what you want, because this is all I can give you for now. I can give you no dreams, no illusions, just this moment."

She understood. No marriage, no future, only there and then. She closed her eyes and pulled him down to her. His breath was hot, ragged, as he said, "I'm not letting you go tonight, Holly. I'm going to make love to you all night long, as long as you want me inside you. . . ."

"All night, all day," she whispered tremulously, wanting him more than she'd ever wanted anything in her life. Boldly, she caressed his swollen member, cupping his firm, rounded buttocks with the other hand, pulling him closer. She opened her legs to receive him.

He entered her, a sword of victory, devouring her

hunger with his own till they found, together, the ultimate glory. . . .

Afterward, he held her tightly in his arms. She broke the silence by whispering, "I'm not sorry, Scott. Maybe I should be, but I'm not. Yet, you promise me nothing."

Gently, he reminded, "You haven't asked me for anything."

They both knew they were skating around the subject. "I think we should just say what we mean, Scott. We should be talking of romance and love, yet we speak only of desire."

He gave her a teasing smile. "Do you expect me to say I love you and I want to marry you?" He shook his head slowly. "Oh, no, Holly, not you. A husband is the last thing you want now—especially a Yankee soldier for a husband. As for love, I think we can both admit we feel something for each other." When she didn't answer, he said bravely, "I do. I feel a great deal."

Holly nodded mutely. After all she'd been through with him, it was too hard to say "I love you."

Finally, she drew in a deep breath and ventured, "I care for you. I admit I've fought against it, fought hard, too." She turned to meet his warm gaze. "I'm still bitter about the war, yes. It does matter that you're a Yankee. But . . . I'm not so stubborn as to say I hate all Yankees. I certainly don't hate you."

She pressed her fingertips against his lips, and he kissed her palm, then clutched her hand against his cheek. Oh, how he wanted to tell her how much he loved her, but the pain of betrayal was still too strong.

Wordlessly, they moved apart to dress, both surprising themselves with sudden shyness. Neither glanced at the other while dressing.

As Scott was buttoning his shirt, he looked up, froze. "Oh, no! Holly! It's your cabin, I'm sure of it. . . ."

She whipped around, half dressed, and saw brilliant orange flames against the black night sky. They seemed a couple of miles away—on her land. Grandpa's land.

Scott quickly put his uniform in order, and she threw herself into her clothes. They reached the house. No one inside had seen the fire. As they rushed through the front doors and into the foyer, all eyes were upon them. The musicians stopped playing as Scott yelled, "Fire! I think it's the Maxwell cabin! Any of my men here, come with me. Anyone else who wants to help, get moving."

He turned to leave, but Holly clung to him. "You have to take me with you," she cried. "It's my home."

Scott stared down into Holly's anguished eyes. An ordinary woman had no business going along, but damn it . . . "Come on," he snapped, pulling her along with him.

Jarvis got to the foyer too late to stop them. Claudia, sobbing, saw Roger coming in from the rear of the house and rushed to clutch the front of his ruffled shirt. "Go bring her back, Roger. She shouldn't be there. Please, go get her."

Very carefully, Roger removed Claudia's clawing fingers from his shirt. He smoothed the front of his coat, lifted his chin ever so slightly and said, "Colonel Colter always thinks he can have his way, Claudia. It's too late to stop him in this instance, but"—he gave her a tight, cold smile—"I assure you, this is the last time."

Roger followed the other men outside, then. After all, it would look most peculiar if he didn't go along to help put out the fire. Actually, he had seen the fire before Colter did, because he'd been standing a way down from where those two animals were thrashing around on the ground. He had a perfect vantage point from behind a tree, having followed them in the shadows from the time Colter had left the house. The fools. He'd seen Holly drunkenly, brazenly, flirting with Colter.

So be it, he decided with bitter resignation. At least now he'd learned there was another obstacle in his way. Scott Colter. And, like all the other obstacles, Scott Colter would be removed.

As for Holly, well, this changed the picture a little. He still wanted her, but now he wouldn't have to be so gentle in his quest.

Roger Bonham was angry. Anyone who knew him understood that he was hell to be reckoned with when he was angry.

Scott and Holly would find out what hell was very soon.

🐚 Chapter Eighteen 🐚

SCOTT and the three other officers who had been at the party sped off on horseback toward the cabin. Scott led the way with Holly riding behind him, arms wrapped tightly around his waist, head pressed against his back, the picture of misery. Knowing what she would see, he warned, "There's probably nothing left, sweetheart. All we can do is try to stop the fire from spreading to the woods."

She made no sound at all, too miserable to speak. Norman had been right. He'd said there'd be trouble tonight, because they knew she'd be away.

Norman! Had he gone against her wishes and been on her land? And where was Sally? She hadn't been seen all evening. "Oh, God!" she whispered hoarsely.

Quickly she told Scott her fears, and they rode even faster through the night, taking shortcuts through the woods while the men in wagons and carriages had to stay on the road.

Smoke stung and watered their eyes as they drew closer, and the sound of flames crackling screamed like an evil, devouring forest creature. They rounded the final bend and reached the cabin.

There was nothing left of it, only burning chunks

of wood amidst rubble and glowing ashes. Holly slid from the horse, running toward the smoke and flames. He jumped off, grabbed her, held her back. "There's nothing we can do for the cabin." He shouted to the three officers just arriving, "Let's get a bucket brigade going from the inlet there. The others will be here in a minute. We've got to stop the woods from catching fire." He gave Holly a shake. "Get hold of yourself, damn it. There's work to be done."

"Buckets in the shed, there," she called to the men.

Within moments the brigade was started, and soon the other men arrived, led by Jarvis, and joined in. Some trees had caught the flames, and had to be chopped down quickly before the flames spread to the tops of others. Several grass fires were burning, too, but these were brought under control quickly.

Holly carried a bucket, working as fast as the men, until Jarvis hollered to her, "You had no business coming out here, Holly. Colonel Colter will hear from me about going against my wishes, you may be sure of that."

In shock, exhausted, his well-meant words of concern sounded like criticism, not like fear for her welfare. He saw the way his words had struck her and came over, awkwardly putting his arm around her. Gently, he said, "I think it's obvious everything's gone, Holly. I'm sorry. But there's nothing more to be done here. I'm going to take you back so you can get some rest. You're dead on your feet."

She shook her head. "We still don't know about Sally and Norman. They might be—"

At that moment, the officer Scott had sent back to

Magnolia Hall to search for Norman and Sally rode up, calling, "Nobody's seen 'em, sir."

Holly began to tremble violently. Scott organized a search party of the men who could now be spared from fighting the few remaining flames. "Remember, they might be frightened and hiding," he barked.

Tenderness and sympathy were gone. He was all military. Two people were missing and nothing else was important just then, not Holly's home, not their lovemaking. He hurried away, snapping orders, and Holly stared after him for just a moment before she turned away to examine the smoldering ashes of her home.

It had never been much, just a rough-hewn cabin, but every one of those boards had been hand-cut and shaped by Grandpa. The furniture had also been lovingly carved by him. As she stood there thinking, she realized that the few clothes she owned, the little bit of money, all was gone. Everything hers was just . . . gone.

The tears began, and simultaneously she felt a hand on her shoulder and someone's arms around her. She looked up at Neil, whose face was twisted in misery. "I just heard. I went to Magnolia Hall, looking for the colonel, and they told me. God, Holly . . ." He looked around, surveying the total destruction of her whole life. "I'm sorry. Oh, *damn.*" Embarrassed, knowing there wasn't a thing he could say, he gave her another hug, then said, "I have to see the Colonel right now, Holly. I'll check on you later and do whatever needs to be done."

He hurried toward the woods, pushing his way into the weeds and brush, moving, he realized, par-

allel to the swamp inlet. Far ahead, he saw the
torches of the search party. As he drew closer, he
saw that they were standing in a semicircle at the
water's edge, torches held high. They were all staring down at the ground, unmoving.

He pushed his way through to stand next to Scott.
On the ground were the bloodied remains of a Negro man and woman.

Scott spoke slowly, voice catching. "They shot
them, or cut their throats. Impossible to tell now.
Threw them in the swamp for the alligators. There's
not much of them left." He drew in his breath, let it
out slowly. "Get them out of here—and make sure
Miss Maxwell doesn't see them." He moved away
from the others, knowing that Neil had something
important to tell him or he wouldn't have come all
the way out there. Out of hearing range of anyone,
he snapped wearily, "Well?"

Neil was swallowing against the nausea that
welled in his throat. He'd never seen bodies look
like that, not even during the war. "Jim Pate's in
town. Says he's got the information you wanted."

Scott whipped his head up, excitement in his
voice. "Did he tell you anything?"

"No. He said he was told to report directly to
you."

"Where'd you take him? Not to the barracks, I
hope. I want him out of sight."

"I know that. I told him to be at the Delta Hotel,
room seven, at midnight. You're going to have to
move fast to get there by then," he warned.

But there was Holly. "I'm leaving now," he told
Neil. "Go to Holly. It's going to be hard on her, but
I'd rather she heard about Norman and Sally from

us. If she doesn't want to go back to Jarvis's, then bring her into town. Take her wherever she wants to go. Just stay with her as long as she needs you, understand?'' Neil nodded briskly. ''Let's move.''

Scott gave his horse full rein. Pate's assignment had been to track down a rumor that the father of one of the gold thieves was ready to talk. It seemed the old man had been ''saved'' at some fire-eating revival and wanted to confess all of his sins—one of them being that he'd sired a son who stole. One night, drunk in a riverfront tavern a few hundred miles north, he'd told his story to a bartender. He'd been overheard by a soldier who remarked to one of his commanding officers that it was strange to hear someone talking about a stolen Union gold shipment when there was no such thing, was there? The officer passed the unusual story along until, finally, it reached the ears of the right person. If the old man knew anything then, by God, things were looking brighter, as long as word of the theft didn't get too far.

Vicksburg was asleep when Scott rode in. He tied his horse to the hitching post in front of the Delta, then went around to enter the building from the alley in back. It was almost midnight. The only signs of life came from the saloons.

He hurried up the creaking stairs, hoping Pate would be waiting. Slowly opening the door to room 7, he took one look, leaped inside and slammed the door behind him. ''Lisa Lou! What the hell are you doing here?''

She was lying on the bed, a sheet pulled over her naked body, her clothes on the chair. Her long golden hair was fanned out on the pillow, an effect she had arranged carefully. Flashing him a practiced smile, she cooed, "Why Scott, you knew I'd be meeting you here, didn't you? That's why you left the door open." She sat up, allowing the sheet to fall away from her thrusting breasts. "Maybe you were just *hoping* I'd come."

"I want," he said slowly, evenly, eyes narrowing, "for you to get dressed and get out of here. I wasn't waiting for you, Lisa Lou."

"No?" she raised an eyebrow. "Then who are you expecting, Scott? Surely not that ragamuffin Holly Maxwell. Why are you here? Who's your whore?"

He wanted to say she was already one whore too many in his life. Gathering up her clothes, he tossed them at her, then stood back and waited, arms folded across his chest.

Lisa Lou stared at him, her fury mounting as she saw that he meant it. "Damn you, Scott Colter," she erupted. "Just who the hell do you think you are? I . . . I've done everything I could to please you." Tears threatened, but he didn't move.

"This has nothing to do with another woman, Lisa Lou. Just get dressed and leave, please. We'll talk later."

She looked at him hard for a second, then knew he wasn't going to relent. He didn't want her. "Believe one thing, Scott Colter. You're going to be sorry about this. You're going to pay."

She pulled on her clothes in furious silence and left. Scott lay down on the bed, then, tensed, waiting. The minutes rolled by.

A half hour passed. He paced the room. Hell, if he'd known Pate wasn't going to be on time, he could've been the one to break the news to Holly about Sally and Norman.

He sighed, exasperated. It was almost one o'clock. Where the hell was Pate?

He turned at the sound of footsteps clattering up the stairs, instinctively knowing Pate wouldn't be so stupid as to make that kind of noise or bring anyone along with him. Drawing his gun, he moved behind the door quickly. It opened, and at once the room filled with men, four of them, each holding a pistol or rifle. Talton Pollock led the pack.

"Drop the gun, you raping bastard!" Pollock growled. "You can't kill us all."

"I'll get a few," Scott said evenly. "Who wants to go first?"

The men began to exchange uneasy glances. It was one thing to go along with their friend in defending his daughter's honor—especially when the odds were in their favor. But nobody had figured on Colter being ready for them. Staring down the barrel of a gun made the picture look different.

"You tried to rape my daughter," Talton said between tightly clenched teeth, his shotgun pointed straight at Scott. "You may think you're the law in this town, but by God, there's law bigger'n you. You took advantage."

Scott knew the man wouldn't listen to reason, but he knew he was expected to try anyhow. "I didn't try to harm your daughter. You've got it wrong." Lord, if he only knew about his daughter! "When you've cooled down, we'll talk. Tomorrow."

Talton looked around, expecting his men to share his outrage and contempt, but they were all moving toward the door. "All right, we'll go for now," he said. "But you ain't heard the last of this. No man hurts my daughter and gets away with it. You're dead, Colter!"

They shuffled out, muttering among themselves, and Scott locked the door. What in hell was going to happen next? And where, damn it, was Pate?

He waited another half hour, and then, finally, he was forced to admit that it was foolhardy to remain there any longer. Pate was way overdue, and Talton would, no doubt, be drinking somewhere and fanning the flames of fatherly rage. He just might get up the nerve to come charging back.

Scott's hand was on the doorknob when he heard the sound of soft, cautious footsteps. Once more, he drew his gun and waited.

But Neil Davis was not so foolish as to slip up on Scott Colter. He called through the door, and Scott yanked it open, pulling him inside. "Where the hell is Pate? I thought you said . . ." Then he saw the expression on Neil's face. "Tell me," he said tersely.

"Someone found his body down at the livery stable," Neil said, spreading his hands helplessly. "His throat had been slashed. Probably been dead since right after I talked to him."

Scott sent his fist crashing into the doorjamb. This could mean only that Jim Pate had indeed had the information they needed. Worse, someone had known he was in Vicksburg, which meant Roger Bonham and his thieves knew someone was on their trail. Did they know it was him? He realized suddenly that Lisa Lou's rape charge might not be all a bad thing. He had a cover now, a reason for leaving the site of the fire without explanation.

He asked Neil what had been done with the body, and his friend shrugged. "What else could I do but treat it like the death of any stranger? I acted like I didn't give a damn, and sent poor Jim over to the undertaker. They'll identify him eventually. I couldn't admit I knew him."

No, it could be no other way. But he and Neil had lost a friend, a man they'd been through the war with, and felt the scorching brimstone with. For now, there wasn't a damn thing they could do to avenge Jim Pate's murder. For now. But later, he vowed in silent fury, later, someone would pay for the death of a good man.

Neither Scott nor Neil looked at the other during the ride back to the post. Why embarrass another man by letting him see your tears—or his?

Chapter Nineteen

ROGER was extremely pleased with himself. It was the next day, Saturday morning, and he sat in his father's study, behind the large mahogany desk, enjoying a cup of coffee laced with brandy. A brilliant sun shone through the windows, birds were singing, and a soft breeze was blowing in from the river. It was a lovely day. Holly's cabin was gone. The Negro troublemakers were gone. It might have been less messy, he recalled with a distasteful sniff, but Barney Phillips had always been a bit crazy with a knife in his hand.

Alex Wellman was out of the way, too, and now Holly was in debt to Roger for having saved her virtue.

His eyes clouded. Her virtue! She'd handed it right over to that goddamn Colter. Well, Colonel Colter was going to be easier to get rid of now. Roger'd been prepared to send a telegram to a friend in Congress who owed him a favor, asking that Colter be relieved of command in Vicksburg, but hadn't planned on giving a reason. Now he had one, thanks to that slut, Lisa Lou Pollock. According to the message he'd received from Phillips, Pollock had caught his daughter slipping into the house after midnight. After he'd given her a sound thrashing, she'd confessed to meeting Colter.

Roger leaned back in the leather chair and propped his boots on the edge of the desk. To top everything, Phillips had succeeded in getting rid of the spy, Pate. That had been a stroke of luck. Linwood Dobbs had heard about his father, Speight, suddenly becoming religious, heard his old man was talking too much. Linwood confided all of it to Phillips, explaining that he was sure he could make his father shut up. Phillips took no chances, however. He sent two of his men to see Speight Dobbs, and when they learned the old man had been talking to a stranger, one of them followed the stranger when he left town. The other remained behind to see that Speight had an accident, a fatal one.

When the stranger came to Vicksburg, Phillips killed him, then decided Linwood had to be eliminated, as well. Once he learned of his father's death, he'd have become a problem.

The trouble was, Phillips had killed Pate before giving him time to make contact with anyone. There'd been no choice. They couldn't risk Pate doing any talking. But *had* he planned to meet anyone? There was no way of knowing, and Roger hated that kind of loose end.

Roger downed the rest of his coffee and got up and stretched. There would be time enough later to worry. Now, he would enjoy the fruits of his labor.

He made his way upstairs, and as he neared the top of the stairs, he heard Jarvis's voice. Drawing closer to Holly's room, he stopped and listened.

"You must attend the party tonight," Jarvis was

saying. "Holly, I understand how you feel, truly I do. They were your friends. It was a horrible thing. But this whole weekend means a lot to your mother—and to me."

Holly's voice was just as firm as his. "I will attend the wedding tomorrow, of course, but out of respect for Norman and Sally, I will not socialize tonight. I want to make sure they have a decent funeral and burial, and I want to be with *their* friends tonight, not sipping champagne with *yours*—some of whom may even know who killed them," she added bitterly.

Jarvis's voice rose. "We can have the funeral late this afternoon. Claudia and I will even attend with you. Then there'll be time for you to dress for the party."

"Maybe their friends don't want to throw them in the ground so fast," she lashed out angrily, "like so much garbage. If you'll leave me now, I want to go and see what plans *their friends* want to make."

Jarvis held on to his patience. "Do as you think best, dear." He left then, Roger meeting him in the hallway as though he'd just gotten there. He nodded to his father, and went into Holly's room. She accepted his condolences in stony silence, then went to see her mother.

Claudia was still in bed, propped on pillows, sipping tea. She looked so pale. She beckoned Holly to sit in the chair beside the bed, and she tried hard to make her smile bright. "I'm just tired, dear. The parties are wonderful, but talking to everyone, dancing till late . . . it's all exhausting, to tell the truth."

Holly said bluntly, "You weren't dancing last

night, Mother. You're worried about me, aren't you?"

Claudia shook her head from side to side, tears sparkling. "Oh, Holly, those men won't stop. Poor Sally . . . Norman . . ." She gave way to sobs, and Holly took the teacup away, threw her arms around her, and sobbed right along with her.

They clung together for some time, each seeking comfort, and then Holly said, "Crying won't help."

"No," Claudia sniffed in agreement, "and I want to tell you something, Holly. I'm not sorry the cabin's gone. Oh, I know how you felt, but now you can't go back there, and *maybe* they'll leave you alone. You will stay here, won't you?"

"Maybe I'll stay with Abby, in town," she said, thinking about being in the same house with Roger while her mother was away on her honeymoon. "When you get back, we'll talk about the future. I just don't want you worrying about me. Put everything out of your mind except your wedding."

"Only if you agree to stay here while I'm gone." Claudia clutched her arm in a desperate plea. "I mean it, Holly. Roger is headstrong and spoiled, I know, and he can be quite unpleasant, but he'll look after you and I won't worry about you. But in town, with Abby . . ." Her voice trailed away as she pictured the two females alone in Vicksburg, one of them a lightning rod for troubles. When Holly did not respond, her mother tightened her grip. "Please do this for me."

Reluctantly, Holly nodded. Her mother's anxiety was, indirectly, her fault, and she couldn't refuse.

They talked awhile, and just before Holly left,

her mother said, "I saw you with Colonel Colter last night and I . . . . I'm sorry if I'm prying, I am curious about your relationship with the Colonel."

Holly couldn't suppress her smile. "I like him, Mother, I really do," she confided. "We had some . . . differences," she said cautiously, "in the beginning, but we've resolved things. He is a Yankee, after all, but he's nice, and I do like him. Do you approve?"

Claudia flung back the covers and leaped from the bed to embrace her daughter. "I'm delighted. He's just about the handsomest man I've ever seen—and so well bred. A real gentleman. Though he strikes me as a man you wouldn't want to cross." She laughed with delight. "With *your* peppery temper, I imagine you *have* had differences! Yes, I do approve. I don't think I've ever seen you look so happy."

Holly welcomed her mother's approval. It meant more than she'd known it could. "It's like a sudden ray of sunshine in the midst of a storm," she told Claudia. "But then the clouds come back, and you wonder how long before the sun is going to shine again. Does that make sense?"

Claudia blinked back fresh tears. "I felt the same way about your father. I'm so happy for you. I love you so much."

Both warmed by their new understanding, Holly left and went downstairs. The next hours were heartbreaking. The caskets arrived, and the undertaker. When the remains were prepared, there was nowhere to take them but the stable because the newly-converted barn didn't have room for all the mourners. So, amidst the soft stirrings of horses and the sweet, pungent odor of hay, the Negroes sang their spirituals, and paid their last respects.

The afternoon passed that way, hours blending together. Roger stopped by but not for long, displaying, he felt, just the correct amount of respect. Later, Claudia came with Jarvis, and as they were leaving, Jarvis whispered to Holly, "Please don't resent me. I'm not a monster. I don't know what's happened between us, but I'm not a bad man, Holly. I love your mother and I want to make her happy. If you'll let me, I'd like to love you as I would my own daughter."

Holly listened, then quietly thanked him. She was grateful when he took her mother and left.

Darkness fell. In the distance was the sound of carriages as people arrived for the evening's festivities. The Negroes continued to sing, and candles were lit, casting eerie lights around the stable. The atmosphere remained reverent and respectful, despite the sounds of revelry drifting out to them from the great house.

Holly was sitting with her head bowed, hands folded, lost in thought, when someone touched her shoulder. Thinking it would be Roger, she looked up with the greatest reluctance. It was Scott.

He knelt, covering her hands with his own, and whispered, "I'm sorry about all of this, and sorry I had to leave you last night, but I had no choice. Is there anything I can do for you?"

She shook her head. Wishing she could say that seeing him was enough, but this wasn't the place for that. Realizing he was in his regular army uniform, she asked, "Aren't you going to the party? You're not dressed for it."

He wanted to tell her everything, how bad things were in town, thanks to Lisa Lou. But he could say nothing with the other mourners so close by. Yet, if he didn't tell her himself, she'd hear it from somebody else. The story was spreading quickly.

He drew her to her feet. "Please. I have to talk to you." Not giving her time to protest, he led her away from the gathering, all the way to the far end of the stable, into an empty stall. He drew her close to him. "There are a lot of things I'd like to tell you, Holly, too many for right now. But there is something you've got to know now, because you're going to hear it soon enough from somebody. I'm surprised you haven't already."

There was almost no light at all, and she strained to see his face, searching for something to dispel her fear. He drew in a deep breath, about to begin, and just then Roger Bonham walked in.

"Well, well, Colonel Colter. From hotel rooms to stables? You're not very elegant about where you take your women, are you?"

"How dare you say such a thing?" Holly hissed at him, enraged. "What right do you have sneaking in here? This is none of your business, Roger, and I'll thank you to leave."

"The honor of this family is very much my business," he bellowed. "I have every right to resent your sneaking off with a rapist."

"Rapist?" Holly echoed, looking first at Scott and then back at Roger.

Scott's arms fell away from her and he stepped back. "Far be it from me to rob him of the pleasure of telling you."

Roger was quick to oblige. "It's all over town,

Holly. He raped Lisa Lou Pollock last night.''
Roger snickered. ''I'm surprised he had the nerve to
leave the post, considering that people are saying he
ought to be hanged.'' He reached over and placed a
possessive hand on her arm. ''Come along, Holly. I
can't allow you to be with him. It isn't—''

He never saw Scott move, but his next awareness
was of a hand around his throat, and he felt himself
slammed against the wall. The wind was knocked
out of him.

''She's safe,'' Scott growled as he squeezed
Roger's wind pipe. *''You aren't.''* He released his
hold, letting him crumple to the floor. ''Get out of
here before I kill you.''

Roger thrashed in the dirt as he struggled to
speak, eyes bulging. He coughed, spat, gasping,
''I'll have your head for this. You can't treat me like
this . . .''

Scott took a menacing step forward and Holly
placed herself between the two. ''Stop it!'' she
cried. ''This is a place of mourning and you've already stopped their singing with all this hollering.''

Roger backed away and left the stable. Lowering
her voice to a whisper, Holly said, ''Let's go outside, where we can talk without intruding on the funeral.''

As they stepped outside, she looked up at him and
said, ''I think you owe me an explanation.''

He smiled slowly. It was not a nice smile. ''I did
not rape Lisa Lou.''

''Then why would she say you did?'' Holly
pleaded. ''I think I have the right to—''

''The *right!*'' Scott echoed. ''I made love to you,
Holly. Is that what gives you the *right* to question

me? I came here to explain, not to deny. I was fool enough to think you wouldn't assume I was guilty. Let's don't talk about *rights,* Holly. Let's talk about trust—something you evidently don't have, or not for me." He was weary. "It's best I go now. We can talk when we've both calmed down."

Holly made no move to leave. "You've slept with her, haven't you?" she said. The pieces were slowly coming together. "You've slept with her, and she came to you sometime later and you rejected her. You made her mad, so she said you'd raped her."

"That's about the way it was, Holly."

She stepped away. "Then go. I don't think we have anything else to discuss, do we?"

"That was before last night, Holly, before our lovemaking." There was a pleading note in his voice.

"I can appreciate that," she flashed him a bitter smile, "but it was also *after* our time in the woods, wasn't it? You didn't waste any time finding another woman, did you? I guess you don't care who you make love to. The trouble is, I do care."

She whirled around and went to the house, leaving him there.

🎐 Chapter Twenty 🎐

SALLY and Norman were buried on Sunday morning, beneath an ominous gray sky. As the first clouds of dirt from the gravediggers' shovels splattered against the wooden coffins, the clouds unleashed cold raindrops. None of the mourners moved to escape the pelting rain. The wind increased, and the rain came down harder.

Finally, his clothes plastered to him, Roger contained himself no longer. "Can we please leave?" he whispered to Holly impatiently. "We're both going to be sick, standing out here like this. It's over now. Let's go."

"Go on back to the house," Holly said crisply. "I'll be along later." Why must he act like her watchdog all the time?

He stiffened, squared his shoulders, and jutted his chin higher. "If you insist on standing here all day, catch cold, miss the wedding, then I'll stand here beside you, damn it."

She wished he would go away, but there was no point in remaining, so she took a final look at the graves and turned toward their waiting carriage. . . .

In a couple of hours, the house was filled with

ebullient guests. Servants scurried through the parlors serving champagne and fruit punch, sandwiches and cookies. Cooks were bustling in the kitchen, preparing food for the buffet luncheon and planning for the feast to be served after the wedding.

The rains did not let up, so the guests couldn't spill out onto the lawn, as Jarvis had planned. The house, large though it was, became stuffy. The day got more and more humid. The flowers decking every available surface were soon wilting. There was a feeling of wanting the day to hurry on. It was not the gala Jarvis had worked so hard to bring about.

Holly, dressed in a gown of yellow lace over green taffeta, was determined to perform her duties as hostess as cordially as possible, but she quickly learned how hard that was going to be. In every room she entered, it was the same, the men on one side growling about that "animal," Colonel Colter, the women on the other side, saying he *looked* like a savage, and they weren't at all surprised. Poor little Lisa Lou Pollock! What the child must have endured! Holly would have to explain all the gossip to her mother, she knew.

An hour before the wedding, Jarvis came rushing to tell Holly that her mother had fainted. "The heat, the closeness," he fumed, as they hurried upstairs together.

Claudia was lying in bed, terribly pale. Two doctors, present for the party, were beside her. "I'm fine, really," she protested over and over. "It's just the heat. Give me a moment to rest, something cool to drink, and I'll be fine."

"You don't look fine to me," Jarvis said, then turned to the doctors. "What do you think? Should we postpone the wedding? Say what you really think."

"No," Claudia cried, tears in her eyes. "Don't you dare say I can't go on with our wedding."

Dr. Burlington, the older of the two, cleared his throat nervously and exchanged a glance with his colleague. The woman was pale, weak, but it was a humid day, after all. The patient's excited state— her wedding day—had to be taken into consideration, too.

Dr. Grant turned to Jarvis. "If Dr. Burlington concurs, we'll yield to Mrs. Maxwell's wishes. After all, her only symptom is that she's fainted."

"Thank you," Claudia said quickly. "I'm going to put on my wedding gown now, and we're going ahead. I feel fine. Holly, help me get dressed, will you?"

The three men left the room, and Holly knew there was nothing to do but oblige her mother. She helped Claudia dress in the beautiful blue and ivory lace gown. Perhaps, she thought, as she stood back to appraise her, it was the soft colors that made her mother appear so pale. . . .

In a twinkling, with Holly standing beside her mother and Roger beside his father, Claudia Maxwell and Jarvis Bonham were married, to the delighted smiles of two hundred guests.

Jarvis kissed his bride, and at that very moment, someone cried, "Look! It's a blessing on the marriage!"

All eyes turned to the south windows and saw the sun bursting from behind thick, gray clouds. A bril-

liant rainbow appeared. The rains tapered, ceased,
and, with many cries of delight, people began spilling from the stuffy house into the cool gardens.

Jarvis held Claudia tightly and said with a grin,
"It's an omen, darling. Heaven will bless us."

Claudia was as radiant as the sunshine streaming
through the doors and windows. "Yes," she whispered, gazing up at him. "Oh, yes, darling. We *are*
blessed."

Holly turned away. It was their world now, and
she must not intrude.

She retired to her room, wanting to lie down, but
she heard some noise in the dressing room and remembered that the room had been offered for use by
the lady guests. There was nothing to do but wait
and hope whoever was in the dressing room would
not be in a talkative mood.

She sat down on her bed. She did not have long to
wait. In barely a moment, she gasped as Lisa Lou
came out of the dressing room. Stunning in a gown
of coral satin, the skirt beaded with tiny gleaming
seed pearls, Lisa Lou's beauty was marred by the
fierce grimace that swept her face. Hotly, she exploded, "What are you staring at me like that for?
I've got a right to be here. My family was invited,
and what am I supposed to do? Hide forever? I'm
sick of people staring at me. I've done nothing to be
ashamed of." Taken aback by the outburst, Holly
continued staring at her in stunned silence. "Well,
say something!" Lisa Lou challenged, hands on her
hips. "You're the one who should be upset about all
this. You *were* chasing him, weren't you? So, you
must find it devastating that he tried to force me into
giving him what you were offering freely!"

"Forced you, Lisa Lou? Scott forced you? But why should he? What about before, when you met him in secret? What happened that he suddenly had to force you? Did you have a lover's quarrel? Were you getting even for something when you cried 'rape'?" Lisa Lou took a retreating step as Holly rose and came toward her. She struggled to recover her balance in the face of this unexpected attack. How did Holly know the truth? How? "Or did you get caught, Lisa Lou, and this was your way of saving yourself from scandal?"

Holly had a flash of memory, lying in Scott's strong arms, his passion melding with hers. Her eyes burned into Lisa Lou's. *She* had experienced the same joy, and the realization made Holly blind with furious jealousy. "Well?" she cried. "Why did you lie about him?"

Lisa Lou blustered, "You have no right to say these things, you bitch! You don't know what you're talking about. You'd better watch your mouth, because my father is pretty upset, and if you go telling lies about me, there's no telling what he might do."

Holly felt her fury collapse all at once. "I feel sorry for you, Lisa Lou. What a lonely person you must be. I was a fool to doubt Scott. His only mistake was getting involved with you in the first place." She turned toward the dressing room. "And I believe I'll just go tell him that right now!"

Lisa Lou laughed shrilly. "Oh! You're the one, aren't you? The slut he was waiting for that night?"

Holly turned around. "What?"

"Come now, Holly. The game is over. Let's settle this now. There'll be no reason for us to hate each other then. You won. I lost. It's that simple. Just admit it was you he was waiting for in the hotel that night. You were the reason he turned *me* down." Holly stayed silent, bewildered, and Lisa Lou grew exasperated. "Oh, come now, Holly," she cajoled. "What difference does it make now? Surely you can understand how I feel. When a woman loses out to another woman, she likes to know who the rival was. Besides, it wasn't so hard for me to figure out. Your cabin burned down that night, so you couldn't meet him. That's what happened, isn't it?"

Holly wasn't going to admit anything, not even the fact that Scott hadn't been waiting for her at all. What he'd been doing at the hotel late at night was beyond her.

Knowing before she even spoke that her words would make no difference, she asked, "Why don't you tell the truth, Lisa Lou? You can't feel very good inside when you know your lies have hurt an innocent man."

"Doesn't matter to me." Lisa Lou smiled with a shrug. "Serves him right for being such a ladies' man. He got what he deserved. Besides, my reputation is more important than his."

Holly turned away. She reached into the wardrobe to find a proper riding dress, wishing Lisa Lou would just go away. "I'm going to Vicksburg, to find Scott, to straighten everything out."

At least Lisa Lou could enjoy a triumph. "You're too late. He ran away during the night."

"I . . . I don't believe you," Holly stammered.

The other girl shrugged. "Go ride into town and see if he's there. Make a fool of yourself. See if I care. I'm tired of talking about it anyway." She whipped around, skirts flouncing, and strode out of the room.

Holly stood rooted, knowing intuitively that Lisa Lou wasn't making it up. Scott had left. But *why?* It wasn't like him to run. Nothing made sense any more, nothing.

Her worried study was intruded on all too soon by Roger, pounding on her door. "Holly, what's wrong? I've been knocking and knocking."

She shook her head. "Nothing. I'm fine. I just needed to be alone."

He laughed. "Feeling left out, are you? So am I. Seems our parents are deserting us, so we should wish them well and take solace from each other. Come on. They're getting ready to leave."

She reached slowly for the hand he was extending, and he clasped her fingers, pressing them against his lips. "Holly, about the scene in the stable yesterday, I . . . I apologize. Please understand that, well, seeing you with that . . . that rogue," he growled, "I admit I went too far. I'm sorry."

"You thought you were protecting me, I know, but believe me when I say it wasn't necessary. I'm in no danger."

"Not any more," he retorted. "The man is gone. Left in the dark of night like the belly-crawling snake he is. He deserted, I guess, with his sidekick, Neil Davis."

She blinked. Scott desert? Never! What *was* behind this nightmare? She wanted desperately to figure it out, but Roger was squeezing her hand, coaxing her along.

Everyone was gathering at the bottom of the

stairs in anticipation of Claudia's tossing the bouquet. Roger left Holly for a moment, then returned with a specially prepared drink for her that would set the mood for the evening he had planned. He watched intently as Holly finished it all. Everything was going to be easier than he'd hoped for.

Claudia walked to the railing, smiled, and gaily tossed her bouquet, which flew directly at Holly. But Holly made no move to catch it. It bounced off her shoulder and fell to the floor. Roger was quick to grab it and thrust it into her reluctant hands. "So," he said heartily, "you'll be the next to get married. I wonder who the lucky man will be."

Holly pressed the flowers against her cheek. Marry? Not she. It seemed the man she loved had left, left without a single thought for her.

Chapter Twenty-one

ONLY with the greatest effort was Holly able to get through the rest of the evening. The single drink she'd taken seemed to have gone straight to her head. She was dizzy, sleepy, having a hard time staying awake. But her mother and Jarvis had left, so the role of hostess fell to her. It was her duty to see that the guests enjoyed the reception and lavish dinner.

Gathering her wits about her, she went to the kitchen and asked one of the cooks to make a pot of very strong coffee, several cups of which she consumed heartily. She felt better afterward.

Never had the hours passed so slowly or more miserably. Damn Scott Colter, she cursed silently, and damn herself for caring so much about him. Damn everything! If this was love, she wanted nothing to do with it. The pain was too deep to be endured.

All evening, everywhere she went, Roger was there, offering champagne or wine. She declined most of the time. She desired only one thing, to be alone with her misery. To think about the only thing that mattered. Scott. He was gone. And he had left thinking she was angry.

Suddenly, she realized she had never felt more alone in her entire life.

Roger appeared toward the end of the party, seemingly out of nowhere, and cried, "Ah, there you are!" He was holding out yet another crystal glass filled with bubbling, sparkling champagne. "My God but you look exhausted. Here. You are going to drink this, Holly, and then you're going to your room to rest. No one expects you to run around here and act like a hostess after all you've been through these past few days. Drink." He thrust the glass at her and she took it and drank. He was right. She was weak, and tired of forcing a smile all the time. "Thank you," she murmured, handing him the empty glass and brushing by him. "I am going to sleep, Roger. The guests can entertain themselves now. As far as I'm concerned, the party is over."

He watched her glide gracefully up the stairs. No, he told her silently, the party was not over. It was only just beginning.

Roger dismissed the servants as soon as the last guest departed, loudly congratulating them on doing such a wonderful job. The clean-up tasks could wait until morning, he said. He even gave them a case of leftover champagne, sending them happily on their way, knowing that within a short while they'd all be drunk or sleeping.

At last, the house was empty. He extinguished the lights and candles, and went to his room, where he changed into silk pajamas and a maroon silk robe. He turned back the covers of his bed, and opened a bottle of chilled champagne, pouring into it the rest of the powder he'd given Holly earlier. He glanced in the mirror and smoothed back his hair, smiling. The house was empty and the night, by God, was his.

He hurried to Holly's room and was pleased to find her lying across her bed, fast asleep, as he'd hoped he would. He carried her back to his room. She stirred only slightly as he laid her on his bed. He removed her clothing, cursing silently at all the stays and complicated fastenings. As more and more of her was exposed, his breath grew harsher, hotter, and he slowed his progress to savor every moment. Her breasts exposed, he kissed each nipple, delighting at the hardness he aroused. Berries, rich red berries. It was only with the greatest of self-control that he restrained from spreading her thighs and plunging deep inside. He commanded himself to take his time, enjoy every touch, every vision.

She stirred, moaned softly, and he reached for the glass of champagne and held it to her lips. She coughed, flung her head from side to side, and the liquid spilled down onto her breasts, but she did not awaken.

He chuckled. It would be nice to feel her response to his lovemaking, but there would be time for that in the future. His desire was getting the best of him. He would wait no longer.

Removing the last of her silky undergarments, his eyes raked over her naked flesh.

A voice called his name from outside the window and Roger cursed. He stomped angrily across the floor to the window. "What in the blue-blazed hell do you want?"

Barney jerked back, surprised. "I need to talk to you," he called. Resentfully, he added, "You said if I was ever in doubt, to ask you, so don't bite my head off just 'cause you got woke up. I don't like being up all night either."

"You ninny," Roger growled. "I'm not alone up here. Understand? Whatever it is can wait till morning."

Barney's temper was rising, matching Roger's. "It ain't gonna wait till morning. It's time we got things settled. There'll be time for fuckin' later," he added insolently. "You come down now or I'm comin' up."

"Son of a bitch," Roger hissed, infuriated. "I'll be down." He tightened the belt on his robe and hurried downstairs.

Jerking the back door open, he found Barney leaning against the house, nonchalantly picking his teeth and eyeing Roger coldly. "Well? What's so important?" Roger snapped, a little wary.

Barney took a moment to answer.

"We had a talk tonight, all of us, and we don't like your orders about takin' the gold out a little bit at a time. The girl ain't around to see us now, and we want to get it all now—and get the hell out of here. We're tired of screwin' around."

Roger's eyes narrowed with fury. "You fool! You know damn well I don't want the men all paid off at one time. I told you to take care of the potential troublemakers, the most restless ones first, get them out of the way and take care of the others later. I don't need a bunch of rich idiots running around blowing their money and causing talk. I told you that from the beginning.''

Barney Phillips did not wither before the angry challenge. He squared his shoulders and continued staring at Roger. ''You ain't listenin'. All the men are restless, including me. What's stoppin' us? The girl's burned out. We ain't got no spies, 'cause I slit that guy's throat. Colter's gone. Your daddy's on his honeymoon. Them nosey niggers is dead. There ain't no reason to wait. So''—he paused—''we ain't goin' to wait no more. I come to tell you that if you want to be there for the big dig, you better come on.''

''Damn you, Phillips! You're pushing too far.'' Roger wished he were not standing there in a silk robe, and he longed for the derringer he always kept inside his jacket. It made him feel secure. Now all he had was bluster. ''There will be no dig tonight. That is my order, and I expect you to see it's carried out.''

Barney laughed. ''Sorry, boss, I'm on their side. Oh, you ain't got to worry about gettin' cheated. Nobody gets more'n what they've got coming to 'em, what was agreed on. You just tell me where you want your share put. You can trust us.''

Roger had known all along the men wouldn't just take the gold and run. How could they, without his ship? Besides, they were scared of him. They knew he could find any of them.

He lunged for Barney, shoving him hard against the wall. ''Goddamnit, leave mine where it is. If you can no longer control your greed, so be it. I'm probably better off without you. But nothing happens till tomorrow night, you hear me? I've got other plans. Tomorrow. Just one more day. Understand?'' Roger released him and stood back, awed by his own bravery. Physical confrontations were not his forte, and he always hired someone else to do any dirty work that came along. Barney Phillips could crush him with one blow, and they both knew it. He'd surprised himself, but it was a good feeling.

Barney peered at Roger, pondering. He finally decided that one more night wouldn't matter. ''All right. I'll tell everybody to hold off.''

Roger stepped back and nodded. ''Good. You'll all see that I'm right. We must be cautious. Tomorrow you can arrange a meeting for all of us, and we'll set a time for the final dig.''

They parted, and as Roger stepped inside, he hesitated. He had depended on Barney for some time. It wasn't a good idea to suddenly have this hostility between them. He went quickly back outside and called to him.

In the shadows Barney turned and waited as his boss hurried toward him.

''There's something I should say,'' Roger began slowly, then allowed his words to spill out in a torrent. ''I'm going to need a good man, a right-hand man—a bodyguard, I suppose you could say. I'd like you to be that man. I'm asking you not to go back to wherever you came from. I'll pay you well. Will you think about it?''

Barney thought only fleetingly about the skinny, nagging wife he'd left in Pennsylvania. He did allow himself a full fifteen or twenty seconds of guilt over the two sons and a daughter he'd be deserting. But what the hell? He was lucky to be alive after the goddamn war, and he deserved to live a little, not

LOVE'S WINE 241

die slowly behind a plow. He reached out and
grasped Roger Bonham's hand, pumped it up and
down. "You got yourself a man. You won't be disappointed."

"Good." Roger nodded but didn't permit himself a smile. It would take some doing to keep this
big idiot in line. "Don't say anything to the others.
They would resent it. As soon as they're paid off
and everything is settled, you can move in here."

Roger went back inside, furious over the inter-
ruption.

Holly was still fast asleep—and still nude. Gingerly, he touched her breasts. He preferred larger,
but hers were beautifully molded and rounded. Her
waist was tiny, and her hips and thighs tapered to
long, gentle lines. Yes, she was a rare beauty. He
would be the envy of every man, having such a
lovely wife. After he had broken her spirit, taught
her ways to please him, then she would truly delight
him.

He shucked off his robe and stretched out beside
her. Turning sideways, he gazed at her, marveling
at her nearness, the warm, sweet scent of her. He
was too enraptured to be alarmed when her eyes
opened.

The sight of Roger Bonham's face leering down
at her, so close, lips parted, birthed a wave of terror
and she screamed one long, reverberating scream.

"No, no, dearest," he protested, pushing her
back down on the bed firmly as she tried to rise.
"You want me as much as I want you. You know
you do. Don't fight. Give, my sweet, give to me as I
give to you."

Holly came to life then, a driving desperation

bringing her out of the drugged stupor. She twisted away, her nails raking painfully down his face. "Damn you!"

Her voice was thick, struggling through the great, swirling cloud of nepenthe. "Have you gone insane? Leave me alone."

Roger was enjoying himself despite her indignant shrieks. He placed one hand over her face to stifle her, and twisted her arms behind her back. "Enjoy me, my sweet. You came to my bed, begging me to love you. Don't play tricks on me now, Holly. You asked for me, and you shall have all of me."

Her insides churned with revulsion. He had to be lying. Never would she have come to his bed, never. She opened her mouth to say so, to ask why she was naked, but he pressed his mouth against hers, stilling her.

After a long kiss, he placed his hand over her mouth. "You surprise me, Holly. I knew how I felt about you for a long time, but I was afraid you didn't return my love. Now I know you do." He kissed her forehead. "It's wonderful. We'll be married at once, of course. I had wanted to court you properly, give you a lovely wedding, but under the circumstances, I think it best that we forgo formalities."

He removed his hand and she sat up, blood raging through her like the angry waters of a river. "You can go to hell. I'll never marry you, Roger Bonham. I didn't even like you before this, but now you've made me *hate* you."

She started to move off the bed, but he grabbed her. "Holly, oh, dear Holly, listen to me. I know you're upset. You're a lady and you're afraid I'll think less of you now. You came to my bed, and now you're feeling guilty, but you shouldn't feel that way. I'm trying to explain that I wanted to marry you before this anyway. You see? I'm not proposing out of a sense of honor. If I didn't love you, I'd just cast you aside. But I love you.''

He tried to kiss her, but she jerked her head away. And then suddenly, he abruptly released her and turned away from her. She stared at him. What in heaven's name did *he* have to be angry about? Amazed, she watched him get up and reach for his robe. "Get out," he said. "It sickens me to have my respect for you trampled. I thought you loved me. I didn't know you were just seeking pleasure, like . . . like a trollop." His eyes swept over her with a mixture of disgust and pain. "I can't believe it. I placed you on a pedestal and look what you've done to me."

Never in her entire life had she been so confused. Surely to God, he was lying, had to be. "I don't . . . understand, Roger. You're lying."

"Lying?" He seemed terribly hurt. "Oh, my darling, I would never do anything to hurt you. Had I know you were so drunk, I never would have touched you. I thought you loved me, as I loved you."

As she began to speak, they heard a man's voice in the hallway, calling out.

"Where is everyone?" the voice boomed, and then the door opened.

Holly and Roger found themselves staring at the face of Jarvis, who paled at the realization of what he had intruded upon.

🎋 Chapter Twenty-two 🎋

JARVIS swayed, stricken with horror. His own son and his stepdaughter. Passing a trembling hand before his eyes, he turned toward the door, unable to face the abominable sight. His voice came out a croak. "Cover yourselves. I have to talk to you. Claudia is very ill."

Holly cried out. "What's happened? Where is she?"

He would not, could not, look at her. "Vicksburg. The hospital." Then the words came tumbling forth in all his wretched despair. "Sometime after we sailed, she became very sick. She fainted, and I couldn't awaken her, so of course we headed back to Vicksburg, the closest port. She's there now, and I"—he shuddered—"Oh, Holly, how could you?"

"I want you to take me to her as soon as I get dressed," Holly said, throwing the bed coverlet around herself and running from the room.

Jarvis slammed the door after her, anger replacing shock. Glaring at his son, his face pinched, tight-set, he felt quaking begin deep within. "How could *you?*" he asked in a raspy voice. "Damn you, Roger, don't your harlots satisfy you? Did you have to pick an innocent young girl?''

Roger began to dress. ''Don't worry. I'm going to make an honest woman of her, for the sake of our family name,'' he added with a sneer.

Jarvis was quick to say no. ''I won't have it. I know you, Roger, for the arrogant, cruel creature you are. You may be my son, but I pity any woman who marries you, and by God, it won't be Holly.''

Roger barely spared him a glance. ''I don't give a damn what you think. I'm going to marry her. Now how about getting out of here and letting me dress so we can get to Vicksburg.''

Jarvis planted himself in front of Roger, his manner implacable. ''I won't allow you to marry her. It grieves me to have to say this, but if you do, you'll never see any of my money again. We both know you worship wealth. So think hard, Roger. I mean what I say.''

Roger looked at him—a long, hard look. ''I don't need your money, you old goat,'' he said finally, enjoying the hurt on Jarvis's face. ''I've got more money than you ever dreamed of having. I don't need you for one damn thing. I can buy you and bury you if I choose.''

Jarvis felt a sharp, unfamiliar stab of pain deep in his chest. His heart hurt . . . ached to hear such abuse from his own son. ''How . . . how can you speak to me this way? I'm your father.''

Roger buttoned his shirt, his eyes riveted on Jarvis. ''My father? You *are* a fool. I suppose it's time for the truth. I can't stand to hear your sniveling.

''Are you really this stupid? You were as ineffectual with my mother as you've been in all your relationships. She couldn't stand you any more than I can. She told me years ago who my real father is . . . was. He's dead now," he said coolly. "No matter. At least I am not the fruit of *your* worthless loins, I'm pleased to say."

Jarvis clutched at his chest, swayed, and stumbled. Roger made no move to help him. "You . . . you're making it up, Roger. How can you hurt me so much? Lies, Roger. Your mother. You lie about her. An honorable woman, and you besmirch her memory."

"Besmirch!" Roger echoed contemptuously. "You *are* an old fool. She laughed behind your back as I laugh in your face. She stayed with you because of your money and your social position. My father wasn't her only lover. There were many. She didn't try to hide anything from me. We were close. I respected her for trying to find happiness despite you. She was what she is, as I am what I am, and I'm glad to at least be able to tell you the truth."

Jarvis forced himself to stand erect. Slowly, very slowly, anger was overcoming the pain. He regained his composure as he faced the son who had suddenly become an evil stranger. "You will remain here. I will take Holly to her mother. Then I'm coming back here and we are going to talk."

Roger laughed. "I don't dance to your tune any more, old man. I am wealthy now, on my own. I don't have to kiss your pompous ass, Jarvis. God!" He rolled his eyes heavenward, sighing exaggeratedly. "How wonderful to be able to say 'Jarvis,' at last, and not the hypocritical name 'Father.' "

"Shut your mouth," Jarvis said furiously. "No more, do you hear? No damn more!" He lunged forward, catching Roger off-guard and hitting him across the face.

Roger reacted with forceful fury. "You don't ever strike me, you pompous bastard!" Roger struck out with his fist as hard as he could, sending Jarvis sprawling backward against the bureau. Roger leaped on him, grabbing him by the collar and jerking him to his feet, then slapped him back and forth with his open palm until blood trickled from the corners of the older man's mouth. "Never hit me again, Jarvis! Understand? I have the power now, not you, not any more. You will do as I say or I'll have you killed. Do you believe me, or must I beat you senseless?"

Jarvis struggled to hold on to consciousness. The pain in his chest was terrible and getting worse, as though a giant fist was opening and closing around his heart. With the last shreds of his strength, he reached out gently and touched this stranger's face. "Tell me . . . tell me you were drunk . . . didn't mean it . . . anything," he pleaded. "I swear to believe you, forgive you. I love you. . . ."

His voice trailed off and his eyes suddenly became transfixed, unseeing. One last convulsion rippled through his chest and he went slack.

Roger released him, allowing him to slump lifelessly to the floor. Then he leaned over, pressed his hand against Jarvis's chest, felt the stillness.

He straightened. Goddamnit, the old fool was dead. He ran stiff fingers through his hair. Damn, damn, damn! Holly would come in soon, dressed and anxious to get to Vicksburg. How was he going to explain this?

He heard the sound of footsteps hurrying down

the hallway and knew he had run out of time. Before he could even cover Jarvis's body, Holly burst into the room. Her eyes went to Jarvis, then to Roger.

He moved quickly, placing firm hands on her shoulders. "I know it's a shock. He's dead. I assume it was his heart. It was just too much for him, I guess, finding us together." He marveled at his own quick wit, his craftiness. The words were flowing easily now. He was in control. "It was bad. The things he said, admitted to. He was my father, but dear God, when he told me about Sally and Norman, and wanting your land so badly—"

"Sally?" She jerked away. "What about Sally? And my land? Tell me everything, Roger. I've a right to know."

The room was spinning, and Roger walked her slowly to the bed, sat her down, and knelt before her. He took her hands in his and squeezed tightly. "I've never seen him as he was tonight," he began slowly. "Like a madman. He said you'd been nothing but trouble since you came, insisting on keeping your land when he wanted it for his empire."

He shook his head mournfully. "My God, I thought I knew him. *My father.* He was a sick, sick man. He admitted he was responsible for everything, the attacks on you, the deaths of Sally and Norman. He flew into a rage and attacked me. I tried to hold him off. Then he just keeled over. Just like that." He blinked back tears.

Holly felt the slow stiffening along her spine and knew what it was—the strength, the courage, to face this new horror and keep going. All that mattered was getting to her mother as fast as she could. Dear

God, how was she going to tell Claudia about Jarvis?

They did not speak as they rode through the night to Vicksburg. Roger took her directly to the hospital, explaining that he would return as soon as he made the death report to the authorities.

She turned away, but he caught her hand, squeezed it, looked deep into her eyes and whispered, "I love you so much, my darling. Somehow, we'll get through all this."

"Love me?" she echoed blankly, stunned. "Oh, Roger, how can . . ." She shook her head wearily and then told him, "Go and do what you must, Roger. I've got to see my mother."

The hospital was very still. At the end of a narrow, dimly lit hallway, a sleepy-eyed nurse sat behind a desk and watched Holly approach, then showed her to Claudia's room. Please, God, Holly prayed silently, let her be all right. Let it be just the excitement of the past few days. And give her the strength to bear Jarvis's death.

The door was closed. Holly stood outside, took a deep breath, and entered. A lantern glowed softly on a table beside the bed. How pale and gaunt her mother looked, how tired. Her eyes were closed and she lay very still. Holly drew the only chair to the side of the bed and sat down, tears rolling down her cheeks. She didn't dare even to clasp her mother's hand, fearful of waking the poor woman. Oh, why did she look so awful?

The night passed slowly, so many thoughts tormenting Holly as she tried to will some of her own strength into her mother. Scott. Where was he?

Would she really never see him again? And Claudia. What would happen to her now with Jarvis dead?

Jarvis. Anger battled with bewilderment as she speculated about him. All along, Roger said, it had been Jarvis who wanted her off her land. Why? Simple greed. But she would have to push this new knowledge aside and grieve for Jarvis, for Claudia's sake. Let Claudia have her happy memories. Both she and her mother would have to be satisfied with only memories now.

Claudia stirred at dawn, eyes fluttering open. She was frightened by the strange surroundings. She was supposed to be on the ship. "Holly? Where is Jarvis?"

"Just rest, Mother," Holly said quietly. "You got sick on the ship, and Jarvis brought you here."

Slowly, it came back. "Yes, I remember. I got so dizzy." She laughed nervously. "I feel so silly. What will people think? Ruining my own honeymoon! Poor Jarvis. Where is he?"

Holly was too frightened of her condition to tell her the truth.

"He was very tired. It's been a long night, and he's gone home to sleep awhile. Now you rest, please," she urged. "I'm going to stay here until I speak with your doctor, and then I'll go home for just an hour or so. I'll come back later."

Claudia drifted off to sleep without mentioning Jarvis again, and Holly went to find her doctor. He was not very encouraging.

"We just aren't sure what the problem is, I'm sorry to say. I don't think she's in any danger now, but I would like to keep her here for several days."

Holly prodded hopefully. "She's been unusually active lately. Couldn't it just be exhaustion?"

"Fainting can be a symptom of many things," he said slowly. "Will her husband be in soon? I'd like to speak with him."

She told him about Jarvis, finishing, "I decided she shouldn't be told yet."

He nodded solemnly. "I agree, but we won't be able to keep it from her for long. She's going to expect to see him. We'll have to tell her tomorrow."

Roger was waiting to take her home. When they were settled in the carriage, he gave her a long, thoughtful stare. "There's something I want you to know. I'll never let you down. Don't feel that you and your mother are all alone, because you've got me to take care of you." She started to speak, but he rushed on. "And about last night," he said hoarsely, "please, please believe me when I say I love you, and I'm not sorry it happened."

She turned away abruptly. "I don't want to talk about that now, Roger. There are things I must consider and—"

"Yes, yes," he interrupted frenetically, "I know. So much has happened. But please realize one thing—that I'm here, loving you with every breath I take. I would be so honored if you would marry me. Allow me to help you through your pain, Holly, and try to bring you some joy."

Holly drew in her breath, let it out slowly. "Roger," she said evenly, "I need a lot of time now, to think. Please don't let's talk about this now."

He nodded, smiled, and started the horses mov-

ing. "It won't take you long to think it all through,"
he said confidently.

But all she could think of was Scott Colter's dear
face. Dear God, where was Scott when she needed
him so?

❧ Chapter Twenty-three ❧

SCOTT Colter sat at a small table at the back of a dimly lit bar on the ragged outskirts of Washington, D. C. His head ached, and his stomach churned, but still he tossed down another shot of whiskey. When was the last time he'd eaten? It didn't matter. Oh, he did his job, did the goddamn, boring paperwork that was his job now, a loathsome desk job. He hated it, couldn't wait for each day to end. By damn, all his days now seemed to roll into one.

Oh, well. It had come as no big surprise when he and Neil were pulled off the assignment in Vicksburg and brought back to Washington. With Jim Pate dead, the investigation was at a standstill. Besides that, the brass didn't like the Scott–Lisa Lou scandal. Bad public relations.

He poured himself another glass of whiskey, staring into the glass and, as always, saw Holly's beautiful face, that elusive wood-sprite face.

Where was she at that very moment? How was she?

He threw the whiskey down his throat, wincing at the sudden burning. Why couldn't he forget her?

During the day, he seemed drunk and withdrawn

from everything around him, but it was different at night. Nighttimes, the clarity he really felt, drunk or not, made itself apparent to Scott and his thoughts focused on one thing—Holly and her power over him. Oh, he could tell himself that he'd get over her in a while, but he knew better than to try fooling his own heart like that. The sprite was different, damn her to hell. He loved her as he hadn't loved in a long, long time, maybe ever. Worse was the fact that *he* knew what Holly didn't know. He knew they were good together, fine together, and probably would always be happy. But until she saw that for herself, he could do nothing but let her dangle him on a string. Or stay away from her. Neither held any appeal.

And who knew how long it'd be before she came to her senses? Who knew whether she ever would, in fact, find her heart?

Neil Davis walked in and scanned the dark room, squinting, then made his way to Scott's table and sat down. "Doing what you do best these days?"

Scott shot him a hard look. "No lectures. I'm not in the mood."

"Thought I'd come to give you the good news right away," Neil said.

Scott grunted, waiting.

Neil leaned back in his chair. He felt good. For the first time in ages he felt good. They were going to see some action. "I just got the word. We've got the chance to go to Jamaica, if you want to."

"Who the hell wants to go to Jamaica?" Scott's voice cracked. "I want to head back to Mississippi and finish what we started."

Neil gestured for him to calm down. "That

comes later. Just listen.'' He then explained that he'd just come from a secret meeting with the person most concerned about the gold theft. "He hasn't given up. We've still got to keep it quiet, 'cause so far, nobody knows it's missing.''

Scott was suddenly sober, alert. "What's it got to do with Jamaica?''

"Roger Bonham is in Jamaica.''

Now Neil had Scott's full attention, and he went on cautiously. "Scott, you've been sort of out of things lately. Brooding. Drinking too much. We've gone on without you. And, to tell the truth, we've kept some things from you till you got yourself together.''

Scott frowned. "Go on. You did right.''

"Jarvis Bonham died right after we left. Shortly after that, Roger left Mississippi. We only just found out he's in Jamaica. There's been no word of activity from the Night Hawks, so we can only assume they got their share of the gold and split up. Naturally, the biggest horde will be Roger's, so that's what we've got to try to get back.

"We go to Jamaica as emissaries of the United States government, to see how things are going now that England is establishing a colony there. Since the uprising of former slaves at Morant Bay, things've needed smoothing over. It's a good cover for us.''

Scott was fired up for the first time in weeks. He was not, by God, going to sit behind a desk and turn into an old man before his time. He grinned, delighted. It was a damn good feeling. "When do we leave?''

Neil laughed, cuffing him on the shoulder good-naturedly. "Great to have you back, Colonel Colter."

They drank in celebration now, not in sorrow.

"After Jamaica," Scott said cheerfully, "we go back to Mississippi."

Neil nodded slowly. *He* was not going to be the one to tell him. Let Scott find out for himself. What Scott was seeking wasn't in Mississippi, not any more. She was in Jamaica. And she was Roger Bonham's wife.

No, Neil vowed. Hell, no. No way on earth was he going to be the one to break the news to Scott Colter.

Two months had passed since Holly and her mother had arrived in Jamaica. Roger had left them no choice about it.

Holly sat beneath a banana tree, staring pensively out at the clear blue waters of the lagoon, deeply grateful for this respite, a little time alone. She could see all the way to the bottom of the water to the white, sparkling sand, the myriad darting fish, like fleeting tiny rainbows.

She now knew the true depth of despair.

The only consolation was that her mother seemed better. Beneath the warm Caribbean sun, she had regained some of her strength. There were even times when Holly found it difficult to believe the doctor's grim diagnosis.

Marveling at the beauty around her, she prayed for time to stand still. Here, knowing her mother was taking her nap under the watchful eye of a native servant girl, and that Roger was making his rounds on the plantation, Holly was allowed a little peace, a brief escape.

Jamaica was beautiful. There were tall, lofty mountains that rose straight up from the white beaches, a contrast to the rolling lands around them. There were forbidding wild areas, with giant forests, strange-shaped rocks, and dangerous, bottomless sinkholes.

Fertile valleys, swamps, hot springs, over a hundred rivers, the island was rich in variety and the crops were abundant—bananas, cacao, coconuts, coffee, sugarcane, and so many fruits Holly couldn't name them all.

Sunshine was perpetual, and cool breezes blew in from the hills at night.

High up on a bluff overlooking crashing, foaming waters, was the pink stucco mansion she lived in—the place she could never call home. Large, airy rooms, lavishly decorated, it was beautiful. But she hated it, hated everything within its walls, especially the bedroom she shared with her tormentor . . . her husband.

At first, Roger had been gentle, vowing he would make her love him. She tried to, with all her heart she had tried. But all too soon came the nights when he drank too much rum, forced her to submit to unspeakable depravities. To refuse always meant a beating.

She clenched and unclenched her fists, letting the sand trickle through her fingers like the days of her life. The only consolation in all the horror her existence had become was Claudia. Claudia didn't suspect the truth about Roger, and the one decent thing about Roger was his promise not to hurt Claudia as long as Holly obeyed in him in every way. He had even kept his word not to tell Claudia the nature of her illness or the seriousness of it.

So Claudia was happy, or as happy as she could be, considering the emptiness Jarvis had left. She missed him, talked about him often when she and Holly were alone. It was all Holly could do not to reveal her terrible secrets as she listened to her mother talk about Jarvis's kindness, his thoughtful manner.

At least my mother doesn't know she is dying, Holly thought a hundred times a day. It was her hold on sanity, that realization. Claudia knew nothing. Claudia would die in peace. For this, Holly had sacrificed herself in every way, waking each day to more pain and despair, knowing she might have to live this way for years.

She'd been forced into this sacrifice by Jarvis's death, and by Roger's grip on his father's finances. Oh, he'd explained after Jarvis's funeral, she and Holly were free to leave, but where could they go where Claudia would get the medical care she needed? Did Holly wish, Roger asked, to build another shack on the ruins of Grandpa's old one, and drag Claudia there to live . . . for the short time she *would* live? Or did Holly wish to think once more about marrying him? Because those two options were her only ones. Claudia had Bright's disease, explained the doctor Roger had summoned from New Orleans. She would weaken, her kidneys would stop working, and she would die. She would never get better, he was firm on that point. But the time it would take her to die, and the suffering she would endure, that was all in the hands of Roger, their benefactor, who could provide the life Claudia needed—or refuse to give them a cent. If he turned them out, what would happen?

And so, Holly said yes to Roger—and turned her back on any hope for herself.

Always, in times of deepest anguish, her thoughts went to the one man she had ever loved. The worst of it was, she didn't even know where Scott was. Was he all right? Dear God, it was all so cruel, and her heart hurt so deeply. Scott was all she had, except for her mother.

A crashing sound in the nearby brush made her jump to her feet. Lilda, the young native girl who sat with her mother, was hurrying toward her, brown eyes wide with fear. Holly ran to meet her. "Is it Mother? Is she sick?"

Lilda shook her head, kinky black curls dancing. "No'm. It's Master Roger. He's back and he's looking for you. Sending men to look for you. Hurry."

Holly quelled the impulse to be frightened. Damn him, anyway. Damn Roger.

Lifting her chin defiantly, she followed Lilda toward the house, understanding when the girl darted away just before they got there. She didn't dare let the master know she had warned Holly, had known where she was. Roger could be brutal with servants.

She entered the house, appearing calm before Roger's icy glare. He was standing just inside the front door, arms folded across his chest. He held a leather riding crop.

"Holly, where have you been?" His voice rolled like thunder through the huge foyer. She started by him, toward the curving stairs, but he grabbed her and spun her around. "I asked you a question. I expect an answer." He towered over her, slapping the leather crop against an open palm. "Or would you rather go in to see your mother and have to explain why there's a welt across your face?"

"I went for a walk on the beach," Holly said. "Surely my lord and master can have no objection to that."

He stepped closer, squeezing her breast painfully. "I'll tolerate spirit from you only in my bed. I have forbidden you to leave this house. Tomorrow you will find yourself locked in your room. Now go on and see your mother. I'll have trays sent in for the two of you, and you can eat your dinner in there. When you have finished, go straight to our room and take off your clothes and lie down on the bed and wait for me. Tonight, I shall give you another lesson in wifely obedience."

She writhed as he continued to squeeze her breast, struggling against him, but the more she fought, the harder he clenched her, and finally she was forced to yield and stand helpless before him, tears streaming down her cheeks as the white-hot pain shot through her chest.

Abruptly, he released her. "Go now. Do as I say. Whether you believe me or not, I do not like having to treat you this way, but you leave me no choice."

She gathered her skirt and ran up the steps, but did not go to her mother's room yet. She couldn't face her like this. She went to her own room to wash her face and dry the tears, and when she managed not to look so tormented, she went to Claudia.

She found her mother sitting near the open window, the gentle tropical breeze causing her hair to blow wistfully about her face. "There's my darling," Claudia cried, holding her arms open to Holly, who went to her eagerly, biting back tears as she sank to her knees before her.

They gazed out the window to blue water stretching endlessly toward the horizon. "Isn't it beautiful here? Back home, it's getting on toward time for winter. Here it's eternal summer. I know Jarvis must have loved it when he lived here. Funny, but I feel so close to him these days. I still think of this as his house, not Roger's house."

Holly saw the sparkle of tears in her eyes and squeezed her hands. "Don't torture yourself, Mother. Jarvis wouldn't want you to grieve so."

Claudia stared down at her thoughtfully, a woeful smile touching her lips. "What else is there for me to do but brood? I . . . don't mean to sound ungrateful, dear. It was kind of Roger to insist on bringing me along, but this is your honeymoon." Holly abruptly dropped her gaze. "And I find myself growing restless . . . missing my friends, familiar surroundings. I don't dare say anything to hurt Roger, but I can't help wondering when we'll go home."

Holly hoped the smile she gave her was bright and convincing. "I don't know, Mother. I can talk to Roger—"

"No, no," Claudia was quick to counter. "Don't say anything, please. The last thing I want Roger to think is that I'm ungrateful. I'll stay as long as he wants to. I want you to be happy, my darling," she added wistfully, "and if you're content here . . ." Her voice trailed off.

Holly simply could not speak.

Claudia searched her face. "You *are* happy, aren't you, Holly? There are times when I think you're hiding something. After all, I know you better than anyone else ever can. There are times when I have a feeling there's something I don't know . . . that I *should* know. Am I right?"

Holly had been fearing this moment all along. She swallowed hard, praying she wouldn't burst into tears. "It takes time to get to know someone, Mother, and you never really know them before you marry them. Roger and I have our difficult moments, but we manage to handle them. Don't worry about me, please."

"I do worry. It's in your eyes. That faraway look I've seen so many times before, when you're in pain." When Holly didn't respond, her mother realized she mustn't pry. If Holly didn't want to talk, she didn't.

Lilda brought supper trays in then, and Claudia confessed, "I do miss the food back home." There was pepper pot soup, made from Indian kale and okra and finely chopped meat. There were vegetables, papaws and granadillas. She wrinkled her nose at the sight of the hard-boiled booby eggs, small and with a pink yolk and a gamy taste. "I manage to swallow most of it, but I'd love some fried chicken and hominy grits."

Holly agreed, reaching for a bowl of cassava pudding and some roasted breadfruit. They shared an after-dinner drink of "sour-sweet," a blend of the crushed pulp of the soursop fruit mixed with pineapple milk, and then Lilda appeared to announce that Mr. Bonham was waiting for his wife.

Holly kissed her mother good-night and left before her pose crumbled.

Roger was scowling. He was wearing a red silk dressing robe, open enough to reveal his nakedness. "Hurry up," he snapped, tossing his riding crop on the bed. "You deliberately dallied, and you've only made it worse for yourself, because I don't like to be kept waiting."

Holly began to undress, using that time to move her consciousness elsewhere. Lately, she had become adept at transporting herself back to those wonderful times in Scott's arms. Not that she could pretend it was Scott holding her instead of Roger, but she could at least take herself away from where she was.

She struggled with her undergarments, and Roger moved forward to rip them away. "Damn it, I'll buy you more. I can't wait any longer."

When she did not move quickly enough to suit him, he put his hand roughly on the back of her neck and slung her forward onto her knees on the floor. "Let's begin this way, since you delight in provoking me tonight. You pretend it hurts you, but you know you love it. Now receive me, my willful whore!"

He thrust himself into her, and Holly toppled forward in a flash of red-hot pain. He wrapped his fingers in her hair and jerked her back up to her hands and knees. "None of that," he grunted. "Enjoy, my darling. Enjoy. The night is just beginning."

✣ Chapter Twenty-four ✣

AS the carriage rolled to a stop, Roger leaned over and squeezed Holly's arm tightly. "Remember what I told you. Behave well, or you'll suffer for it later."

She wrested her arm away furiously. "You don't have to tell me how to act, Roger."

He glowered at her. "This will be a very important party for us. A lot of important people are coming. The governor doesn't invite peasants to the King's House. I *intend* for us to be invited back, understand?"

Holly stared straight ahead. In truth, she wasn't really miserable at all. Getting out of the house, seeing other people . . . she looked forward to it. They were staying in a hotel for the night, too. But she couldn't let him know she wasn't unhappy. He'd find some way of ruining the evening for her.

Their carriage was lined up behind nine or ten others, waiting to reach the brick-columned entrance, with its tall, burning torches. Coachmen resplendent in red satin waistcoats and crisply starched white pants were helping the ladies to alight from the carriages. Groomsmen took the carriages away to hitching posts just across the street.

The King's House was the residence of the governor, and was now occupied by Sir John Peter Grant. It was impressive, in an austere fashion. Offsetting the austerity was the lawn. Lanterns glowed beneath thick clumps of banana and coconut trees, giving the appearance of a playground for wood sprites and fairies.

Music reached them as their carriage moved forward. "That's the royal military band," Roger said. "They were sent all the way from England just to play for this occasion." He sighed. "It's good to know we're accepted. One never knows about society, even if you're quite wealthy. I like living here, so I'm glad I've been accepted."

Holly could not resist asking, "But how much longer before we return to Mississippi? Mother seems homesick, and I must admit I'd like to see some familiar faces."

It was the wrong thing to say. A scowl replaced his peaceful expression. "I don't give a damn about your mother. She should be grateful I'm taking care of her. As for you," he snorted, "I imagine you *would* like to see familiar faces—men you've been to bed with." Holly shook her head, but Roger delighted in ridiculing her. "You know, Holly," he went on, "I have tried to be good to you. I don't *like* having to be so heavy-handed, but you would try the patience of a saint. You *make* me treat you roughly. It's really all your fault. When are you going to learn to be obedient to your husband? Then I'll be able to be nice to you."

He searched her face. She said nothing.

"I have no plans to take you back to Mississippi," he said. "I will be returning soon, on business, but you will stay here. I can control you pretty easily here."

It was like being struck in the stomach with an iron fist. Her only hope was to return home. For there, surely to merciful God, there would be someone to help her escape the nightmare her life had become. Here, among strangers, who would help her? She had even thought of telling her mother the truth, asking Claudia to run away with her. But how? Even if Claudia had the strength, they had no money. Roger saw to it that Holly never had any money of her own, and he kept her locked in her room most of the time. When she was out, he often had spies watching her, and she had no way of knowing whether she was being watched or not.

"So," Roger was saying, "now you have a special reason to behave yourself tonight. Since you are going to remain in Jamaica for the rest of your life, these people are going to be your neighbors and friends. You'd be wise to make them like you, so we can be invited out often."

She glared at him then, no longer caring whether she made him angry or not. He would punish her later, but at that particular moment *he* had no choice but to endure *her* fury for a change. "I hate you, Roger," she said very quietly. "I hate everything about you. You are evil, and I wish you were dead. When you take me in your arms, I wish for my own death. I loathe you. You make me sick." She gave him a little smile, enjoying the white-hot rage that had taken over his face. His eyes were glowing like hot coals, and his hands were clenching and unclenching at his sides. "I wonder why you don't have any pride. A woman tells you that she thinks you're disgusting, that she hates you, and you still want to keep her around?"

There was a deadly silence.

"You will pay for this," he finally said hoarsely. "When we get back to the hotel tonight, I'm going to tie you to the bedposts and strip you naked and beat the flesh from your contemptuous body, you bitch."

Holly knew he was capable of starting to do just that, but he wouldn't finish. He might start to beat her, but he'd lose control of his desire and fall on top of her to pummel away until he released himself. And she, meanwhile, would take herself away mentally, to oblivion. Or, if she could manage it, to another time . . . another place . . . and other arms.

"Get out," he growled as the carriage rolled to the final stop before the entrance. "Get out before I turn around and take you back this very minute."

She knew better. Roger was a miser, and he'd had to spend a great deal on their clothes for this party.

A coachman helped Holly to the ground, and she was at once aware of the admiring stares of the other women. She supposed she did look nice, but there was no reason to care. Her hair was curled in ringlets, with tiny strands of pearls intertwined among the tresses. Her dress was of lime-green satin, setting off the red in her hair. The bodice dipped so low she was embarrassed.

"I want to show you off," he had declared when

she protested the design of the gown. "Let the other men see what they will never possess."

He took her elbow and whispered, "Stand up straight. Thrust your bosom out. Everyone is staring, and I want them to envy me."

Holly bit back tears of frustrated fury. "You make me feel like a whore. Please, Roger, let me have my shawl." She had brought the lace stole along in hope that Roger would yield and allow her some semblance of decency, but he snatched the garment away angrily.

"You stupid little Southern imbecile! You know nothing! Why, that dress style is the rage in Europe. You should be proud of your bosom. Jesus Christ, why was I stupid enough to make you my wife instead of my mistress?"

How she had hated him then . . . hated him now . . . loathed him more and more with every beat of her heart.

He hissed, "Stand up straight, I said. Start walking, Holly. People are beginning to stare."

Suddenly, the spirit that, by God, he would never destroy, erupted. Looking him straight in the eye, she said, "Roger, go to hell!" Hooking her thumbs into the bodice of her dress, she yanked it up as high as possible and began to walk up the walkway as fast as she could without actually breaking into a run.

He was right behind her, grabbing at her arm, at the same time turning his head to flash artificial smiles all around. It was a joke . . . nothing serious.

Inside, Holly forced herself to be poised as they passed through the receiving line, saying and doing the proper things. But every time Roger attempted to touch her, to clasp her arm or take hand, she jerked away.

"You're going to pay for this," he seethed over and over. "So help me, before this night ends, you'll wish you'd never been born."

"I already do, Roger. Believe me, I already do."

She took only passing notice of the opulent furnishings and made her way to the refreshment table, quickly downing the glass of champagne a hostess handed her, reaching for another in a second.

After several glasses, a pleasant buzzing took over. It was her only relief, and she partook only when desperate. Perhaps she would become a hopeless drunk one day. She hummed a little tune, wondering if she would ever escape the hell of her life.

She had drifted back to the refreshment table when a firm hand clamped down on her bare shoulder. A masculine voice said quietly, "Holly, I think you've had enough."

A familiar voice. But not Roger. She turned, disbelieving when she found herself staring up at Neil Davis.

It could not be so. *Neil*. In Jamaica? He was in United States Army full-dress uniform. What cruel trick was her mind playing on her? She turned without a word and ran.

Neil caught her arm and led her from the room, out a side door and onto a patio enshrouded with fragrant blossoms and vines. A quarter-moon peered down on them as Holly dared to look up at that wonderful face.

"Why?" she whispered. "Why are you torturing me?"

He gave her a gentle shake. Lord, despite her beauty, she looked terrible. The gauntness, the shadowed eyes.

"Holly, I knew you were in Jamaica somewhere, and I've been trying to find you. I didn't dream you'd be here tonight, but thank God, you are."

Doubts disappeared. "It is you! Oh, Neil . . ."

She stepped into his arms and he embraced her, holding her close. He began to speak, to tell her why he was in Jamaica—a military assignment, more or less based on goodwill. But he interrupted himself. "What the hell is the matter, Holly?"

"There is nothing you can do for me, Neil. Nothing anyone can do," she said.

"Not even Scott?"

There was a long pause before she dared say, "Scott? Is Scott in Jamaica?"

He smiled, inclining his head toward the sound of revelry. "Somewhere in there. I'll go get him."

He turned, but she stopped him. "It's too dangerous, Neil. Roger—"

"Yes, I know you're married. But Scott doesn't know, Holly." He explained. "He knows you're in Jamaica, but I didn't want to tell him you were married. He probably thinks you and your mother just came over with Roger on family business."

"Has he said anything about trying . . . to find me?" she asked very hesitantly.

"Scott keeps things to himself, Holly," he said.

"You know that. He hasn't said anything, but I know he's been looking. We're leaving day after tomorrow to go back to Mississippi and clear up . . . a few matters there. I figured if he didn't find you this time, he'd come back to Jamaica and keep on searching. He loves you," he went on matter-of-factly, as though it were all quite simple and there was no reason not to say it. "You love him. Fate would have brought you together again, sooner or later."

Time was so short. Roger might find them any second. "We are living in Roger's house on the bay in Ocho Rios," she whispered rapidly. "Tonight we're staying in a hotel in Kingston because it's too far to ride home. Tomorrow we'll be going home, and—"

"No," he interrupted firmly. "You're going to meet with Scott tonight. I'll arrange it."

Was he joking? She shook her head wildly. She had to make him see. Roger was already planning to beat her. She had dared too much as it was. "Neil, listen. As much as I want—"

Taking her hand, he pulled her to the end of the patio. An opening in the thick shrubs and vines led to narrow steps and a path leading into the darkness. He pointed, saying, "Go straight down the path to a small duck pond at the bottom of the slope. I've seen it in the daytime, because Sir Peter had us here for an afternoon tea when we arrived. There's a lot of planting there, bushes and shrubs, and you'll have privacy. There're no lanterns down there either. You won't be seen. Go now. I'll find Scott."

She hesitated, and dear, sweet Neil gave her a little push. "Go, Holly, now," he said sternly.

She hurried down the steps and disappeared into the shadows.

Neil stared after her a moment, then turned and went inside. He didn't see Roger anywhere. Scanning the room, he spotted Scott talking to a trio of men in a far corner, men Neil recognized as government officials assigned to Jamaica from England. Approaching the group, he exchanged nods and forced himself to wait for a chance to interrupt.

"I think," one of the men was saying, between puffs on an odorous cigar, "it's the banana trade with the United States that will bring prosperity back to Jamaica."

"That, and the indentured labor being brought here from India," another interjected. "It makes my blood boil every time I think about the uprising in Morant Bay. It would suit me if we never put those damned Jamaicans back to work. Serve 'em right."

Scott smiled, sipping from his brandy glass. "Gentlemen, I can understand your feelings, and the United States is very interested in Jamaican export, not only bananas, but sugar, rum, cocoa, coconuts, coffee. But let's not get carried away taking revenge on the natives. The Civil War in America and the discontent among the ex-slaves here combined to bring about Morant Bay. Keep in mind that the natives here didn't *ask* to be brought from their homeland to Jamaica in the first place. They didn't wish to be slaves, you know."

The three men exchanged glances, and Neil

chose his moment. "I've got to see you, Colonel Colter. It's important."

Scott frowned. He was doing what he'd been sent to Jamaica to do—soothe ruffled feelings and negotiate.

He nodded politely to the men. "Excuse me. We'll continue this conversation later." He followed Neil to a distance where they could not be overheard.

Neil took a deep breath and said simply, "Holly is waiting for you down by the duck pond."

Just as Neil expected, Scott turned and headed straight from the room without a word.

From a distance, Roger Bonham stood and watched as Scott met Holly by the pond. He had seen her leave with Davis, saw Davis return without her. He'd put it all together easily enough.

The bitch. His eyes narrowed. The conniving bitch. He had given her marriage, yet she still . . .

Also boiling inside was the question of why Colter and Davis were in Jamaica. No matter, he told himself. His cache of gold was waiting for him. He had Barney Phillips looking after things, and the two army men weren't going to find out any more here than they had learned in Mississippi. He was too smart for them.

He was also no cuckold.

By god and be damned, it was one thing for Colter to take his pleasure with Holly when she was single. It was another thing now. She was Roger's wife—till death did them part.

He signaled discreetly to one of the men in his employ, one of his ever-present henchmen.

Roger wasn't going to sully his hands by playing the role of the jealous husband. It was unnecessary. He had someone to do that for him.

℘ Chapter Twenty-five ℘

HOLLY stepped inside the ring of fragrant, flowering shrubs bordering the small pond. In the faint light, she found her way to a marble bench and sat down, pressing her trembling hands together in her lap.

Her heart was pounding with excitement, near-hysteria. Did dreams come true sometimes, even for her? Was she actually going to see Scott?

Suddenly she stood up and started back toward the path as her brain began to command her to leave, run, go back to the party before Roger found her out.

Scott was standing in the path, tall and stalwart in the lacy patterns of moonlight that fell across his handsome face.

Holly whispered his name. The sound was the softest of anguished moans, and it melted into the gentle night wind.

At once, his muscular arms wrapped around her, folding her against his broad chest.

He didn't speak, but held her in a deep embrace that left them both breathless. Then he drew her back into their nocturnal haven, past the bench where she had waited, on to a secluded spot beneath the thick, draping branches of a jasmine bush.

He laid her on the ground, hands gently tracing the contours of her face, that face he had never been able to forget, as though he needed to prove she was real.

They lay on their sides, facing each other, and Holly drank in the sight of him until their lips met in the sweetness of silent, desperate longing.

Holly began to unbutton his uniform coat, then boldly unfasten the starched, white shirt beneath, as well. She pushed the shirt open to dance her fingers in his thick, dark mat of hair. Then she rested her cheek against his warm chest.

Caught in a driving longing to express the maelstrom within her, she cast aside any semblance of inhibition. Boldly she caressed his manhood, then undid his trousers, taking him in her hand eagerly. Within the dizzying throes, the burning hunger, she thrilled to feel the liquid of his pulsing desire against her flesh—evidence that he wanted her intensely.

"I want you," she whispered, "deep, deep inside me. I need you . . . must have you. . . ."

Taking one more long look at her exquisite face, he removed his trousers and hooked his fingers in the waist of her undergarments, pulling them away in a single swift movement. He quickly maneuvered himself on top of her, and she wrapped her legs around his back. He moved them higher, till they were around his neck.

A hard thrust and he was inside her, and she gasped. He whispered urgently. "Tell me if I'm hurting you, beloved."

"No, no," she whispered, flinging her head from

side to side, her nails digging into his back. "Make me your own, Scott, please."

The passion that engulfed them stopped time altogether. A gentle nightbird called out to them. Two spirits igniting as one . . . two bodies entwined . . . two loves becoming one love, forever and eternal. Their love carried them high, higher, beyond the horizon, and they soared as one into that rainbow that only those who know true love can reach. . . .

They lay locked in each other's arms for a long, long time. Holly squeezed back her tears. Soon, oh, so soon, the truth would have to be faced.

Scott rolled to the side, smiling at her in the dim moonlight. "We're both a mess, Holly. We can't go back inside tonight."

Her response was hardly more than a moan.

"We will do what we should have done long ago," he offered lightly, but with unmistakable meaning. "We leave—together. My ship sails day after tomorrow. That's enough time for you and your mother to be ready to travel."

When she did not, could not speak, he raised himself up on one elbow to stare down at her. "Well, Holly?"

No longer could she hold back the tears, and she began to weep, pressing her face into the cool, damp grass.

Scott made no move to touch her.

With a deep sigh, he gently asked of her, "Holly, what's wrong? Tell me."

She drew in her breath and then pronounced the words. It was like a sword slicing into her soul. "I can't leave with you, Scott. I'm married."

He drew away, sat up. "Married? Holly, what the hell are you talking about?"

The black man stepped from the shadows.

Scott and Holly got to their feet and Scott made a move toward him, stopping abruptly at the sight of the revolver. He shoved Holly protectively behind him. "What's this about? I don't like having guns pointed at me, mister."

"I do not like to point the gun," the Jamaican said in a clipped British accent. "Please do not make me use it. I am Mrs. Bonham's bodyguard, and her husband has asked that I escort her to her hotel. Do you mind?" He grinned broadly, flashing shiny white teeth.

The thought registered with Scott, a thought he didn't accept. "Mrs. . . . *Bonham?*" he echoed. "Mrs. Bonham? Holly, you *married Roger?*" His flesh was turning icy cold.

The Jamaican took a step backward, gun unwavering lest the American allow his building rage to explode.

"Damn you, Holly," Scott snarled. "What kind of woman *are* you? How—"

He threw on his uniform, then disappeared into the night.

The Jamaican watched as Holly struggled into her clothes. Half-dressed, she started after Scott, but the Jamaican grabbed her arm and twisted it hard behind her back. "Do not make me hurt you, Mrs. Bonham. I feel your husband has enough pain in store for you without my inflicting yet more."

She twisted, writhing against the agony. "Get your hands off me," she screamed, hoping someone would hear. "Get away!"

The man gave her arm such a jerk that a white-hot flash shot through her body, blacking out her consciousness. When she came to a few moments later, she found herself leaning against him. He released his hold.

"That is better," he said softly. "Now you will go with me. Your husband told me to take you directly to the hotel, to your room, and keep you there until he arrives. I have a carriage waiting around the side of the house. No one will see us leave. Please walk slowly and not cause me to hurt you further.

"I saw you, you know," he went on, chuckling. "You should thank me. I did not wish to interrupt such beautiful lovemaking, even though I could have. Mr. Bonham should pay me more for having been so thorough in my 'body-guarding.' " He threw back his head and laughed.

That was when Holly saw her chance.

Catching him off-guard, she whirled around to bring her knee up into his crotch, at the same time jerking the gun from his hand. As he doubled over in agony, she grasped the revolver with both her hands and brought it smashing down on the back of his head with all the strength she possessed.

He fell to the ground and lay still.

She stood over him, gasping for breath, heart pounding. Where could she go? Roger would come looking for her when she wasn't brought to the hotel. Besides that, what about her mother? Roger still had that power over her. She could not run away as long as her mother was back at Roger's house.

She heard someone running and she pointed the gun toward the sound.

"Holly, don't shoot!"

Neil. She dropped the weapon and threw herself into his arms.

He glanced down at the Jamaican, retrieved the revolver, then forced her to meet his gaze. "Listen to me," he said harshly. "I just ran into Scott. He didn't tell me what happened, but I've never seen him so furious. Let's get out of here. You can explain everything later."

"No," she told him. "You must listen *now*, Neil. That man was hired by Roger to—"

He gave her arm a tug. "Tell me later."

"No!" she said again, furiously. "Neil, I can't just run away. My mother is at Roger's house, near Ocho Rios."

She explained, and Neil rubbed his forehead.

"How far to Ocho Rios?" he asked.

Lips quivering, she said, "I don't even know the way. I'm sorry. With all those curving mountain roads, and the brush and trees, the whole island looks like one big forest to me, Neil."

He stared down at the Jamaican, whose eyelids were fluttering slightly. "Well, that leaves us one choice. He'll have to lead us."

"And what then?"

He gave her a smile. "Why, darlin', then we go to Mississippi, what else?"

A lavender mist hovered over the eastern sky as Holly and Neil approached the Bonham mansion. A ring of gold clinging to the last wisps of night promised a clear day, and the wind that blew across their tired, dirt-streaked faces was warm and gentle.

The native, who had grudgingly told them his

name was Bon, rode just ahead of them on one of
the three horses Neil had managed to get for them.
As the house came into view, Bon began to plead,
"Let me go now. Mr. Bonham, he will kill me
when he finds out I brought you here."

"Bon, you just keep on riding," Neil said. "You
don't have to tell him anything. By the time he figures out what happened, we'll all be gone. Now
shut up and keep riding."

"We are here," Bon persisted, a worried crease
on his forehead. "You can let me go now. Please."

Neil shook his head. "You might decide to be a
hero to save your own hide."

During the long ride, Holly had told Neil everything, and he had listened quietly, nodding now and
then, hiding his revulsion. He knew she didn't need
pity, she needed help. He assured her that, once
Scott calmed down, she could tell him everything
and he would understand. "Believe me," he told
her, "there are some things *he'll* need to tell *you*
about, too."

She pressed for an explanation, but he declined.
It wasn't his place to tell her.

Lilda spotted them from an upstairs window, and
by the time they reached the grassy slope of the
lawn, she was running toward them, smiling and
waving her arms. Holly dismounted quickly to embrace her, asking about her mother. Then she explained what her plans were, knowing Lilda was to
be trusted.

The girl cried, "But I will go with you as far as
Kingston. If I stay, he will beat the truth from me."

"Yes, you come with us," Holly told her. "Now
please, start packing our things. Quickly. Not

much, just enough to get by." Lilda ran toward the house.

"Hurry," Neil called out as Holly started after her. "We can't waste a second, Holly!"

Outside her mother's door, Holly prayed for the right words.

Claudia was sitting at her usual place by the window. When Holly entered, she glanced up without undue surprise. "Darling," Claudia said with a smile, "you look so tired. You aren't ill, are you?"

Holly crossed the room and knelt before her, placing her head on her knees, reveling, as always, in the rush of warmth and love she felt at her mother's touch. Could she just break it to her? How could she explain in a way that wouldn't alarm her?

She took a deep breath, "Mother—"

"We're leaving," Claudia said quietly. "I've known it would be soon. I'm ready."

Holly jerked her head up, staring at her. "What . . . what are you talking about?" she stammered.

Claudia smiled broadly. "You think a mother doesn't know what's in her daughter's heart? You think I have not sensed how unhappy you were? How cruelly Roger treated you? Oh, Holly, Holly"—she shook her head from side to side— "there are so many things I know about you, and one of them is how much you love me. I will do my best not to be a burden to you. I wish I could have prevented all of this, but what could I have done?"

Holly continued to stare up at her in utter amazement. She had known. All this time. Yet she had given Holly the right to hide within herself what Holly didn't want seen. She had allowed her daughter that rare thing, pride.

"Mother, I never dreamed—"

"There's no time for talk," Claudia said firmly. "Let's just say I knew that, when the time was right, when your mind was made up, we would leave. So let's be on our way."

❧ Chapter Twenty-six ❧

THEIR ship sailed and they were safe.
  Soon the tall mountain peaks became small
hills, then disappeared from view. Holly watched
from the deck, finally turning away from Jamaica.

She went belowdecks and peeked in at her
mother. Satisfied that Claudia was sleeping
soundly, she went to her own cabin to keep her
vigil. Where was Scott?

There had been no sign of Roger nosing about the
dock, so he did not know her whereabouts. *Was* she
as safe as she was tempted to feel?

"By the time he wonders whether you're off the
island, we'll be on our way," Neil had told her.

If only there were not this other trouble tearing
away at her.

Standing in her cabin, searching Neil's face
hopefully for a sign that things were not as bad as
they seemed, she asked him about Scott.

Neil dropped his gaze. "I just haven't been able
to approach him, to explain. I've never seen him so
mad. God help anybody who tries to talk to him."
He sighed. "All I can do is wait till he calms down

enough to hear about Claudia being so ill. Then he's bound to understand.''

It didn't look good, but at least Neil would try. Dear Neil. Whatever would she have done without him?

She heard her mother calling out to her, and rushed across the hall to Claudia's cabin.

"I'm fine," Claudia said as her daughter's anxious face appeared in the doorway. "I just wanted to talk to you. How are you, dear?"

Holly sat down on the bed. "I wonder," she said, "since you seem to see straight through me, whether I even have to *tell* you what's wrong."

Claudia smiled. "No, you really don't. Since it was Captain Davis who helped us escape, not Colonel Colter, it doesn't strain my imagination to figure out there's a problem. I assume it has something to do with your marrying Roger. Colonel Colter must be quite upset."

"I think he hates me. Neil says he's so mad he hasn't even dared to tell him I'm on this ship."

Claudia nodded. "It will all work out, I know it will. Right now, I think you'd better concentrate on what we're going to do once we get to Vicksburg. Sooner or later, Roger will return." Sorrow overcame her. "Oh, Holly, I can't bear the thought of you being that man's wife. You'll never know how I suffered, because I knew *you* were suffering. I couldn't say anything, but I wanted so much to let you know I understood. I wanted to beg you to leave. I was sure you were only putting up with him for my sake, but I couldn't let myself say anything." She eyed Holly shrewdly. "We must do something to keep him from ever touching you again. No more nightmares.''

Holly smoothed her mother's hair back from her face. Even in illness, she was a lovely woman. ''As soon as we get home, I'm going to see a lawyer and find out how to straighten everything out. I want a divorce, of course, but I also want to make sure you receive everything you're entitled to as Jarvis's widow, and not have to go through Roger to get it,'' she proclaimed resolutely. ''There has to be some way.''

''I'm not a complete invalid, Holly. I can stand up for myself. I'll be right there beside you.''

Holly mused, ''We'll go to Abby's house and—''

''No!''

Holly was stunned by the sudden strength in her mother's voice.

''I'm going to live in *my* house, Holly. Jarvis built that house for me, not for Roger. I'm his widow. It's my right.''

Holly didn't want to go into a long, tiring explanation of how that particular subject had been the means by which Roger had manipulated her into marrying him in the first place. He would not allow her mother to live in the house except as his mother-in-law. ''He is the administrator of Jarvis's estate,'' Holly ventured. ''The first thing we must do is get a lawyer and find out just what your rights are, Mother.''

''He may be administrator, trustee, or whatever,'' Claudia snapped, ''but there has to be a way for me to be allowed to live in that house without his approval. We will take whatever steps are necessary, but we are not moving in with Abby, by God, we're going home!''

Her eyes glittered with spirited tears, and Holly embraced her, smiling through her own tears. Claudia was so angry and so determined. Was this the emotional lift she needed to bring her back to health?

But Holly knew, even as she wistfully dreamed it could happen, that the disease could only worsen. There was no cure. Please, Lord, let her have as happy and as peaceful a time as possible until she dies. Had Claudia, with her astonishing intuition, sensed the seriousness of her condition? No! Don't let her know she's dying. . . .

Claudia was staring at her daughter. "There's something else I want to talk to you about," she declared. "You never did lie very well, you know. You didn't marry Roger because you wanted to. You didn't even marry him because you thought you loved him. He caught you at a very vulnerable time. I think he used my sickness to get to you, maybe even making it sound worse than it is.

"And," she held up a finger for silence, "we will talk about Jarvis now, and your feelings about him. He was a good man. A kind man. He cared very much for you, Holly, and he wanted to be a father to you. He hated what was happening to you. Do you know he cried when he told me about Sally and Norman?"

Holly told herself to just keep silent. Let Claudia have her dreams about Jarvis.

"Jarvis," Claudia continued, "was worried about Roger. He said Roger was resentful because he didn't have wealth of his own. Oh, Jarvis was generous with him, but he refused to finance his gambling. However, toward the time of our wedding Jarvis noticed that Roger seemed to have money. Roger refused to talk about it, but he seemed to have money for anything he wanted, and he and Jarvis were having arguments because, more and more, Roger wanted to take over, run things.''

''So where did Jarvis think he was getting this money?''

''That's the point. Roger wouldn't say. He just hinted that soon he'd have more money than Jarvis ever dreamed of having. And you know Jarvis was a very rich man. Jarvis didn't want to come right out and accuse his own son, but he hinted to me that he thought there was something illegal involved. It worried him so terribly, Holly.''

''Mother, it doesn't matter any more. I know Roger for the despicable hypocrite he is. I'll divorce him as quickly as I can and try to forget I ever knew him. I'm sorry I wasn't able to feel closer to Jarvis. I'm sure if you loved him he wasn't all bad, and—''

''He was a good man,'' Claudia said firmly. ''And I don't know why you feel the way you do. There's something you aren't telling me, and if you say you're not hiding anything, I'll know you're lying.''

''All right,'' Holly admitted. ''I have my reasons, but I'm not going to tell you what they are. Jarvis is dead. I am sorry he's dead, for your sake, and I will be respectful and not speak unkindly of him. So now, can we just drop the subject?'' She stood up, pitching sideways and throwing out her arm to steady herself as the ship rolled. ''I think I'd like to go for a walk and get some air.''

Claudia leaned back against the pillows and closed her eyes. "He was a good man, Holly. Remember that. One day, you'll realize it's true."

Holly tiptoed quietly from the cabin and climbed the stairs to the deck. She took great, drinking gulps of the pungent salt air and instantly felt refreshed. Picking her way over rigging and ropes, she made her way to the railing and stood marveling at the water glimmering blue in the sunshine. The ship pitched and rolled, but Holly only found the movement melodic, not upsetting. It lulled her.

It was short-lived.

Neil appeared at her side, grim-faced. "Holly, I hate to sound like a tyrant, but you don't have any business up here. Please go back down to your cabin."

What was she doing wrong?

He understood her confusion, and nodded toward the sailors working nearby. "They aren't used to having a woman on board. This is a cargo ship, not a passenger ship. They're a rough bunch, Holly, to put it bluntly. The captain sent word he wanted to see me, and he said to get you below. He doesn't want his men getting notions." He smiled. "Come along now. Spend the day with your mother, or rest. The captain has invited both of you to dine with him tonight."

Vexed, Holly jerked away. "Men! It seems women have to gear their every thought to what makes life comfortable for men." With a swish of her skirts, she moved by him and went below to her tiny cabin. . . .

The day passed slowly, and late in the afternoon,

Claudia said she would like to remain in bed for the evening.

"I'm afraid I'm not much of a seafarer. Tea and soup will do fine for me, but you go on to dinner with the captain."

Holly did not try to change her mind. The sea did seem to be getting rougher.

Holly rummaged through the valise that Lilda had hastily managed to pack, choosing the one really pretty dress. Mauve silk, it had a dipping bodice edged in delicate lace. It was strapless, and there were slip-on puff sleeves reaching from elbow to wrist. The skirt was a smooth sheath, the tight-fitting waist coming to a point over her flat stomach.

She brushed her hair to hang straight and shining about her bare shoulders, then touched lilac cologne to her neck and ears. Staring at her reflection in the small, silver-stained rectangular wall mirror, she was satisfied with her appearance. Attractive, sophisticated, but not too elegant. Elegance would have little place on a cargo ship.

Neil knocked on her door promptly at seven to escort her down the passageway, then down a short flight of stairs to the galley. A small room off to one side served as the officers' mess. Upon entering, she saw two men politely stand in greeting. "First Officer Harold Pearson," Neil nodded to the taller of the two. The other he introduced as Second Officer Malcolm Perryman. "Miss Holly Maxwell," he finished, deciding for her that "Mrs. Roger Bonham" no longer had a place in her life.

Officer Pearson gestured to her to take the seat next to him. "We're sorry your mother couldn't join us," he said. "I hope she isn't seasick."

Holly exchanged a glance with Neil, then said, "Mother's been in poor health for some time. I'm anxious to get her home."

Officer Perryman chimed in, "Jamaica is a beautiful island, but if I were sick, I'd prefer to be home."

Captain Weyman Dubois walked in then, and Neil made the introductions. Holly found the small, rotund man polite and charming. He surprised her immediately by apologizing for sending her to her cabin earlier.

"I don't want to create problems," she told him, "but I find it disconcerting when a woman has to hide, Captain."

"Not *hide*, Miss Maxwell," he smiled brightly. "I'm afraid my crew are not all men of honor, as my officers are. In the future, should you feel the need for a walk, merely ask one of the officers to escort you. A lady as beautiful as you are should always be escorted," he added with a friendly wink.

Officer Perryman nodded to the only empty chair. "And where might Colonel Colter be? Don't tell me he's seasick," he laughed.

"He'll be along," Neil commented, then whispered to Holly, "I'm sorry. I went by his cabin again to tell you were on board, but he just wasn't . . . approachable. I've never seen him so . . . so . . ."

"Don't worry about it," Holly responded lightly, holding out her glass for Captain Dubois to fill with crimson wine. "I think Colonel Colter's problem is *his* problem alone. I'm not concerned."

Brave words. But twenty minutes later, when the door finally opened and Scott appeared, there was no denying the flush that crept over Holly's entire body from head to toe. Massively handsome, as always, his brilliant dark eyes fell on her, and tiny red fires of rage sparked in those eyes. He shot an accusing glare at Neil, then turned around and left the room.

Officer Perryman was the first to speak in the startled silence. "What was that about? Granted, I found the Colonel quite moody on the journey over here. But what he did just now was downright rude."

The others exchanged murmurs of agreement, as Holly leaned toward Neil to ask, "How do I find his cabin?"

He hedged, "Holly, I don't think—"

"I'm not asking for your thoughts, just some help," she snapped, standing so quickly that her chair clattered. Embarrassed, sorry she'd snapped at Neil, she apologized to the captain and the other men.

Neil sighed. Maybe it was best she and Scott fight it out. "He's on the same deck you are. First door on the right."

She hurried from the room and, reaching Scott's door, pounded on it.

"I don't want to see anybody," was Scott's roaring response.

That only infuriated her further. Using both fists, finally giving in to utter frustration, she began kicking the door as well. She was not going to put with this any longer.

The door jerked open and Holly fell forward into his arms. Shaking with a deeper rage than any she'd known before, she faced him, then slammed the door shut.

Hands on hips, she began, "You pompous, arrogant, bastard! Just who the hell do you think you are? You think I *deceived* you? I will remind you, *I* am not the one who walked away from Vicksburg without a word.

"Tell me," she shrilled, long hair bouncing around her face as she tossed her head, "who was bedding Lisa Lou Pollock all the time he was fawning after me? Begging me to forgive you for tricking me into thinking you fought for the South, while all the while you were a no-good, yellow-bellied, goddamn Yankee dog!"

His eyes went darker and darker with fury. "Holly, I'm warning you to get out of here."

"I'll leave when I'm through telling you what kind of man you are. *Man!*" She spat the word contemptuously. "You're nothing but a sneak. A liar.

"Yes," she rushed on. "I married Roger Bonham, and many a night he made me wish I was dead. But *I had no choice,* you bastard. My mother is dying. He was going to kick us out of the house, maybe put her in an institution, let her die there." Tears began streaming down her face, and she brushed them away furiously. Damn it, tears were a sign of weakness. "I never," she said evenly, "stopped loving you, Scott Colter, until you turned your back on me and I found out just what an egotistical, insensitive monster you really are." She turned toward the door. "I'll go now. I pray I never have to look at your arrogant face again."

He caught her, pinning her arms to her sides.

Smiling, he whispered, "If I had a bar of lye soap, I'd wash your mouth out."

He threw her on the bunk and fell on top of her. "I'm sorry, Holly. I truly am. I guess a lot of the things you said about me are true, but . . . there's much you don't know." He took a long breath. "Right now, we both need . . ." He kissed her and the fire was ignited. The flames spread, and neither could stop those flames. She pulled him close, closer.

The ship rolled and pitched, gently moving Scott and Holly into their union, rocking them as they moved together into the love that could not, would not, be denied.

🐾 Chapter Twenty-seven 🐾

A PERFECT golden moon, framed by silver clouds, threw its light across the water, making the sea sparkle as though dusted with diamonds.

A gentle wind caressing them, Scott and Holly stood at the railing. His arm was around her, and she pressed her head against his chest. "Are you happy?" he whispered.

"I never knew I could be so happy," she whispered back, "never dreamed I could feel this way."

The rolling sea lulled her, and she sighed, "If only Mother could get well, everything would be perfect. I'm afraid she's getting weaker. She never says a word, but I know she's more tired than she was a week or so ago. She even seems to be swelling, despite being so thin."

Scott tightened his arm around her. "I don't know anything about Bright's disease, but from what you told me, I'm afraid you can't expect anything different."

Her entire body began shuddering, and she said, "I want her at home, Scott. She shouldn't be anyplace except home. Will it be much longer?"

"Two days," he said, "maybe three."

She pressed closer, enveloped by his warm glow.

Their first night together, they'd stayed awake talking until dawn. Holly explained how Roger had managed to enslave her, vulnerable as she was. She had not, however, confided the depth of degradation and misery suffered in his bed, for these nightmares would never be trespassed on, even by her.

When it was his turn, Scott confided everything about himself and his secret army mission. She was horrified. "Why didn't you tell me before? You *knew* why those men were trying to run me off my land. Why, Roger even had me believe it was poor Jarvis! He told me Jarvis was responsible for Sally and Norman's murders." She stared at him, wide eyes glimmering. "How could you have kept that from me?"

"Because you were in enough danger without having that knowledge. I couldn't risk either the investigation or you."

He went on to confide that, when they arrived in Vicksburg, he and Neil were going to have a few trusted soldiers with them and be ready when Roger returned, which he would eventually do.

On another subject, he stated, "I'm not going to apologize for anything between me and Lisa Lou, but you may sure there wasn't any rape. I don't deny I have a past. Yes, there have been other women—and none of them had anything to do with you."

Yes, Holly told herself silently, gazing out at the sea, other women had loved him, answered the hunger in his body. But that was the past. It was today and tomorrow that mattered, and she wanted to be the only woman he wanted.

He brought her out of her reverie with a kiss. "I don't have to ask. I know what you're thinking. I can *feel* your jealousy." He smiled. "Come on. I am going to prove to you once and for all that I will never need any woman but you."

He took her to his cabin, closed the door, and locked out the world.

She was wearing a simple, pale green muslin dress, the collar reaching nearly to her chin. He lowered his head, and, as his fingers deftly unfastened each tiny button, his mouth and tongue touched her throat, setting her on fire.

She closed her eyes, yielding to his every caress, and when she was naked, he carried her to the bunk and quickly removed his own clothing.

She watched him, marveling once again at the perfection of his body—the broad chest, wide, muscular shoulders, long, strong legs.

Her gaze went to his rock-hard thighs, then, slowly, to his swollen, eager manhood, the epitome of his perfection.

She held out her arms to him eagerly, but he shook his head. "No," he whispered huskily. "You give me so much of everything, my darling. Tonight, I intend to give to you."

He spread her thighs and lowered his head. At the first thrust of his tongue, she gasped, "Scott, no, please."

"Yes," he said fiercely. "Yes. Tonight you are mine, to love any way I want to, and this is how I want to love you. I want to taste the sweetness of your body, kiss every inch of you, drink the nectar of your love. Relax, little one, and take everything I have to give."

She felt the pulsation begin deep within, and then it was rushing forth, exploding in a sensation never felt so intensely. Her fingers wrapped in his thick black hair as he devoured her, her back arched with the spine-wrenching force of orgasm. But he mercilessly continued his onslaught, savoring her as though she were a delicious fruit, consuming her again and again.

"No, no, I can't take any more, Scott, *please.*"

He ignored her protests, taking her to the ultimate crest again and again, and still he did not relent. His driving hunger was to satisfy her totally.

Holly was utterly spent, unable even to raise her head from the pillow. Finally, she mustered her strength and raised herself, pushing him from her. She lowered herself to him and took him with her warm mouth, driving him to his own frenzy, till he had no choice but to mount her and drive them both to the summit.

Afterward, he held her against him fiercely.

"Now do you understand?" His voice seemed to light up the dark cabin. "There's nothing left for me to give another woman. You are all I want, and I love you."

When Holly entered her mother's cabin, she frowned at the breakfast tray. "How can you expect *not* to feel weak when you won't eat, Mother? I asked the galley to prepare your eggs just the way you like them, but you've hardly eaten a bite."

Claudia shrugged, teasing, "Look at you. You're positively glowing, Holly. Has someone captured your heart at last? I do wonder who that someone

was not about to give in until then. Until that time, there was something she had to do. What? Why did she have the certain feeling that she was being kept on the earth for a purpose?

❧ Chapter Twenty-eight ❧

HOLLY wearily pushed a strand of hair back under her bandanna. Autumn had a steady grip on the temperature, but she was perspiring nonetheless. It had been a hard day. Not only were there chores to be done outside the house, there was plenty to do inside. She had spent several hours giving the newly hired help their instructions, and then there was Artie, the new overseer, to be shown around.

Beside her, he questioned, "You got anybody to do the shoddin'?" He gestured to the stalls and the expensive thoroughbreds within.

She glanced at him apologetically. "I don't know. When we left for Jamaica, Mr. Bonham just closed the house and left Barney Phillips in charge of the stock. From the looks of things, Phillips did a good job, but I don't know exactly what he did, or who did what."

Artie nodded. "I'll check on it." His face softened. "Don't worry, in a few days, we'll have everything running smoothly, Mrs. Bonham."

"Maxwell," she corrected crisply. "I prefer that you call me Miss Maxwell."

302

"Yes'm," he murmured, without further comment. He knew the gossip, but he didn't figure it was any of his business. He was glad to have the job, glad she had confidence in him. Artie had been a good friend of Norman's, and he knew Holly Maxwell's fine reputation.

Wearily, she asked, "Is there anything else we need to go over, Artie? I need to get back to the house."

"No'm," he responded. "I'm going to ride into town and order some things we need. I won't get back before dark anyway, so I was thinking about just stayin' in town and visitin' my sister—if it's all right. I'll come back first thing in the morning."

"Of course. Take all the time you need, Artie." She gave him a hurried smile and headed back to the house.

It had been three days since their return to the house. What a strange arrival it had been. After spending one night with Abby, her mother and she had simply come home. No fanfare. No fireworks, either. Scott checked the house and grounds thoroughly, but there'd been no one around.

Holly sent word to Betty, one of the servants who had worked at the mansion before Jarvis's death, and the next morning Betty and a full staff had arrived, a couple of the white servants and several Negroes. So Scott left, and Holly took up the running of the house.

Early the next morning, Barney Phillips had showed up.

"Where's Mr. Bonham?" he demanded as he planted himself in the entrance foyer, glancing around with narrowed eyes. "He didn't tell me you were comin' back."

When she told him she was in charge, he had looked her up and down nastily. "You gotta be kiddin'. I don't take orders from nobody but Mr. Bonham. I don't know what's goin' on around here, but I goddamn well don't take orders from you."

"You will," she had told him coolly, "or else you are fired, Mr. Phillips. Quite frankly," she added, "it would suit me if you did remove yourself from my property."

That infuriated him. "You let me tell you somethin', miss uppity, I work for your husband, not you, and you ain't tellin' me what to do."

"Mr. Phillips," she said very quietly, "I gave you a chance. Now leave. You don't work here any longer."

"I told you," he had taken an advancing, menacing step, "you ain't got the power to fire me. I'll run this place as I see fit, and you'll keep your mouth shut. When Mr. Bonham gets back, he's gonna be plenty pissed at you."

Holly didn't lose her temper. No, she was beyond that particular weakness. With one swift movement, she swept up the hem of her skirt and whipped out the knife strapped to her calf. Moving so lightning fast that Barney Phillips was caught completely unawares, she pressed the tip of the blade beneath his chin and told him, "I said, Mr. Phillips, to get off my property. Now move!"

His arms shot high above his head in surrender, and he leaped backward. "I'm goin', I'm goin'," he assured her, backing toward the door.

But when he reached the door, and was, he felt,

out of her reach, he yelled, "One thing I do know, bitch, when Mr. Bonham gets back, you're gonna get what's comin' to you, and I damn *sure* want to be around to see it."

He had bolted from the house. Holly returned the knife to its sheath and lowered her skirt, sighing. The knife was necessary. She was no longer going to be defenseless, not ever.

Now, walking toward the house, she hoped Phillips had packed up and left the area for good.

She had almost reached the house, anxious to see her mother, when she felt a sudden chill. It was twilight. Why were there no lights burning inside the house? She came to a full stop while her gaze swept the mansion, top to bottom. Then she quickened her steps, hurrying through the back door.

The kitchen was empty and chilly. There was no smell of dinner cooking. What had become of Betty? Holly's worried calls brought none of the other servants, either. A staff of six, and nobody was there.

She went down the hall, into the foyer, and on into the study. A candle was burning on the desk, but that was the only sign of life. "Betty?" she called again.

There was no answer, only the rustling of curtains at a partially-opened window.

She ran from the study. She did not see the movement in the shadows in a far corner of the room . . . did not see anyone follow her up the stairs as she ran to find her mother.

Pushing the door open slowly, Holly made her way to the bed. Leaning over, she found her mother sleeping. But why, she wondered, had Claudia not

been served her dinner tray? There was no sign of
anything on the bedside table, not even the usual
teacup. Damn it, where was everyone? If she'd
known her mother was all alone in the house . . .

She gently pulled the sheet up to her mother's
chin, straightened the covers, then tiptoed out of the
room.

Walking along the gallery, she moved toward the
stairs, then froze.

Light was spilling from the study into the foyer,
not the scant light of a single candle, but much
more. Holding to the railing, she moved cautiously
down the staircase, trying not to make a sound. She
reached the foyer, bent and lifted her skirt, pulling
the knife from its sheath.

Suddenly a strong hand shot out of the shadows
and grabbed her wrist. The knife clattered to the
floor.

"Phillips told me about your goddamn knife,"
the voice growled as she was pushed roughly to her
knees, then kicked to the floor.

"Roger," she spat. "You bastard!"

He grabbed her arm, snatched up the knife, and
jerked her upright, dragging her to the study and
flinging her inside. She fell on the sofa, started to
rise, but he yelled, "Stay, damn you. You've got a
beating coming, but not now. We're going to settle
things."

He tossed her knife onto his desk, locked the
study door, pocketed the key, and poured himself a
drink. Then he sat down behind the desk.

"What are you doing here?" she cried, knowing
what an idiotic question it was, but unable to stop
herself.

"I live here," he said, eyeing her over the rim of his glass. "I'm so disappointed that you left Jamaica without me. Had I known you were this anxious to return, I might have been persuaded to bring you back here myself. You just never learned how to coax and wheedle your way with me, did you?

"Actually," he went on without pausing, "I returned two days ago. Not far behind you and your . . . abductor. Of course, I had a larger ship, so we made better time than you did. I've been around, watching you. I talked to Phillips. Thank heavens, he warned me about that disgusting knife. Really, Holly!"—he made a clucking noise, downed his drink, poured another—"We will have to do something about your behavior. I can't have my wife—"

"I'm divorcing you, Roger."

He turned to stare at her, stunned more by her calmness than by the information.

While she had the chance, she spoke. "We both know I never loved you, that you caught me in a helpless situation. I not only do not love you, Roger, I hate you," she said emotionlessly.

He waved a hand. "Makes no difference, Holly. I don't care how you feel about me. You're my wife. You will remain my wife."

He reached for the bottle again. "Would you like to join me? We have time before we have to sail."

"What have you done with the servants?"

"Told them to go to their quarters and keep quiet if they valued their lives," he replied matter-of-factly. "They were no problem. I wish I could say the same of you. Now, if you'd like a drink, don't be stubborn. We have a few minutes before we have to be on our way. And," he added, smiling, "don't worry about packing. I brought enough of your clothes that you can get by on the return trip.''

She struggled to keep from screaming at him. ''I'm not going anywhere with you, Roger.''

''Well,'' he gave a mock sigh of resignation, ''then you leave me no choice but to drag you out of here. That might awaken your poor mother. It would upset her. That would be most unfortunate, don't you think? It will be startling enough for her to find you gone, without her having to witness an unnecessary scene. But that's all up to you.''

Holly's teeth were clenched so hard her jaws ached. ''I am not,'' she repeated tightly, ''going with you. I will fight you every inch of the way.''

He yawned, looked at the large grandfather clock in the corner. ''Well,'' he said airily, as though it were really no great inconvenience, ''I'll just have to go ahead and put your mother out of her misery. She's going to die soon, anyway, so I suppose it doesn't matter all that much.''

Holly pressed her hands together, praying for the strength to act calm. ''You would, wouldn't you? You are capable of killing. It was you who murdered Sally and Norman.''

He looked at her as though she had gone insane, then chuckled. ''Oh, good heavens, woman, no, I surely didn't. I would never bother killing Negroes. That's beneath me. I had my men do it. But,'' he said thoughtfully, ''I must admit to being responsible for Jarvis's death. The bastard asked for it. He pushed me too far, so he had only himself to blame.''

Holly suddenly felt all of the strain, and she began to shake. ''Your own father?''

He snorted. "Father! That spineless ninny was *not* my father. My mother might have been stupid enough to marry him, but she wasn't so hopeless as to have a child by him. My father, she told me, was an earl, a man of great wealth and power, who was killed in an accident before he could take her away from the misery of her life. She had no choice but to pass me off as Jarvis's son, but she never tried to fool me. She used to talk to me for hours about how wonderful my real father was."

"I'm glad," Holly told him sincerely, "glad to hear that Jarvis Bonham was not your true father. From what I've learned of him since his death, it would be difficult to believe so fine a man could sire a cowardly, worthless piece of scum."

His eyes narrowed, face tightening into a mask of uncontrollable fury. "Watch your tongue, you fiery little bitch, or I will kill that simpering mother of yours just to watch her die and teach you what happens to people who try to cross me."

Holly pressed on, knowing it was a risk, but she had to take it. "You ordered the Night Hawks to try to frighten me away. You were behind all of it. Why?" She knew why, but she couldn't give away the fact that Scott was on to him. She was hoping he wanted to brag about his triumphs, and she was right, he did.

His face took on a glow and he announced, "I have a fortune in gold buried in various spots on that land." She managed to look suitably shocked, and he was gratified. "You complicated things when you retained title," he confided, "because I had picked that site very carefully. I was sure Jarvis could buy this land and everything surrounding it."

"Why didn't you have me killed so you could get the land?" she asked bluntly.

He shrugged. "That would have raised a lot of questions, and I wanted everything to go smoothly. Then I became attracted to you and I decided I might as well marry you. It didn't take me long to realize I would have been better off if I'd just made you my mistress." He shook his head. "You're a lot of trouble, Holly, and sometimes I wonder if you're worth it. But, I suppose, like a prize horse, once your spirit is broken, you'll be good stock for breeding and pleasure."

He laughed, a nasty sound that brought to mind slime and muck.

He stood. "Now then. It's time for us to go. Which will it be? Will you go peacefully, or shall I put your mother out of her misery? It really matters not at all to me, my dear."

Holly made no move. She couldn't go with him, knowing what awaited her, but was there any alternative?

He picked up her knife from the desk and examined it. "I think," he said thoughtfully, "that we've tarried long enough. I really don't want to kill Claudia, you know. I have nothing against her."

Suddenly he looked toward the open terrace door and called out, "Barney, we've wasted enough time."

Before Holly could react, Barney Phillips charged inside from the terrace. He was upon her in an instant. A gag was stuffed into her mouth and her arms were bound together. She struggled, but the gag and bonds held.

"Damn right, we've wasted enough time," Bar-

ney grunted. "That sentry of Colter's we bought off
has had plenty of time to ride to Vicksburg and tell
Colter the big dig is under way tonight. I've got to
get over there and be ready if we're going to get rid
of Colter tonight."

"And your other men?" Roger asked, his eye on
Holly's face. "They'll take care of the rest of Colter's bunch?"

Barney snorted. "Ain't that many of 'em, but we
got 'em covered. Our men are handling that. They
ought to be out of the way by now. When Colter
can't round 'em up, he'll head out on his own, and
that's the way I want it, just me and him."

"Take care of Colter, and when the rest of our
men get there, dig up all that's left of the gold and
take it to the barge. We'll take it on board, then
head for Jamaica."

Outside, in the dark foyer, undetected, Claudia
stood clinging to the stairway newel post. She held
on for dear life. She could not give way to the oblivion that offered to take her way. No matter that she
knew she was dying. No matter that Roger had admitted to so much evil. All that mattered was that
Holly was in Roger's grasp and Colonel Colter was
about to be killed.

What could she do? Already a cold, clammy
numbness was creeping up her legs. She felt so
weak, she could barely keep herself upright.

She knew there was no point in dragging herself
to the servants' quarters and begging for help.
Those poor Negroes were terrified, would never interfere in a white man's business. Whatever could
be done, she would have to do. Please, she prayed,
give me the strength I need.

She loosened her grip on the newel post and took a faltering step toward the front door. On the next step, she pitched forward onto her knees, consumed by weakness, by sickness, by terror.

🎀 Chapter Twenty-nine 🎀

THROUGH that black night rode the two men on horseback, their horses' hoofs thundering against the red Mississippi clay. They rode hard out of Vicksburg, but as they neared their destination, they slowed to a canter, then to a walk. They strained, nerves on fire, desperate to make as little noise as possible.

Neil Davis spoke softly, "I don't like it, Scott. We need men with us. How do we know what we're riding into?"

Scott shared his partner's anxiety, but he had learned in war that when men are faced with danger, one person's fear could spread. Neil Davis was no coward, but he had reason to be scared. "All we know is that when Sparkwell was on sentry duty he overheard a couple of men making plans to get the gold out tonight."

"Hell, there might be a hornet's nest in there," Neil said. "They might have twenty men, or a hundred. Unless Sparkwell rounds up the few men we can trust and gets them here in time, it'll be just you and me."

Scott shook his head. "Bonham won't have that

many men. Remember, from all we've managed to find out, the Night Hawks are gone. That means they've taken their part of the gold and headed home. I figure a half-dozen, a dozen at the most, and they'll all be roustabouts Bonham picked up for a few hours' labor. They'll run if there's any shooting. Whatever they're being paid won't be enough to make them risk their lives. And remember"—he reached over and touched Neil's shoulder for emphasis—"we've got surprise on our side."

Neil sighed. "I just hope Sparkwell is able to find those men. How they got so scattered, I don't know."

"Saturday night." Scott flashed him a grin in the moonlight. "They're doing the same thing you'd be doing if you weren't out here—drinking and chasing women."

Neil grinned back. "Me? Chase women? The other way around, my friend, *they* chase *me.*" He decided to seize the chance and ask, "What are you going to do about Bonham? About Holly getting a divorce, I mean."

"I don't see any problem, especially when Bonham is going to prison. She'll get the divorce because of that."

"Prison? On what charge?" Neil asked sardonically. "All this has been kept top secret. Nobody knows the gold is missing. How can you send a man to prison for a crime nobody is allowed to know was even committed? All we can hope to do is get back whatever gold hasn't been doled out. But Bonham'll go free. You can't charge him with anything, can you?"

"You're forgetting Talton Pollock."

"What can he do for us?" Neil asked, truly bewildered.

"He's running scared. Now that Lisa Lou admitted she lied, admitted everything about us, even said she'd slept with Bonham, Talton isn't too happy. He's found out his daughter is about one step shy of being a whore. He also isn't sure how much I know about his activities back when Lisa Lou was meeting me. Remember, the man was a spy once. He's got a lot to fear. Apply a little pressure, and he'll tell us anything. In exchange for his freedom, he'll finger Bonham for all the killings. We'll have Bonham for murder without bringing out the gold theft."

The two fell silent, each with his own thoughts. Soon they were approaching the remains of Holly's burned cabin, and in a barely audible whisper, Scott ordered, "Dismount. We'll go the rest of the way on foot."

Not far off, Claudia Maxwell lay in the scrub brush, unconscious. Making her way to the swamp, stumbling, crawling, had taken all of her strength. Her clothes were shredded, her knees and hands bloody. Her breathing was shallow, labored.

Somewhere, deep within Claudia, was a stirring. The hourglass of time turned itself upside down. She was no longer an older woman but a young woman, a new mother, holding her baby. Tears of joy ran down her cheeks and splashed softly on the infant's face. The baby smiled. Babies smiled when angels talked to them, Claudia had been told that by her own mother. Surely a baby so lovely would be in touch with angels all her life.

Painfully exhausted, lying on the cold ground, Claudia's hands moved as she yearned to hold that baby again. She gasped, begging God for the strength she needed, knew she didn't have. Her lips parted to speak, but there was no sound. The words wouldn't come.

Then, miraculously, she felt contractions within her, contractions like the ones she'd had when Holly was born, so many years ago. Only this time, the contractions brought no pain, only a deep, exulting joy.

Scott and Neil crouched in the brush. They dared not speak or move. Each carried Winchester .44 rimfire rifles, as well as Neil's Smith & Wesson .44-40 and Scott's Colt .38-40 Peacemaker.

After what seemed an hour but surely wasn't, a flickering light appeared in the dense forest of cypress and vines. Behind the light were three men all talking urgently as they approached. Soon they were only about thirty feet from Scott and Neil. The officers were sure they'd seen none of the three before. All were strangers.

"Get them lanterns hung and let's get started. I ain't wantin' to be here all night," one growled.

"Hell, we need more help. It's gonna take a long time to dig up that much gold if it's just us diggin'."

"Quit jawin' and start diggin'. You're wastin' time," the tallest man spat.

Scott waited until they had chosen limbs on nearby trees on which to hang their lanterns. Then, when they'd picked up their shovels and begun to dig, he motioned Neil forward. They stepped from cover together. "Hold it right there! You're under arrest," Scott yelled.

There was no way to stop what happened then, for Barney Phillips had planned everything too well. The lanterns had been placed strategically, according to his orders, and the clearing was ringed by light so that Scott and Neil offered perfect targets. In the shadows, Barney raised his rifle, aimed at the back of Neil's head, and fired.

Neil pitched forward. Scott dropped to his knees and whirled toward the sound of the shot, ready to shoot back. But Barney was ready, too.

Two more shots rang out. The first kocked Scott's rifle from his hand and the other smashed into his thigh. With a gasp, Scott's hand flew to the fiery pain, and his remaining gun fell to the ground.

He pressed his hand against the wound, trying to slow the bleeding. His mind was racing feverishly. He had one chance, and he took it. Commanding everything within him, he lunged for the pistol and aimed just as Barney fired.

Neither saw Claudia in the brush. She stood, screamed Scott's name as the bullet intended for Scott ripped into her back.

In that instant, Scott fired, felling Barney with a shot between his eyes. Seeing their leader die, the other two men fled as fast as they could.

Fire stabbing his thigh, Scott struggled across the ground to Claudia. He gathered her tenderly in his arms, beseeching her, "Why? Why'd you get in the way?"

She lifted her hand, pleading. "Holly," she whispered. "Roger has her on a ship. Save her, Scott. Save her. She loves you so."

"Don't try to talk," he said fiercely, holding her as tightly as he dared. There was nothing he could do for her. She was dying and he couldn't stop it.

"Must . . ." She struggled to speak above the black mist enveloping her. "Must tell you. Heard them talking . . . Roger, Phillips. Knew what they were going to do. Save her, Scott."

"I will," he promised, his voice cracking. "You damn well know I will, Claudia."

She lay very still for a moment, eyes closed, and Scott feared she was already dead. But she spoke again, very feebly at first, her voice getting stronger as she talked.

"I am giving birth," she told him. "The Bible says a woman walks in the valley of the shadow of death at the moment of birth. I will not return from the valley. But I give birth, in death, because I am giving Holly the one thing that can make her happy —love. Your love, Colonel Colter. I can die in peace now, giving birth to my child all over again. . . ."

Claudia Maxwell Bonham closed her eyes and died.

Scott laid her gently on the ground. He closed her eyes and silently offered a prayer of thanks. He examined his wound and found that the bullet had gone clean through. With no qualms, he tore a piece from the bottom of Claudia's robe, wrapping it tightly around the bleeding hole. Then he stood and made his way to Neil's body. There was no time to bury his friend, no time even to pray over him.

Pain knifing down his leg, he limped down to the water, gasping as the sudden, icy chill of the water hit him. Beyond, in the distance, were the lights of a ship. That ship was where Holly was being held prisoner. He was sure of it.

He waded waist-deep and then lunged forward into the water, swimming out to the ship. Claudia, he promised her silently, you didn't die in vain.

❧ Chapter Thirty ❧

HOLLY lay, bound by ropes, on the bed in Roger's spacious cabin, hoping that all the venomous hatred she felt for him was in her eyes. "Goddamn you, Roger," she whispered. "I hope you burn in hell."

He was drinking straight from a bottle of rum now, no longer bothering with a glass. "One day, maybe I will," he shrugged, "but that won't be for a long, long time. No, precious wife, but there may soon be times when you wish you were dead, because I am going to break that spirit of yours. I am going to make you crawl to me on your hands and knees." He burped. "Starting now."

He began to undress slowly, watching her face carefully.

"Do you know what I see before me?" she asked evenly. "I see nothing before me but a naked monster." She hoped none of her fear showed.

But he knew exactly how frightened she was, and how best to torment her. "By now, your friend Colter is dead. But don't think about him, dear wife, think of other things, like the ecstasy I am going to offer you in a moment or two."

Using the knife he had taken from her earlier, he sliced through the ropes that held her. "Don't try anything you shouldn't, my sweet," he warned as he slowly cut her clothes off of her, his eyes glowing. "Holly, this is a new beginning for us. Be glad for this chance to renew our love."

As Holly stared at him, her entire life seemed to pass before her. She remembered once condemning her mother for being weak, for depending on a man. Now Holly found herself truly alone. If Scott were dead—and she prayed with all her strength that he was not—then she knew she'd be alone forever. But she was damned if she would surrender.

Death would be better than Roger's love. She would take her chances with death.

She whispered lustily to him, "You think you're man enough for me? You think you can satisfy me? Colonel Colter was ten times the man you are. He took me to glory so many times I lost count." She laughed tauntingly. "You aren't fit to lick his boots, you bastard."

Incensed, Roger leaped for her, pawing at her till she cried out in pain. Blind lust had taken him, and he'd dropped the knife on the bed, just as she'd hoped he would.

Roger grunted, panted, telling her in the basest terms what he was about to do to her, and all the while, she was moving her arm slowly toward the knife.

"Now!" Roger moaned suddenly, ready to plunge himself into her. "Now!"

Her fingers closed over the knife and she plunged it downward.

The blade caught him in his shoulder and he

shrieked in pain, rolling to the side. She leaped to her feet, holding the knife before her and making wild, slicing motions in the air. "Enough, Roger!" she screamed, her whole body trembling with rage and despair. "I will kill you, I swear I will."

He came at her, and she slashed out, the blade cutting into his face. He yelped, leaping backward, blood pouring from his cheek and his shoulder. He lunged for the door and ran out into the narrow corridor and up the stairs, screaming for help.

Holly was right behind him, fearless. She followed Roger's trail of blood up the stairs, naked, oblivious to the stares of the crew gathering on deck. The men stood as still as statues, staring at the woman who had gone berserk.

She swung with the deadly knife, slicing air, walking toward Roger, who backed away from her, screaming, "Stop her! She's crazy! Kill her before she kills me."

One brave soul, or fool, dared to move toward her. He was about to draw the pistol tucked in the waist of his trousers when she brought her knife down, slicing into his arm. With a cry of pain, he stepped back, but not before she grabbed the pistol. She faced the others, pointing the knife in one hand and the gun in the other. "Anyone else care to flirt with death?"

No one spoke, and no one moved.

"Overboard," she said tersely, waving the gun at them.

One of the men cried, "We ain't goin' overboard."

She fired the pistol at his feet. "Then move."

Running as one large body, they left the deck and made for the stairs.

Roger was backed against a mast. Breathing heavily, hands pressed against his bloody face, he snarled, "You're going to have to come after me, you bitch. You're going to have to kill me. So shoot—if you dare."

She eyed him coldly, emotion gone. "This will be for Sally, and Norman, and poor Jarvis, and all the others you've killed. And for my mother, for Scott, for me. For all the hell you've caused on this earth."

Neither of them had seen Scott laboriously, painfully, pull himself over the railing. They believed themselves alone until, at the moment Holly pulled back the pistol hammer, Scott called out, "Don't!"

She froze.

"Don't," Scott called again. "You've never killed, and you might not be able to live with it."

Leaning against the railing, stooped, his hand on his oozing wound, he glared at Roger, whose face had frozen into a mask of hatred and contempt.

"You goddamn, worthless son of a bitch," he hissed. "Do you know the misery you've caused, you and your goddamn greed? You've killed the best friend I ever had in this world."

Too numb for feelings, Holly merely registered Neil's death. There would be time for mourning later. "Scott," she asked, almost conversationally, "what shall we do with him?"

Scott limped forward, straightening as best he could as he reached her. He took the gun and knife from her and embraced her gently. "Your mother is dead, Holly. I'm sorry."

Holly nodded silently. It was no surprise.

"She gave her life for me," he said quickly. "She took the bullet that was meant for me." He related Claudia's last words about giving birth again, and then told her, "She asked me to save you. But whatever happens now is up to you."

She understood. "Then what do we do about him?"

"I think," Scott answered, "we'll give him the same chance he gave other people."

Holly looked at him quizzically. "And that will be . . . ?" Her voice trailed away.

Scott barked his final orders at Roger. "Overboard. Alligators may have been following me, after my blood. If so, you can feed them." He paused long enough to cock his gun. "Or else feel this bullet." He pointed the gun at Roger. But Roger had made his decision. He preferred anything the sea had to offer to letting Scott Colter take his life. His gaze flickered briefly over Scott, then rested a moment on Holly. Then he walked to the railing and hurled himself overboard.

There was the sound of his body hitting the water, then the thrashing of alligators as they fought over the evening's offering.

Roger Bonham's screams of terror were soon garbled by the water rushing into his lungs, then disappeared altogether as he was pulled beneath the surface.

Scott and Holly held each other tightly. "I'm sorry," he said quietly.

She knew he meant her mother.

"She loved you," he said somberly.

"Yes," she whispered. "And she did give birth

to me again, because she gave me my life when she gave me you.''

Misery and anguish lay in their past. Joy awaited them.

His lips pressed against her face. ''I told you once that your kisses should taste of warm, sweet wine. Let's find the wine, my love, and drink to the future. It's time to say good-bye to the past.''

Above them, clouds dusted with gold moved apart, allowing the moon to shine down on them. Enraptured, Holly murmured, ''There's a poem I always loved.'' She looked up at Scott and recited, '' 'The wine of love is music . . . and the feast of love is song . . . and when love sits down to the banquet . . . love sits long.' ''

''Then we begin the banquet now,'' Scott said huskily, wrapping his arms around her more tightly, ''for we have the wine of love.

''We have,'' he smiled down on her enchanting face, ''love's wine.''

The Blazing Romances
of *New York Times* Bestselling Author

JOHANNA LINDSEY

BRAVE THE WILD WIND   89284-7/$3.95 US/$4.95 CAN
In the untamed Wyoming Territory, a fiery young beauty is swept into passionate conflict with a handsome, arrogant Westerner who has vowed never to love.

A GENTLE FEUDING   87155-6/$3.95 US/$4.75 CAN
A passionate saga set in the wilds of Scotland, in which a willful young woman is torn between tempestuous love and hate for the powerful lord of an enemy clan.

HEART OF THUNDER   85118-0/$3.95 US/$4.75 CAN
Set in the untamed West of the 1870's, this is the story of a headstrong beauty and of the arrogant outlaw who vows to possess her father's land—and her heart.

SO SPEAKS THE HEART   81471-4/$3.95 US/$4.75 CAN
When a beautiful heiress is betrayed into the bondage of a powerful and passionate knight, a love as mighty as the sword raised against their enemies is born between them.

Also by Johanna Lindsey:
GLORIOUS ANGEL	84947-X/$3.95 US/$4.95 CAN
PARADISE WILD	77651-0/$3.95 US/$4.95 CAN
FIRES OF WINTER	75747-8/$3.95 US/$4.95 CAN
A PIRATE'S LOVE	40048-0/$3.95 US/$4.95 CAN
CAPTIVE BRIDE	01697-4/$3.95 US/$4.95 CAN

AVON ROMANCES